"PALPABLY EXCITING."
—David Morrell

W9-BRI-266

Salvation
and
annihilation
meet at
one degree...

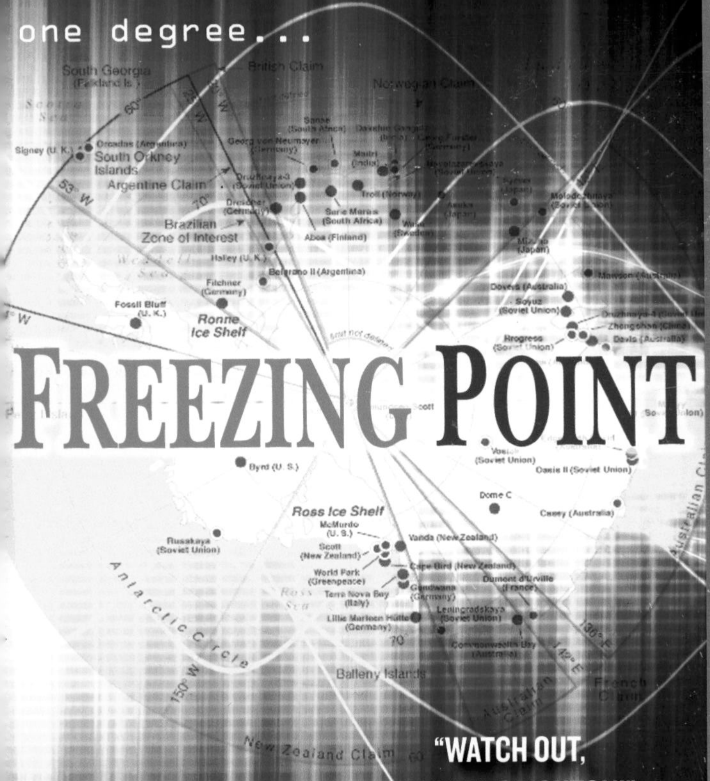

FREEZING POINT

"WATCH OUT, MICHAEL CRICHTON!"
—Gayle Lynds

Praise for *Freezing Point*

"Palpably exciting. A scientific thriller about a looming global crisis far more critical than oil. Karen Dionne is the new Michael Crichton."

—David Morrell, bestselling author of *Scavenger*

"Fascinating and action-packed, *Freezing Point* by Karen Dionne is a riveting tale of cutting-edge science, boardroom greed, and the triumph of those who respect nature. Dionne's voice is authentic and fresh. Watch out, Michael Crichton!"

—Gayle Lynds, bestselling author of *The Last Spymaster*

"Karen Dionne's *Freezing Point* has everything. Exciting to read, highly original in plot, provocative in subject matter, and peopled with engaging characters. What a very promising debut!"

—John Case, bestselling author of *The Murder Artist*

"From the pulse-pounding beginning to the intrigue of multibillion-dollar corporate shenanigans, this is a tale of corporate greed and the triumph of one good man. Readers won't be able to put it down."

—David Dun, bestselling author of *The Black Silent*

FREEZING POINT

Karen Dionne

JOVE BOOKS, NEW YORK

THE BERKLEY PUBLISHING GROUP
Published by the Penguin Group
Penguin Group (USA) Inc.
375 Hudson Street, New York, New York 10014, USA
Penguin Group (Canada), 90 Eglinton Avenue East, Suite 700, Toronto, Ontario M4P 2Y3, Canada
(a division of Pearson Penguin Canada Inc.)
Penguin Books Ltd., 80 Strand, London WC2R 0RL, England
Penguin Group Ireland, 25 St. Stephen's Green, Dublin 2, Ireland (a division of Penguin Books Ltd.)
Penguin Group (Australia), 250 Camberwell Road, Camberwell, Victoria 3124, Australia
(a division of Pearson Australia Group Pty. Ltd.)
Penguin Books India Pvt. Ltd., 11 Community Centre, Panchsheel Park, New Delhi—110 017, India
Penguin Group (NZ), 67 Apollo Drive, Rosedale, North Shore 0632, New Zealand
(a division of Pearson New Zealand Ltd.)
Penguin Books (South Africa) (Pty.) Ltd., 24 Sturdee Avenue, Rosebank, Johannesburg 2196,
South Africa

Penguin Books Ltd., Registered Offices: 80 Strand, London WC2R 0RL, England

This is a work of fiction. Names, characters, places, and incidents either are the product of the author's imagination or are used fictitiously, and any resemblance to actual persons, living or dead, business establishments, events, or locales is entirely coincidental. The publisher does not have any control over and does not assume any responsibility for author or third-party websites or their content.

FREEZING POINT

A Jove Book / published by arrangement with the author

PRINTING HISTORY
Jove mass-market edition / October 2008

Copyright © 2008 by Karen Dionne.
The Edgar® name is registered service mark of the Mystery Writers of America, Inc.
Text design by Kristin del Rosario.

All rights reserved.
No part of this book may be reproduced, scanned, or distributed in any printed or electronic form without permission. Please do not participate in or encourage piracy of copyrighted materials in violation of the author's rights. Purchase only authorized editions.
For information, address: The Berkley Publishing Group,
a division of Penguin Group (USA) Inc.,
375 Hudson Street, New York, New York 10014.

ISBN: 978-0-515-14536-6

JOVE®
Jove Books are published by The Berkley Publishing Group,
a division of Penguin Group (USA) Inc.,
375 Hudson Street, New York, New York 10014.
JOVE® is a registered trademark of Penguin Group (USA) Inc.
The "J" design is a trademark belonging to Penguin Group (USA) Inc.

PRINTED IN THE UNITED STATES OF AMERICA

10 9 8 7 6 5 4 3 2 1

If you purchased this book without a cover, you should be aware that this book is stolen property. It was reported as "unsold and destroyed" to the publisher, and neither the author nor the publisher has received any payment for this "stripped book."

For Jeff, for everything

Acknowledgments

No author writes in a vacuum, but when it comes to assistance and encouragement, I am more indebted than most.

My deepest thanks go to my husband, Roger, for his love, support, and fabulous gourmet meals.

To my agent, Jeff Kleinman, whose unwavering faith in a raw talent and keen editorial eye turned an aspiring writer into a published one.

To my editor, Natalee Rosenstein, who took a chance on an unknown, and to Michelle Vega, who answered my questions with patience and grace.

To a terrific author and my most trusted reader, Dr. Jeffrey Anderson, for helping me get my science right. Any errors in the text are most definitely my own.

To the experts who offered assistance: Dave Rutledge, David Jefferies, John Dunn, Ed Niehenke, Richard Bowen, Stan Lippincott, and Paul Miller. You may have forgotten about the help you gave me, but I haven't.

To Christopher Graham, a true friend and the best business partner ever, and to Mark Bastable, Simon Burnett,

Jon Clinch, Eileen Cruz Coleman, Keith Cronin, Tom Davidson, Susan Henderson, Harry Hunsicker, Jessica Keener, Kelly Mustian, Kristin Nelson, and all of the other fabulous writers at Backspace. It's impossible to list you all here, but know that I appreciate the help and support of each and every one. Everything I know about publishing, I learned from you.

To the marketing, promotion, production, and art departments at Berkley, whose combined talents turned the manuscript into a real book.

To my parents, Dwite and Marian Walker, for instilling in me the conviction that I could do anything I put my mind to.

And to my children, Sarah, Daniel, Carolyn, and Deanna, who grew themselves into such fine adults while I was gone.

We thought, because we had power, we had wisdom.

—STEPHEN VINCENT BENÉT

PART ONE

Access to a secure, safe, and sufficient source of fresh water is a fundamental requirement for survival . . . yet we continue to act as if fresh water were a perpetually abundant resource. It is not.

—KOFI ANNAN,
UNITED NATIONS SECRETARY-GENERAL

Chapter 1

St. John's, Newfoundland

The wind howled around the solitary trawler like an angry god. Inside the wheelhouse, Ben Maki braced his feet as an errant wave hit broadside and the trawler listed heavily to starboard. Sleet spattered the windows on the port side. White patches of sea ice told him they were close. He gripped the back of the first mate's chair and glanced at the captain. In the hurried introductions, Ben hadn't caught the captain's name, and the guy was so intimidating with his overshot brow, deep-set eyes, and unruly salt-and-pepper beard that Ben was afraid to ask him to repeat it. The captain grinned—at least, Ben hoped it was a smile; the expression could have been a grimace as it wrapped around an unlit cigar.

He shifted his feet again when the trawler finally righted herself, thanking God he'd eschewed his oxfords this morning for a pair of Doc Martens. He peered out at the forward deck. Derek MacCallister, the *Arctic Dawn*'s owner and the man Ben had flown 3,400 miles to see, stood at the open prow, nylon jacket flapping furiously in the wind, bare hands gripping the icy rail. Ben shook his head. He'd entrusted his life to a madman. Only a lunatic would leave port in this kind of weather. Dark clouds in the east promised more snow, the St. John's fishing fleet were safely tucked into their berths, and yet here they were, out here all alone, battling waves the size of small mountains with the harbor two hours behind them. Back at the dock, the trawler and her crew looked like something out of *The Perfect Storm*, and now that they were out to sea, the resemblance hadn't diminished. The lawyers who'd flown up with him were probably sitting in a bar or a pub or whatever they called them up here, laughing at Ben's impulsive decision to play iceberg cowboy and sucking back beers while Ben tried not to upchuck and to stay out of everyone's way.

"Where's Derek?" Jack, the first mate, climbed the narrow gangway to the bridge.

The captain jutted his chin toward the ice-glazed window. "Where else?"

"*Out there?* Can't he watch the scope?"

The captain shrugged.

Tyler, a skinny kid they'd hired for the season, joined them from the galley below. His eyes grew wide as the ship rode the crest of another swell and fell with a sickening thump. Ben's stomach plummeted with it. Swallowing hard, he held on more tightly to the chair.

The handle on the wheelhouse door turned, and Derek stepped through. The cabin temperature dropped ten degrees in the time it took to dog down the door behind him with a clang. Derek pulled off his toque and shook the ice crystals out of his hair like Ben's Jack Russell after its bath. His cheeks—what could be seen of them above his curly brown beard—were bright red; each with a white patch in the middle the size of a quarter where the skin was just beginning to freeze.

"It's there! Three hundred yards dead ahead!"

The captain nodded. "I got it on the scope."

"Okay. Start circling around. Jack, you and Tyler get ready to pay out the cable."

"How's she look?" Jack asked.

"Big," the captain answered grimly. "Maybe seventy thousand tons."

Jack's brow puckered. Ben's mirrored his concern. You knew you were in trouble when the first mate looked worried.

"Not to worry," Derek said. "Sure she's big, but we know what we're doing, eh? And snagging a berg this size means we won't have to come out for the rest of the season. You'd like that, wouldn't you, Tyler?" Giving the boy a good-natured shove that sent him sprawling into the opposite wall.

"Aye, sir!" Tyler scrambled to recover the proper seaman's attitude of attention. Derek guffawed, and the boy added a nervous grin.

"All right!" Derek pulled on his toque and turned to his men. "Let's *do* it!"

The captain spun the wheel, and the *Arctic Dawn* swung around, rolling and pitching as she turned sideways to the waves. The crew donned safety harnesses and survival suits, then stepped out of the wheelhouse onto the icy deck.

A hundred yards ahead, the berg towered fifty feet above the ship. "Icebergs calve off the Greenland glaciers," the captain said to Ben as he leaned forward to wipe the condensation off the windows with his shirt sleeve. "Tabular bergs are the most stable, but this far south, we hardly ever see 'em. By the time they get to us, the bergs've eroded into all kinds of shapes. Domed and wedge-shaped are the most unstable. They can roll over in seconds, just by looking at 'em."

Ben studied the craggy, gray mountain looming off the starboard bow. The berg looked stable enough. Was the captain trying to frighten him on purpose?

The captain cut back on the power to let the drift carry them closer. "No way to know what she's like under the water. The *Arctic Dawn* was retrofitted with a three-inch steel-reinforced hull when we changed from fishing trawler to ice hauler, but there's not a ship afloat that could survive that kind of collision."

Hardly reassuring, but Ben didn't figure it was meant to be.

As the craft made its slow circle, the crew paid out the towline: A yellow-and-black polypropylene rope as thick as a man's arm that floated conspicuously atop the rolling sea. The captain kept a watchful eye on his men, cringing when Tyler tripped over a coil of rope and a wave nearly washed him off his feet.

"Boy needs another hundred pounds on him. Skinny ones are too easily swept into the sea."

Another unlucky thought. What happened to the much-vaunted sailors' superstition? Ben's seafaring experience was limited to working weekends as a teenager on his grandpa's Great Lakes fishing boat, but even he knew that a sailor foolish enough to voice misgivings invited disaster.

The captain turned back to the task at hand, chomping on his cigar until forty-five tedious, stomach-churning minutes had passed. Ben sighed his relief when they completed the circle without incident. Jack snagged the towline with a grappling hook while Tyler worked the winch handle and Derek made the junction and added cable. Once the pelican hook snapped into place, Derek gave the signal, and the captain began the long, slow turn that would take them home.

A clear patch of sky opened directly overhead. Instantly the iceberg transformed into a shimmering celestial blue, its faceted surface reflecting the sunlight like a thousand mirrors. Ben shielded his eyes. He had just decided the sun was an omen of success when a flock of seabirds resting on the berg's peak took flight, their raucous calls audible above the wind. The iceberg leaned to the right. It hung undecided for a moment, like the stuck secondhand on a clock, then tilted even more.

The captain flung open the door. "She's going over!"

Out on deck, Jack was already shoving the boy toward the wheelhouse. Ben held the door as the captain regained the helm and pushed the engines for power, desperate to put distance between them and the collapsing berg.

"Where's Derek?" he bellowed when Jack and Tyler burst inside.

"Out there!" Tyler pointed toward the stern. "He's still trying to unhook the cable!"

"Mother of God!" Jack cried. "Back off! Give him slack!"

The captain jammed the engines into reverse. The ship groaned in protest, and Ben's gut wrenched along with it. As long as they were connected to the berg, their fates were irrevocably tied. If it rolled, they were going with it, and the *Arctic Dawn* would be flipped into the air as easily as a child's toy tied to the end of a string.

Jack leaned out the door. "Hurry!" he called to Derek.

"I'm trying!" Derek yelled back. "The hook's jammed!"

He stripped off his gloves to fumble barehanded with the ring release.

The captain's hand twitched on the throttle as the seconds ticked by. At last Derek waved the all clear and they started forward—just as the iceberg split in two with a thunderous crack and roar.

"Inside!" Jack screamed to the deck. *"Now!"*

"There's no time!" Derek wrapped his safety line around the rail, yanked the survival suit hood down over his head, and hugged the rail in a death-grip, bracing for the killer wave they all knew was coming.

Seconds later it crashed over the ship, engulfing them in icy white.

The captain pulled Ben toward the ship's wheel. "Hold on!" Ben barely had time to hook his arms through the spokes before the ship yawed leeward at an impossible angle, leaving his legs dangling in midair. The crew smashed into the opposite wall, map charts and coffee cups raining down on them like confetti.

"The door!" the captain yelled as the ship foundered. "For God's sake, somebody shut the door!"

"I can't reach it!" Jack called back. "It's too high!"

"I can do it! Boost me up!" Tyler scrambled on all fours across the canted floor. Jack linked his hands and lifted the boy to his shoulders, gripping Tyler's ankles with both hands as he fought to keep his own footing.

Tyler strained for the latch. "Move to the *left*! The left! Hurry, *hurry*!"

"I'm gonna fall!" Jack let go with one hand to brace himself against what used to be the floor.

"More, *more*! Okay, I got it!" Tyler pressed his shoulder against the door as water poured in around the edges.

Ben tightened his grip. No way could ninety pounds

win against the sea. Still, the door slammed shut. Jack lowered the boy to the floor. Tyler put his head in his hands. Jack patted his shoulder. "There, there, lad. Give her a minute, and she'll quick put herself ta rights, you'll see."

But the ship rolled even farther. The cabin lights flickered and went out. Ben squinted through the watery half-light, trying to discern if they had passed the point of no return, but with no true vertical reference it was impossible to tell. If his feet were acting as a plumb bob, they were at 45, maybe 50 degrees. The trawler could probably do 60 and still recover—they had plenty of ballast; the insurance company had seen to that—but any more, and—

Suddenly his feet found their purchase. He thanked God and started to stand, but his feet slipped out from under him and he smashed to the floor. He put out a hand to raise himself, then snatched it back as though he'd been burned.

Mother of God. It couldn't be. He extended both hands again, feeling about cautiously as if slow, deliberate movements could somehow change the truth—but no. Instead of the raised-patterned, sheet-metal floor he'd been expecting, the surface beneath his palms was smooth as baby's skin.

He was sitting on the ceiling.

JesusMaryandJoseph they were turtled; the ship's underbelly exposed to the sky; her antennas pointing uselessly toward the pitiless depths below. It was all over now. The *Arctic Dawn* would float upended for a few minutes, maybe five, maybe ten. Then her holds would fill, and the sea would claim five more. He closed his eyes. He supposed he should do something—break out a window to swim for the surface or try to open the door—but if ever a ship and her crew needed help from above, it was now. He tried to call up an appropriate prayer from his childhood, then remembered the supplication to Saint Elmo his grandpa had framed and mounted in his fishing boat.

Almighty God, he prayed, mouthing the words that had been uttered in every church nave and every household and every candlelit vigil since the first sailor had been lost at sea, *you bestowed the singular help of Blessed Peter on those in peril from the sea. By the help of his prayers may the light of your grace—may the light of your grace . . .* damn—how did the rest of it go? "Shine forth"—yes, that was it—*shine forth in all the storms of this life and enable us to find the harbor of everlasting salvation.* He drew a deep breath and began again. *Almighty God, you bestowed the singular help of Blessed Peter on those in peril from the sea. By the help of his prayers—*

"Derek," Jack whispered.

Tyler sobbed.

Ben squeezed his eyes shut tighter. "Almighty God," he prayed aloud, as if the force of his entreaty could effect an answer, "you bestowed the singular help of Blessed Peter on those in peril from the sea. By the help of his prayers—"

"May the light of your grace shine forth in all the storms of this life," the captain joined in.

"—and enable us to find the harbor of everlasting salvation," they finished in unison.

"We ask this through the name of our Lord Jesus Christ," Tyler added, his youthful voice cracked with terror. "Amen."

"Amen."

The men fell silent, listening to the *Arctic Dawn* creak and moan as if she were already mourning her crew. Ben opened his eyes, but this time, instead of praying, he willed the iceberg to shift, to roll, to split again—anything that would generate another wave like the first one—a monstrous, rogue wave that would slap them with all the force the Atlantic could muster and knock them upright again. It could happen. Miracles could happen. Miracles *did* happen . . .

Almighty God, you bestowed the singular help of Blessed Peter—

The ship shuddered. He blinked, then blinked again as a coffee thermos rolled slowly across the floor. It picked up speed, finally clattering into a corner, and Ben clenched his fists. *Yes,* by God. *They were moving.* He grabbed hold of the ship's wheel.

"Hang on!" the captain cried. "We're going up!"

"Hold on *where*?" Tyler asked as he slid across the ceiling and cracked his head against the window. He scrambled to his knees, then fell again. "Is it really true? We're saved?"

The captain didn't answer.

More, more, Ben urged, *a little more . . . come on . . . keep going . . . keep going . . .* It *wasn't* his imagination; the water outside the windows *was* getting lighter . . .

The ship continued to roll, straining for the surface like an Olympic swimmer after a high dive, until at last they burst up from the depths into the middle of a shaft of sunlight so ethereal Ben would have thought he'd died and gone to heaven if his arms weren't so sore.

He extricated himself from the ship's wheel and looked around the cabin in speechless amazement. Tyler was on his knees retching into the corner, but Ben couldn't fault him for that. He didn't feel so well himself.

Most unbelievably of all, when he stood up on trembling legs and crossed the wheelhouse to look out the door, he saw Derek still strapped to the stern, his hair and beard dripping, his clothes freezing stiff as he grinned back like a madman and gave a big, victorious, double thumbs-up.

Chapter 2

The protesters were waiting when they returned.

As the captain eased the trawler past the breakwater and into the harbor, Ben squinted through the sleet to study Derek's daily welcoming committee: a dozen men and women huddled against the wind, singing and chanting with their arms linked, their SAVE THE EARTH banners flapping so hard they could barely hang on to them.

"Idiots." He'd done his share of picketing back in the day, but he was in no mood for a confrontation—particularly one that would put him on the wrong side of the stick.

"You got that right." Derek took another slug of Jack's whiskey and shuddered. It was going to take more than a bottle of Lord Calvert to make him feel warm again. "I suppose I should be glad it's only the POP people picketing me, and not some extremist group like the Environmental Liberation Front. Those guys are seriously whacked."

Ben agreed. Torching Hummer dealerships and ski resorts and shopping malls under construction and whatever else the ELF thought the earth would be better off without was beyond crazy. Destruction in the name of saving the environment—what kind of logic was that? The Preserve Our Planet people were babes by comparison. The worst they'd admitted to was an incident in Arizona where a member poured soda pop down the gas tanks of construction equipment. The ELF was listed at the top in the United States as a domestic terrorism threat, but the POP people didn't even register. That, along with the cardboard pop-gun cutouts they carried as a symbol of their acronym, made the group seem almost silly.

"Still don't figure why they're targeting me," Derek said. "Compared to outfits like Evian and Perrier, I'm a drop in the bucket. Even my six-year-old understands that turning icebergs into drinking water does no more harm to the environment than plucking a fish out of the sea."

He polished off the last of the whiskey in one long pull and stuffed the empty in his rucksack. As the others made the trawler fast, Derek hung back. Ben couldn't blame him. The rest were riding their adrenaline rush, but Derek had used up all of his surviving. Ben still couldn't believe he'd made it. Riding out a three-sixty wasn't without precedent—coastguardsmen routinely rolled their cutters intentionally during rescue practice—but most men did it *inside* the wheelhouse, and not outside tied to the rail.

Ben flexed his shoulders. Everything hurt. His arms felt like they'd been ripped from their sockets and stuck back on again backward, and cold—what he wouldn't give for one of the protester's down anoraks. Give him a striped cashmere scarf to go with it, and a pair of color-coordinated Thinsulate gloves, and don't forget the mukluks, like the sheepskin pair that tall, blond woman was wearing. He snorted. Mukluks. Where did she think she was, Antarctica?

"*Arctic Dawn* is the tip of the iceberg!" the woman shouted. She jogged her sign in the air. "Pre-serve—our—plan-et! Pre-serve—our—plan-et!" The others joined in, clapping and stomping out the rhythm.

"They've got a new sign." Tyler pointed to a poster featuring the cartoon cub from Derek's bottled water label, only in this version, the little fellow wasn't smiling; he was on his back with his feet trussed and his tongue lolling with a fishing spear protruding from his side.

Derek blew out his cheeks. "Don't react. Don't respond, no matter what they do." He picked up his rucksack, wincing at the weight of it, and led his entourage toward the gauntlet.

Halfway down the dock, a bottle flew past their heads. Derek stopped short and ducked, even though by then the bottle had gone wide and plopped into the sea. He dropped his rucksack and lifted his fists, but instead of shrinking back, the protesters began to laugh. Ben looked to where they were pointing and saw that Derek's rucksack had fallen open, and the empty whiskey bottle had rolled out onto the ground.

Derek's cheeks flamed. As Ben stooped to retrieve the bottle, he noticed a hand holding another pop bottle inches from his nose. Slender fingers curled around the neck; foam oozed from beneath a polished thumbnail. The fingers flexed, and the hand gave the bottle a shake.

He looked up. It was Mukluk Woman. He straightened, and for the first time in his life, he wanted to hit a woman. The feeling shamed him, but his anger was greater and he let it boil. Who did she think she was, coming here to harass Derek? This was his town, his dock, *his life*. He'd just survived the worst experience imaginable, and this woman thought she could intimidate him into quitting by threatening to spray him with soda pop? Ben glared at her, daring her to do it, but something of what he was feeling must have shown in his face because she looked away and let her hand fall, spilling the soda on the ground.

The others took her cue, and Derek and his men walked unmolested the rest of the way to the parking lot. Ben trailed Derek to his pickup.

"Where's your car?" Derek asked as he tossed his bag in back.

"At your house."

Derek gave him a long look. "Get in," he said at last.

Ben climbed into the passenger seat. Derek started the engine and dialed the defroster to high. As soon as a fist-sized area on the windshield cleared, he put the truck into gear and headed inland toward the bluff.

When the heat kicked in, Ben leaned forward to direct the vents toward his face. The movement triggered a twinge in his side. It wasn't a pain exactly; more like a stitch, but it was still enough to make him suck in his breath. He wondered if he shouldn't have asked Derek to swing by a clinic first. His arms and legs seemed to be working just fine, but after the beating he'd taken, you never knew what might be going on inside.

For that matter, they were all pretty well banged up. The knot on Tyler's forehead promised one if not two black eyes, Jack's hands and face looked like they'd been worked over by a pair of Mafia goons, and the captain sported a limp worthy of a Caribbean pirate. Ben closed his eyes, listening to the sleet hit the windshield and the slap of the wipers, marking their progress by the engine sounds as Derek negotiated the switchbacks that led to the top of the bluff. The *Arctic Dawn*'s survival was going to become the stuff of legend, but at the moment, all this particular legend wanted was to go to sleep.

He opened his eyes when they turned off the highway onto a rutted two-track.

"You're wasting your time," Derek said.

Ben sat up. "Maybe, maybe not. You don't know what we're offering."

"Doesn't matter. The Antarctica plans aren't for sale. You know that."

"Everything's got a price."

"I didn't spend ten grand to patent the process just so's I could give it away. The bottled water business is just a lead-in, a trial run. The Antarctica plans are the real deal."

Ben let the statement stand. He wasn't worried. Derek's house was mortgaged to the hilt, and tomorrow, his notes were due.

Derek turned in alongside a picket fence enclosing a turquoise clapboard house and parked next to Ben's dark blue rented Lincoln. As he reached for the door handle, Ben stopped him with a hand on his arm.

"Five minutes. Just listen to what we have to say." He nodded toward the house. "What've you got to lose?"

Derek's wife Aimee met them at the door. She looked tired, and the crusted baby spit-up on her flannel shirt and the smears of what Ben hoped was chocolate on her jeans told him she probably hadn't had the best of days, either. Derek Junior stood behind her, sucking noisily on his thumb as he clutched a wad of his mother's shirttail and stared at the two strangers sitting on the sofa.

Derek gave her a cold kiss.

"You're wet." She reached up to touch his hair and relieved him of his rucksack. "Your bag's wet, too."

"Rough day." He took off his coat and hung it on a peg.

"Papa!" Derek's six-year-old came running. She wrapped her arms around his waist. "I missed you!"

"Ooof—not so hard." He ruffled her hair. "I missed you, too."

"That didn't hurt!" she laughed and squeezed him again.

Derek's wife pried their daughter loose and steered her toward the kitchen. "Go finish your supper," she told the girl. "Papa and I will be along in a minute. Derek—" she nodded toward the lawyers who had stood up when Ben and Derek came into the room "—these men want to talk to you."

"Is that so." He sat down on the chair beside the door and pulled off his boots, frowning as he methodically examined his toes.

Ben knew enough about frostbite to realize that three white toes on Derek's right foot and two on his left wasn't good. Still, considering what Derek had almost lost today, Ben supposed forfeiting a toe was relatively insignificant.

Derek eased on his slippers and got to his feet. "What's for supper?"

"What's— We're having steamed cod."

"Potatoes?"

"Mashed. Derek, these men are from—"

He held up his hand. "I know where they're from, Aimee, and I know why they're here. But right now I'm just a wee bit tired and a whole lot hungry. They can wait." He plucked the baby from his pen and carried him into the kitchen.

So much for the bond of shared experience. Ben found a

seat in the living room. Judging by the empty coffee cups bracketing the sofa and the deep depressions in the cushions, waiting was what the lawyers had been doing for most of the afternoon. He selected an orange plaid recliner with a view of the kitchen.

"You can't just ignore them," Aimee was saying in a low voice as Derek settled the baby in his high chair. She passed him the plate of fish. "They came all the way from California. They flew here on a private jet."

"And did I ask them to come?"

No answer.

"All right then." He forked another mouthful of fish.

There was a cardboard box beside the sofa with a pair of boards over the top so it could double as an end table. One of the lawyers was drumming his fingers on it as he waited. Ben wondered if Derek's Antarctica plans were inside. He didn't see any other evidence of an office or a desk.

The concept was pure genius, born from a small feature item in the newspaper. Last year when Derek called Soldyne to consult, he told Ben that as soon as he read about the 1,250-square-mile, 650-foot-high section of the Larson Ice Shelf that had broken off the previous November, inspiration struck. While the average iceberg floating past the Grand Banks was about the size of a fifteen-story building, the Antarctic berg the scientists had named Larson B contained an incredible 700 *billion* gallons of pure, fresh drinking water—enough to supply the water needs of 4.6 million families *for an entire year*.

Environmentalists saw the breakup of the Antarctic ice shelves as evidence of global warming, but Derek saw dollar signs. He dreamed of a freshwater factory set up on the iceberg itself. Forget the dangerous towing; there were twenty-four beautiful hours of daylight during the long Antarctic summer—plenty of available solar power to melt the ice into drinking water. The trick was to focus all that energy somehow—geostationary satellites and micro-waves and mirrors eventually became the backbone of his process—and melt a lake in the middle of the berg. Pump the water into waiting tankers, send it out to thirsty cities, and make a fortune.

As soon as he heard about Derek's microwave concept, Ben had to have it. Every day, 1.1 billion people in under-developed areas around the world had no choice but to consume contaminated water. Every year, between 40 and 60 million of them died—5 million children under the age of five. Derek's project embodied a happy conflux of two disparate concepts that was so rare, Ben couldn't think of a single other instance in which a commercial venture had the potential to make money *and* benefit humans and the environment.

Unfortunately, thanks to Patent #4,686,605, "Method and Apparatus for Melting Antarctic Icebergs into Drink-ing Water," the concept was wholly Derek's. Ben looked at the MacCallister family gathered around their kitchen ta-ble, at the worn Formica countertop, the doorless cup-boards, the woodstove in the corner, the stained plywood floor. If Derek had any sense, he'd take Soldyne's buyout and use the money to keep his bottled water business afloat—though considering the day's near-disaster, he'd probably be better off cashing the check and moving the family to the Bahamas.

At last Derek pushed back his chair and strode into the living room. Ben and the lawyers scrambled stiffly to their feet.

"Good evening, Mr. MacCallister," the taller one said

as if Derek had only just now arrived. "I'm Trevor Johnston, and this is my associate, James Everett. You already know Ben. We represent the Soldyne Corporation."

Derek shook the two proffered hands, pulled up a chair, and motioned them to sit.

"No doubt you're tired after a hard day on the water," Johnston went on, "so I'll get right to the point. We're here because we've heard great things about your water business. *Great things*. It's not every man who can come up with a business as unique as yours and turn a profit. And your process for melting Antarctic bergs is absolutely inspired. But we're not the only ones who think so. Soldyne's engineers, and more important, our investors, are eager to be a part of this, too. That's why they've authorized us to offer you a buyout. Right here, right now."

Everett opened his briefcase and handed Derek a folded cashier's check.

Derek opened it, read the amount, and whistled. Ben tried not to grin as Derek gaped at the men waiting for his answer, and again at the check.

"One point two million dollars?" he finally said, and Aimee's face blanched. "This isn't a joke?"

"It's no joke," Ben said. "We want that process. Our accountants have determined this is a fair price. What do you say? Do we have a deal?"

Derek didn't answer. Maybe he was praying—maybe he was reciting the alphabet backward or the names of the provinces or counting slowly to ten—anything to keep from saying yes too quickly.

At last he refolded the check, tucked it into Everett's breast pocket, and sat back with his arms over his chest.

"Two million."

Aimee gasped.

Derek sent her a look.

Ben's expression didn't falter. Everett returned the check to his briefcase and replaced it with another. As Derek verified the preprinted amount, he looked dismayed. Probably wondering what would have happened if he'd said three.

They exchanged the check for the box and shook hands all around with a promise to meet Derek at his lawyer's in the morning. As Ben shut the door, the MacCallisters' voices carried clearly through the single-pane window.

"Now what will I use for a table?" Aimee asked as she looked at the empty spot next to the sofa.

"Sweetheart, I'll *buy* you a table!" Derek crowed as he danced her around the room.

Chapter 3

Ben leaned back in his office chair and laced his fingers behind his head. Every square inch of his desk was covered with printouts: geodetic data, syntax tables, temperature gradient graphs, stress differential scatter plots, line plots, elevations—an impressive disarray that amounted to nothing but another nail in his career coffin. When Adam called to say that another batch of ICESat scans had finally come in, Ben had known right away that the results weren't going to be good. He took a deep breath. Devising a plan of action that would allow him to keep his job without having to sell his firstborn or make some similar pact with the devil was going to take all the extra oxygenated thinking power he could get.

"Okay," he said as he eyed the latest addition to the mound. "What've we got?"

Adam Washburn, a crew-cut blond ten years Ben's junior, leaned forward to rescue a stack of transparencies threatening to spill off the desktop and handed the summary page to his boss. He dismissed the question with a wave. "Same as yesterday, and the day before that, and the day before that. Nada. Zip, zilch, zero. Nothing's moving."

"What about this?" Ben traced a thin blue diagonal line across one page.

"Nope." Adam overlaid a handful of transparencies on top of the graph he'd charted from the latest ICESat composite. "Look here. You see? The scans are identical, every blessed one, and yet look at the dates. October 7 . . . November 23 . . . December 29 . . . all the way up to today. Three freaking months with no change."

"All right." Ben took off his glasses and dragged a hand over his head. The information on his desk was stolen, though he preferred not to think of it that way. The scans came from the National Snow and Ice Data Center, and as a nonscientific interest, Soldyne had no right to this information. Ben didn't know how Adam had arranged to get his hands on the printouts; all Adam had told him was that he'd struck a deal with a scientist working out of Antarctica's Raney Station. Ben presumed the debt must have been considerable for a scientist to assume the risk, but he wasn't about to press for details, and Adam didn't offer. Besides, it wasn't as though Soldyne was misusing the reports. They were only monitoring the ice shelves, exactly as the scientists were doing, and short of sending up their own observation satellite, this was the most practical way to go about it.

"You're right," he conceded. "There's no change."

"Of course there isn't." Adam practically spat out the words. "I just wish I knew what's going on. Scientists have been predicting the collapse of the ice shelves for decades: 'The ice caps are melting; sea levels will rise; Florida will disappear.' Yet now that we actually *want* a piece to break off—nothing. I feel like we're the butt of some great cosmic joke."

"Then how come I'm not laughing?" Ben stuffed the summary page into his briefcase, snapped the case shut, and crossed the room, then stopped at the door. "You know," he remarked over his shoulder, "there's only one thing worse than having no iceberg."

"Oh yeah? What's that?"

"Having to break the news to Gillette."

Donald Gillette was a big man. At six-feet-four he towered over Ben, forcing Ben to tip his head back to look up at his boss whenever they were standing together as though Ben were a child. Everything about the man was large. Gillette's '77 Eldorado had been restored at an appropriately exorbitant cost; his neighbors in the San Bernardino foothills pointed to his sixteen-thousand-square-foot mansion with jaw-dropping awe; even the Hermès watch encompassing his left wrist was as big as a silver dollar. The pair of Pollocks on the opposite wall were each easily ten-by-ten, and the floor-to-ceiling windows behind a desk the size of a Ping-Pong table framed a view of Los Angeles expansive enough for a man who conducted his business on a cosmic scale.

"No change?" he repeated after Ben broke the news.

"No change," Ben parroted from the other side of the desk. Unlike the rest of the furnishings, his chair was of normal size, perhaps even shorter than regular seat height; a trick of perspective Ben was convinced was designed to make even the most esteemed visitor feel inferior to the office's owner. Not that the ploy was necessary in his case. The only time he'd come out ahead of his boss during the six years they'd been working together was when the executive board had selected his microwave method over Donald's H.A.A.R.P. technology. But after three years of R&D and enough dollars to have fed several African nations several times over, even that victory had turned hollow. As long as they continued without an iceberg, there was no way to put the board's decision to the test.

"You promised come November we'd see something big break off." Gillette turned his desk calendar around to face Ben and pointed to the condemnatory "Jan. 6." "I believe we've gone just a bit beyond that."

Ben gripped the arms of his diminutive chair and forced his heart rate to slow. Was he expected to conjure up an iceberg like pulling a rabbit out of a hat? They were working with forces of nature; climate change and global warming—not fluffy pigeons or furry rodents.

"Something could break loose any day," he heard himself saying, mouthing words even he had long since given up believing. "Last month we flew a helicopter over the Larson and dropped a man down. Fournier is a climber and an Antarctic expert. He said he'd never seen so many cracks in the surface of an ice shelf. And he was surprised at the number of lakes. Some of them are bigger than a football field. He predicts the whole thing will collapse within two years."

"Two years is a little long to wait." Gillette flicked a finger at the report. "How good is your data?"

"It's solid. Straight off the ICESat feed."

Gillette leaned back in his chair. "The investors are getting anxious," he said, rocking slowly to give his words weight, "and frankly, I don't blame them. They want results. All you've given them to date is a list of expenditures."

Ben didn't answer. Once they started making water, the months of waiting would be forgotten and the investors would go to bed with dollar signs in their eyes. He thought about the Canadian, Derek MacCallister. For a while he'd felt bad about the way he'd taken the guy's idea and run with it, but considering everything Soldyne had invested to date, there was no way MacCallister could have put it into practice. At any rate, he'd cashed Soldyne's check readily enough. Ben hadn't heard from him since last Christmas, when the card he'd sent came back with no forwarding address. Maybe he really did move his family to the Bahamas.

Abruptly, Gillette stopped rocking. "The board's made a decision. This isn't for general knowledge, but I wanted you to know. We've decided who's going to get first water." He gestured magnanimously toward the windows. "It's us, Ben. L.A. Sixteen million Californians are draining the Colorado dry. As soon as they heard about our Antarctic project, the Metro Water District was more than happy to sign up for ours. Forty-seven trillion gallons to be delivered to the city's system as soon as we can make them, with a standing order for more."

"Wonderful." It was the expected answer, but Ben realized he actually meant it. He'd been hoping the first recipient would be a needy Third World country, but California was undergoing its worst drought in decades, and it would be great to have plenty of water again. Naturally the water had to go to the highest bidder. Soldyne wasn't a nonprofit or a charitable trust, they were a business, and right now, they were in the business of making water.

Or rather, they were supposed to be.

Chapter 4

That evening, Ben ran the hose over the pocket-sized lawn of his three-bedroom ranch in a thin stream, training the trickle back and forth, back and forth, a human lawn sprinkler, holding the nozzle as close to the blades as possible to minimize evaporation. The diminishing sun turned his skin as golden as a Buddha's, suffusing the brick houses and asphalt driveways with a warm yellow glow. A hot breeze ruffled his hair, bringing the distant odor of smoke from the fires in the Santa Ana Mountains.

His neighbors had given up on grass years ago, opting for Zen-like yards of black lava rock or raked brown gravel, artfully accented with boulders and saguaro. Ben could never get used to them. A house wasn't a home without a real lawn, he insisted, though in truth *he* needed the green, just as he needed the slice of Pacific blue barely visible between the houses across the street.

Behind him, the screen door banged. Ben turned off the water as Paula crossed the lawn carrying two glasses of iced tea. She handed one to him and linked her arm through his.

"Smell the fires?" he asked.

"Uh-huh. How close do you think they'll get?"

"It's going to be a while before they put them out, but they're not supposed to come this way. Is supper ready?"

"Just about."

"Where's Sarah?"

"She's at Cassandra's. They're supposed to be studying, but they probably snuck off to the mall."

"I thought we agreed to eat as a family."

"I know; I'm sorry. It's just that she makes such a scene when she doesn't get her way."

"I'll talk to her."

"Anyway," Paula laid her head on his shoulder. "Is it really so bad, us eating alone?"

Half an hour later the front door slammed, followed by the rustle of shopping bags and the scurry of footsteps down the hall. Ben stabbed another meatball. Apparently the threat of a 50 percent cut in her allowance wasn't sufficient motivation for his daughter to deign to join them promptly at the table. What was next? Withhold her allowance entirely? Take away her computer? Lock her in her room until she was eighteen? He sighed. Someone should have warned him when he became a father that the job included the role of Gestapo.

When Sarah finally padded barefoot into the dining room, she slid into her chair and helped herself to a serving of spaghetti without looking at him. Her cheeks were flushed, but whether it was due to remorse or a session at the makeup counter was hard to say. Ben watched her wind noodles onto her fork as if nothing could possibly interest her more and wondered if there was anyone more willful than a thirteen-year-old.

For ten minutes the clink of silverware against china was the only sound. From across the table, Paula sent him a *do something* look.

"How was school today?" he asked brightly. Paula rolled her eyes, but to their surprise, Sarah answered.

"It was cool. We got a new assignment from Mr. Mc-Murtry's brother-in-law, you know, the scientist down in Antarctica." She took a folded piece of paper from her back pocket and smoothed it open on the table. "'Scientists say that within fifty years, Saudi Arabia's groundwater will dry up,'" she read. "'Some people have suggested that Antarctic icebergs could be towed to the Middle East to relieve the problem. Is this crazy? What do you think? How would you get an iceberg to the Middle East? Think about it, and then try this: Take some ice cubes and float them in a tub of warm water to see how fast they melt, then see if you can figure out a way to protect your iceberg as it gets closer to the equator.'" She grinned. "Isn't that awesome? Cassie and I already tried it, and wow, the ice cubes melted fast. We can send him questions too, and he answers them. This one's mine." She turned the paper over and handed it to her father.

"'Dear Iceman,'" he read, and looked up. "He calls himself 'The Iceman'?"

"Yeah. Isn't that just so totally cool?" Sarah hugged herself and sighed.

"Totally." Ben smiled, then continued: "'I've been thinking about what Mr. McMurtry told us, about how every year the ice gets a little thicker at the poles. So what I'm wondering is could it get so thick that the earth starts wobbling and gets knocked out of orbit? Is this crazy? What do you think? Your friend, Sarah.'" He refolded the paper and handed it back. "That's a good question."

"I hope he answers tomorrow. He sent Cassie a e-mail today. He signed it 'love.'" She blushed fiercely and looked down at her plate.

So *that* was how it was. Ben sagged. His work centered on the Antarctic, and Sarah had never shown the slightest interest in it, but let her get a few e-mails from some scientist who just happened to be working there and she was mooning over him as though he were a rock star.

The Iceman. What kind of reputable scientist would call himself *that*?

Chapter 5

Raney Station, Antarctic Peninsula

A strip of sunlight leaking from the edge of the aluminum foil–covered window spilled across Zo Zelinski's face. It was enough to wake her, which was no surprise considering that was the reason she'd torn away the corner in the first place. She slid out from her husband's embrace and dressed quickly, layering two pairs of wool socks, blue jeans, a flannel shirt, and a wool sweater over the long underwear she wore as pajamas. Mukluks in hand, she stepped into the hallway, pausing to listen to Elliot's steady breathing before closing the plywood door.

In the kitchen, she sat down on one of the long benches flanking the picnic-style table and pulled on her boots. She zipped up her parka, tucked a bottle of water and a handful of saltines into one pocket, and went outside. The cold, dry air froze the moisture on the hairs inside her nose. She sneezed.

To the east, a crayon box's worth of red and orange streaked across the sky, rimming the pressure ridges along the shore with neon pink. The katabatic winds sweeping down off the glacier were fierce. Shielding her face with one arm, she tucked the other mittened hand into her pocket and hurried away from the station.

Every time she trekked toward the glacier, Zo had the same thought: that in a continent as vast and as empty as Antarctica, it was ironic she had to go to such lengths to be alone. But with twenty-five researchers and support staff packed into two undersized sheet-metal buildings like proverbial sardines, she didn't exactly have options. It was only because they were married that she and Elliot rated a private room. The rest lived dormitory-style in six small bedrooms, sharing a minuscule kitchen and rec room crammed without thought or design among the labs and support systems equipment. At Raney, science was paramount, living quarters an afterthought, and no one ever questioned the arrangement.

Her stomach twisted, and she broke into a run. There was a small ice cave at the base of the glacier; a bathroom-sized cavern with cerulean walls and a torrent of meltwater running down the middle that was perfect for her needs: far enough away that she couldn't be seen, yet close enough to run to in a hurry if the need arose.

Today, she almost didn't make it. Reaching the entrance, she ducked inside, tossed back her parka hood, tore off one mitten, held her long blond hair out of the way, and vomited.

Finished, she wiped her mouth on her coat sleeve and sat down on a flat rock overlooking the bay. Far out on the ice, a pair of elephant seals snorted. A flock of Adelies answered, sounding like braying donkeys. She nibbled a cracker and looked back at the station to where Elliot was presumably still sleeping and kicked at the gravel, sending a shower of scree skyward. To say life wasn't fair didn't begin to cover it. After two years of filling out enough paperwork to have been responsible for the destruction of the entire Costa Rican rain forest, no sooner had she managed to snag a grant with enough funding to allow her to spend the next three Antarctic summers in the field *with* her husband instead of ten thousand miles apart, and her birth control defaults the first week.

Her stomach roiled. She swallowed, then swallowed again. Clapping a hand over her mouth, she dashed back into the cave.

"So it's you."

She coughed to disguise the sound of her gagging and whirled around. The speaker was backlit by the sun, but she knew who it was by his height and by the way he'd said "you"; a lilting, sing songy cadence that managed to pack enough disdain into a single syllable to do a lesser person's self-esteem serious damage. She pushed past him, positioning herself in front of the entrance, and forced a smile.

"Hey, Ross. You're up early."

"I was about to say the same of you."

She pointed skyward. "Hard to sleep when the lights are on twenty-four/seven."

He laughed. "Don't worry; after a few seasons, you get used to it. What are you doing back so soon? Forget something?"

As if. She'd done a great job of setting up her research camp on the other side of the peninsula. She had an old whaling hut for shelter, a kerosene heater for comfort, and enough cases of food and bottled water to last two seasons if necessary. The bottled water part of her shopping list bothered her; she hated to give even a penny of support to the water-sucking megacorporations, but melting snow like they did at Raney for their water needs was too time-consuming a chore for just one person. Because she'd elected to spend her time in the field rather than tending a cookstove, she was stuck with the compromise in the same way every environmentalist was who flushed a toilet or drove a car.

"Elliot radioed that another tour ship was on the way, so I came back to help." Let him make of that what he wanted. Everyone else seemed to think because she was married to the station director, she sublimated her research to his needs; why shouldn't he? At any rate, she wasn't about to tell him the real reason: She needed to send out another batch of ICESat scans asap, and the tour ship afforded the perfect excuse to make an extra trip back to the station. Technically, the scans were for scientific purposes only, but in view of the large amount of good her one small disobedience would accomplish, she didn't see the harm in sharing. A person had to be willing to act on what they believed, and as far as clandestine operations went, hers was definitely low risk: Cull the information, compress it into a zip file, e-mail it to L.A., and delete the record of the transaction from the computer logs. There were plenty of reasons why Soldyne's iceberg water project needed to succeed—not the least of which was that the alternative was unthinkable.

"So you don't mind the station's being overrun by tourists."

"Not at all," she said. "I know some people think the Antarctic should be set aside as a scientific preserve, but I believe tourism is a good thing. When people can see for themselves how special the continent is, it gives us a chance to sell them on the idea of preserving it."

He held up his hand. "You can spare me the lecture; I'm with you on this one. The planet can't save itself, and Mother Earth needs all the help she can get."

"Is that why you set up your Internet classroom? To educate kids about Antarctic issues?"

"How'd you hear about that? I only started last week."

"It's no big mystery; it's all in the e-mail logs. Don't get me wrong, I think an electronic classroom is a great idea; I'm just surprised Elliot agreed to give you satellite time." Communication had improved dramatically over the old days thanks to e-mail and satellite phones but because of the low satellite angle, transmissions were limited to two four-hour periods a day, with reception sporadic at best.

"I usually get what I want." He paused. "And right now, I want to know when you're going to tell Elliot."

So he *had* heard her. Of all the people to figure it out, it would have to be him. "Tell him what?" she asked on the off chance that she was wrong.

"That you're pregnant."

"I'm not. I mean, I— Oh, geez. Okay, so I'm pregnant. How'd you know?"

"I knew someone was." He pointed to the station, then to the ice cave. "Doesn't exactly take an Indian to follow the highway you made to Puke's Peak. Next time you might take a few minutes to cover your trail." He clucked his tongue. "So you're pregnant, and you're keeping it a secret. Brilliant."

"It's no big deal. Women get pregnant every day."

"Not in Antarctica they don't. Not diabetic women."

"Are you the expert on everything? What can you possibly know about diabetes and pregnancy?"

"I know that a woman with diabetes is more likely to miscarry; that the baby's likely to be born overly large or with a serious defect; that other complications such as still-birth and jaundice are possible. There's a high incidence of diabetes among Native Americans," he explained in answer to her raised eyebrow. "My sister has it. She also has three kids. Please tell me you've told Rodriguez."

Dr. Luis Rodriguez comprised Raney's entire medical staff. Like everyone else who'd elected to live and work at the bottom of the earth, he was of above-average intelligence, self-sacrificing, and, most important, good at improvising in a pinch. Zo had considered confiding in him more than once, but the only sure way to keep a secret was to keep it to yourself, so she'd settled for a consultation with his medical books instead. Thanks to *Harrison's Principles of Internal Medicine* she knew how to manage the early weeks of her pregnancy; she also knew that Ross had dredged up the worst-case scenarios to make his point. The complications he was so worried about were all end-stage events; she'd only be four months along when the season was over; plenty of time to seek medical attention then.

She shook her head.

"Are you *crazy*? You're going to have a baby. How long do you think you can keep *that* a secret?"

"As long as I have to. And just in case you're thinking of taking the law into your own hands, you should remember I'm not the only one with a secret."

"I have no idea what you're talking about."

"Maybe this'll help: P. O. P."

"P-O-P?"

"Exactly. What do you think would happen if people found out you were a member? Greenpeace, the Sierra Club, World Wildlife, sure, but *Preserve Our Planet*? No one in the scientific community would take you seriously if they knew. There's a big difference between being an activist and being a terrorist." Which was exactly the reason she'd quit the organization three years ago, after Rebecca Sweet took over and the group turned radical. That protest up in Newfoundland where she'd almost sprayed that guy with soda pop—what had she been thinking? He was just trying to make a living—probably had a wife and family. It wasn't his fault the megacorporations were bleeding the planet dry, and it wasn't fair or even reasonable of POP to target him. Now POP had graduated to firebombing SUVs and blowing up construction sites, but that wasn't Zo's style. She supposed that was the legacy of having been born the change-of-life baby of aging hippies: The tenets of nonviolent protest had been bred into her genes.

"What in the world makes you think I belong to POP?" Ross's bemused expression and open palms were innocence personified.

Oh, he was good. Zo might even have bought his O. J. act if she hadn't seen the evidence for herself.

"If you don't want people to know you're chatting with ecoterrorists," she said, adopting his trademark condescending tone. "You might take a few minutes to erase your e-mail trail."

Chapter 6

For the fourth time in as many hours, Zo shoved the Häg-glunds tracked ATV into park, opened the door, and jumped to the ground. The moment her feet touched down, she bent double, retching her peanut butter and jelly sandwich onto the snow. Straightening, she wiped her mouth on her jacket sleeve and leaned against the vehicle's track to catch her breath. Then another cramp seized her, and she bent forward again.

Once her stomach was empty, she climbed back into the driver's seat, still hungry, still nauseated, and leaned her head against the steering wheel, thinking how ridiculous it was that something as normal as pregnancy should make a woman so sick. At least now that she was on the road, she could throw up wherever and whenever she liked. During the past few days at the station, she'd choked down so much bile she felt as though her stomach had gone permanently sour. Add to that the stress of having to keep her pregnancy secret, and it was no wonder her gut was a wreck. Ross seemed to have accepted the terms of her blackmail and was keeping his mouth shut, and hiding her condition from the others under the bulky sweaters everyone wore was a no-brainer, but keeping it from the man who expected her to climb naked into his bed was another matter. There were two kinds of lies: sins of omission and blatant, overt untruths, and faking her period to avoid having sex with her husband definitely had her guilty of the latter.

She eyed the remaining half of her sandwich; then looked down at the brown-and-purple Rorschach blot in the snow and sealed the sandwich in a Ziploc bag—force of habit, since the Antarctic climate was so dry, an open bag of chips stayed fresh for months. Shifting the Hägglunds into gear, she started forward with one eye on the flag line and the other on the GPS, the mountains on either side rising up out of the snow like miniature Himalayas. She hummed the theme to *Star Wars* as she drove, tapping *dum, dum, da-da-da DUM dum* on the steering wheel and wondering if when Lucas created Hoth, he'd had Antarctica in mind. The peninsula was definitely inspiring: a geographic extension of the Andes, just fifty miles wide, rugged and desolate, with nameless, majestic peaks rising to five thousand feet under a china blue sky.

A pterodactyl-shaped shadow passed over the ground. Zo traced it back to an albatross flying overhead. Seabirds never came very far inland, which meant she was close. She was tempted to roll down the window to sample the salt-smell in the air, but the exterior readout of minus two degrees Fahrenheit and the frequent spindrifts of snow counseled otherwise. She reached down to pick up her thermos of hot chocolate instead—correction: "lukewarm chocolate," since even the best Stanley steel couldn't compete with Antarctic cold—and poured half a cup, sipping it slowly to give her recalcitrant stomach time to acquiesce. When she finished, she licked the cup dry and screwed it back onto the thermos using both hands, steering the Hägglunds expertly with one knee.

After half an hour of jostling and bumping during which she somehow managed to keep the hot chocolate down, she arrived at the Larson. In front of her, the glacier pooled between two rocky promontories like melted ice cream, spilling carelessly out onto the ocean where at some point it ceased being a glacier and became the Larson Ice Shelf. Viewed from a distance, the surface was deceptively smooth, but ice shelves floated up and down with the tides, grating against the rocks and opening up cracks and fissures capable of swallowing an entire fleet of Hägglunds. Icebergs the size of apartment buildings regularly broke off from the leading edge in a process that was as natural as the seasons. It was only in recent years that chunks as big as small countries had begun falling into the sea. Laymen pointed their confident fingers at global warming as the cause, but lacking definitive empirical evidence, scientists were divided. Zo's physical survey was intended to add to their body of knowledge; unfortunately, one season's data wasn't going to amount to much of a contribution.

As she drove out onto the glacier, she followed her previous tracks closely, fully aware of the sacrilege she was committing by scarring the face of the object she'd come to study. For all its harshness, Antarctica's was a delicate ecosystem where change came slowly and even a footprint lasted for decades. The whalers' hut she'd commandeered for her research base was a case in point. The first time she entered was like opening a time capsule. A cast-iron skillet lay on the stove exactly where it had been left a hundred years before; wooden boxes held candles; fur sleeping bags covered the bunks; stoppered glass medicine bottles containing the previous century's latest high-tech remedies lined a high shelf. Faded photographs of King Edward VII and Queen Alexandra presided over a cache of food tins with appetizing labels like "Lunch Tongue" and "Pea Powder." The exterior boards were so wind-scoured, the nail heads that had once been pounded flush stuck out half an inch, but the walls were sound. Quaint as it was, the National Science Foundation assured her the hut had no particular historical significance, and she was free to make any changes she wished. Mac, her best friend at the station and the one who had mapped out the flag line for her, had suggested swaddling the whole thing in plastic to up its R-rating, but Zo preferred the natural look, even if it was a little drafty.

To her left she saw movement, the usual welcoming committee of dark shapes scurrying low to the ground. She tapped the horn in greeting and congratulated herself for not shuddering. The rats weren't the only ones capable of adapting.

When she'd first realized she was sharing her summer home with creatures other than penguins and elephant seals, she'd been appalled to think that once again man's introduction of nonnative species had ruined what was supposed to be a pristine part of the planet. The rats had to have come off the whaling ships, surviving and flourishing by learning to hunt as a pack. Zo postulated they did their hunting at the ice shelf's leading edge, and while she had no direct evidence to back up her theory, an Internet search supported her conclusion: brown rats *had* been known to develop pack behavior under extreme circumstances, particularly when they were descended from a single pair. She had no idea how many infested the continent, but suspected the numbers weren't high; while rats were prolific breeders, conditions weren't exactly conducive to multiplication.

The rats paced her as she drove, running faster when she sped up, slowing down when she did the same in a cross-species game of follow-the-leader she had actually begun to look forward to. Rats were highly intelligent—it was one of the reasons they were such successful survivors—and lacking more ordinary amusements, Zo got a kick out of playing animal trainer.

Eventually the rats disappeared behind an ice hummock and she turned her attention back to her driving. Off in the distance she could see open water and the speck that was her hut on the pebbled shore. The hut seemed to shimmer against the horizon. She blinked, thinking it was a trick of the distance and the low angle of light, but the effect continued. She checked her watch. No wonder she couldn't see straight—all those extra unscheduled vomit stops had stretched the five-hour trip out to seven. She massaged her neck, then rolled down the window, preferring the possibility of frostbite over the certainty of falling asleep at the wheel.

Above the Hägglunds's usual metallic clatter came a low rumbling reminiscent of faraway thunder, or a highway busy with trucks. She cocked an ear, hoping the noise wasn't coming from the engine. Sam, the maintenance guy, was a fanatic about keeping the vehicles in shape, but the cold was a difficult enemy, and something was always breaking down. The way things had been going for her lately, it would be just her luck for the Hägglunds to quit when she was as far from the station as possible.

The rumbling grew louder, accompanied now by regular, concussive thumps. The vibrations thrummed through the floorboards, making her thermos jump up and down as though it were possessed. She shut off the engine. The Hag clanked to a stop, but the thumping continued. She climbed out onto the track and cupped a hand to her ear, rotating slowly to pinpoint the source, but could see nothing out of the ordinary.

As she reached for her binoculars, there was a sharp *crack* and a huge crevasse opened directly alongside her. The Hägglunds slewed sideways. Zo scrambled into the driver's seat and turned the key, wrenching the wheel to the right and away from the flag line. She jammed the pedal to the floor. Earthquakes in Antarctica were as rare as parrots, but whatever seismic activity was brewing, she had to get off the ice shelf, and fast.

Suddenly there was a tremendous jolt, followed by an Armageddon-like *boom*. Zo gripped the wheel as the Hägglunds spun a full 180 degrees, pointing her back in the direction from which she'd come. Off in the distance, a miles-long spume shot up from the surface like jets in a fountain. The vapor cloud rose high into the air until it had covered the sun and the water turned to ice, the ice crystals refracting the sunlight in a kaleidoscope of rainbows before falling like hoarfrost to the ground. Gradually, the atmosphere cleared. Zo realized the booming had stopped.

Hands shaking, she turned the vehicle around. Things happened differently in the southern hemisphere: Water drained in reverse and the man in the moon dangled upside down, but this was something else. She reached for the gearshift, then hesitated. Something about the ocean didn't look right. She picked up her binoculars and squinted, then wiped the condensation off the lenses and tried again. The surface was definitely bulging upward, building and swelling like a fast-growing cancer into a huge, tsunami-like wave. As she watched, the wave crested and spilled over in a furious gray froth, heading straight for the shore.

She jammed the Hägglunds into reverse, then stopped again. *The crevasse.* Certain death behind her; the outcome in front only slightly less so, with seconds to choose. She couldn't outrun the tsunami any more than had Thailand's doomed thousands, and with the crevasse yawning behind her, where would she run to? When the wave reached her—*if* it reached her—at least she'd still have a chance. The Hag was a monster of a truck, solid and heavy, and with luck by the time the wave hit, the worst of its power would be spent.

She closed her eyes and made her decision. Curiously, what came to mind as she waited were not thoughts of her husband or her unborn child, it was her research. Not "who would carry on" if she were to die, but "what did it matter?" She'd been so sure she was making an important contribution by studying the ice shelf, but her altruism had been misplaced before. There were so many things wrong with the world—so many causes, but in the end it wasn't the cause, it was the people who mattered, the ones who—

She stopped, suddenly realizing that the time of her death had passed. Apparently her name was written in her Maker's appointment book for another day. She opened her eyes. Aside from a few small ripples, the ocean was calm. There was no more rumbling, no water spraying like geysers into the sky, no ice shelves splitting apart, no monster waves barreling toward the shore. Everything was as before with one exception.

Her hut was gone.

Chapter 7

Los Angeles, California

Ben buttoned his shirt and knotted his tie as he stood outside his bathroom door, waiting. Built back in the sixties, the house was an anachronism; one of the few left in the neighborhood that had been constructed in the era before two or more baths were de rigueur. Predictably, the lack of multiple facilities hadn't been a problem until Sarah hit her teens. Now he shifted from foot to foot like a two-year-old and wondered if he could get away with sneaking a leak in the laundry tub.

"Sarah!" he shouted for the third time and rapped his knuckles against the door. "That's long enough!"

"You know she can't hear you," Paula said as she squeezed past him carrying a basket full of dirty clothes.

"She's been in there for . . ." He checked his watch. "Eleven minutes! Sarah! Turn off that water this instant!"

Silence followed. Then the toilet flushed and Sarah emerged, steam billowing around her like dry ice on the set of a low-budget space movie.

He shook his finger. "Eleven minutes, Sarah! You had that water blasting for eleven full minutes. You should know better. Think how many gallons you just wasted. Your mother could have done another load of laundry. I could have watered the yard." He paused to catch his breath and search her face for signs of repentance.

She knotted her robe tighter around her waist. Her face was pink. "I'm *sick* of talking about water!" she shouted, and flounced off down the hall. "Why don't you just go make some more!"

"She's only thirteen," Paula said as she sprinkled a handful of fat-free cheese over the scrambled-egg substitute sizzling on the stove.

"Exactly." Ben popped two slices of whole wheat out of the toaster and reached for the tub of soy spread. "Old enough to know better."

"All she knows is that she wants to wash her hair."

"Well, she can't go on wasting water like that. One day she's going to turn on the tap and nothing will come out."

"Yeah, and she should think about all the poor people in other parts of the world who don't have it as good as *she* does," Sarah said as she clomped into the kitchen wearing a tie-dyed T-shirt and bell-bottom blue jeans, teetering like a stilt-walker on three-inch platform heels. Ben bit back his usual comment. Paula had promised him Sarah's pseudo-hippie look was just a phase, but he hated to see the clothes his parents' generation had worn as a symbol of their idealism mutated into a fashion statement. Sarah had adopted their music as well: the Stones, the Doors, Joe Cocker. Ben sometimes felt as though he were living in a time warp. He couldn't get used to Joplin's harsh, sexy vocals leaking out from under his daughter's bedroom door. And just the other day he'd caught her downloading pictures of Jimi Hendrix off the Internet. A part of him was proud that his parents' music had stood the test of time, but as her father, he felt obliged to point out that both Jimi and Janis had died young of drug and alcohol abuse.

"Yeah, and what about the girls my age who can't even *go* to school because they have to spend *hours* and *hours* every day walking *miles* to fetch the family's water?" Sarah folded a napkin around the raspberry Pop-Tart her mother had toasted for her and took a bite. "Oh yeah, and don't forget to tell me how heavy the jugs are and how hot the sun is!"

Ben opened his mouth to reply, but Sarah was quicker. Grabbing her lunch sack from the counter, she escaped out the door.

Ben spent the next hour trapped behind the wheel of his white Toyota Prius, inching along with the other commuters in the bottleneck that passed for L.A.'s morning rush hour. *Rush hour.* What a misnomer. When he'd first come to Los Angeles, Ben had been outraged at the smog, the congestion, the pollution. Growing up in Michigan's far north, all he had known were towering pine trees, and vast blue Great Lakes, and the glorious red of swamp maples in the fall. The air was pure, the water clean. In his hometown, a half dozen cars waiting to pull onto Main Street constituted a traffic jam, and started the locals arguing about the need for a traffic signal.

At UCLA, it hadn't taken long to find his niche. He and a handful of other engineering students formed a loosely knit group that had strong sympathies to Greenpeace.

After a year of sit-ins and protests, their glory moment had come when a select twelve chained themselves to the gates of a nuclear power plant to mark the anniversary of the date on which twelve brave others sailed a small boat into the U.S. atomic test zone off Amchitka Island. Ben kept a folder of newspaper clippings detailing his group's exploits in the bottom drawer of his desk. He had always intended to show them to Sarah when she was old enough to grasp the fine line that differentiated lawlessness and conviction. Now, recalling the morning's argument, he wondered if he ever would.

He lifted his foot off the brake, idled forward, braked, then crept forward again, keeping an eye on the taillights in front of him as he reached for the bottle of water in the cup holder and smiled at the rainbow-colored label in his hand. *Charlie MacLean.* Now there was a man with big ideas. While everyone in his hometown knew theirs was the best-tasting water on earth, only Charlie had taken the initiative to bottle and sell it. His business was reasonably successful, too, though in Ben's opinion, Charlie's could never be more than a regional product. Consumers liked their water packaged with trendy names like Virgin Kiwi or Bad Frog Pond Water, not something as obscure and unpronounceable as Tahquamenon. In fact, he sometimes wondered if Charlie's business would have gone under without his support. Ben had the water shipped out to L.A. by the caseload. It was all he drank. A small indulgence, it reminded him of home.

He took a swallow. Water. Without it, there would be no life. Every animal and plant on earth needed it. Viewed from space, the globe was an ocean of blue, 70 percent of it covered with water. Most of it was saltwater and therefore undrinkable, but even if the 1 percent that was fresh and accessible was evenly distributed, it would still be enough to sustain two or even three times the world's population. And there was the irony. Despite the abundance, the earth was in crisis. Uneven distribution, pollution, abuse of the aquifer—it all amounted to a global water shortage that had scientists and politicians around the world on the verge of panic. The Ogallala Aquifer was being depleted fourteen times faster than nature could replenish it; Silicon Valley had more water-polluting EPA Superfund sites than anywhere in the United States. Thirty percent of the groundwater beneath Phoenix was similarly contaminated, and the Colorado River was so oversubscribed that by the time it passed though the seven states tapping into it, there was virtually nothing left to go out to sea. Even Ben's beloved Great Lakes were down twenty-two inches.

And yet on a global scale, the situation was even worse. The world's population was exploding, and the demand for water was increasing along with it—only at twice the rate. The average American used 130,000 gallons every year; industry claimed another 100,000 to make his car. The cropland that was paved over to make the highways he drove on and the lots he parked in resulted in the continents losing an astounding 6,400 *billion* cubic feet in runoff every year. Joni Mitchell had gotten it right when she sang the warning decades earlier, but no one was listening. Admittedly, Ben's iceberg water project was only a stopgap measure, but like the Dutch boy with his finger in the dike, he had to do *something* to forestall disaster.

He recapped the bottle and returned it to the cup holder. Paula always said he tried too hard to carry the world's problems on his shoulders, and it was true he had enough trouble right here at home. That argument this morning with Sarah. He hated being at odds with his only daughter. She used to worship him; now he'd gladly settle for a little respect. Not that he was so unworthy. He worked hard to be the cool dad: He took her to karate class every Saturday morning, and last Christmas, he'd included Cassie when the family went snowboarding at Vail. At thirty-nine, he had a full head of thick, Finnish-blond hair, and while he was short, he was fit—even if he was a myopic engineer who spent his days behind a desk.

"Make more water," Sarah had said. The remark had stung at the time, but now he smiled. It was actually rather clever. She was so smart. He wanted to tell her that you couldn't really make water, that the total amount of water on earth neither increased nor decreased. It was finite. It just circulated endlessly, from the oceans, to the atmosphere, to the land, to the rivers, and back to the oceans again.

Maybe he could have gotten her attention if he'd told her the water she wasted in her shower that morning had once quenched the thirst of a dinosaur.

"Congratulations!" Adam burst into Ben's office moments after Ben's arrival, brandishing a sheet of paper and an unlit cigar. He victory-danced across the room, pumped Ben's hand like a politician, stuffed the cigar into Ben's shirt pocket, and handed him a fax.

"One thousand square miles?" Ben dropped into his chair. "This is incredible! The biggest one yet!" He grabbed his calculator and started pushing buttons. "Seven hundred *billion* gallons?"

Adam grinned.

"Okay." Ben traded the calculator for a legal pad. "Now we get busy. Call Eugene down in Chile and give him the coordinates. Tell him to drop whatever he's doing and take his team right out. Then call Atlantic Transport. Tell them we need their tankers to begin hauling water in two weeks. No—make that ten days. And if they're already scheduled, make sure they know it'll be worth their while." He looked up. "Does Gillette know?"

"Not yet. I figured you should be the one to do the honors."

Adam had that right. After all the guff Ben had taken over the past few months, it was about time he got to deliver good news. "What about Quentin?" Quentin Fairbanks was Ben's on-site operations director. A fellow University of Michigan graduate (engineering; aerospace science), Quentin would have been Ben's first choice for the job even if he hadn't been Gillette's brother-in-law.

"No one knows," Adam said. "Just you, me, and that little piece of paper there."

"Good. In that case, bring Quentin up to speed as soon as you get through to Eugene. Tell him to notify his team, and I'll have Janice call with the details as soon as she's booked their flight." He put down his pen. "That should do it for now. Meanwhile, make sure everyone understands we need to keep a tight lid on this. We don't want word to get out until we're actually making water."

"Uh, sorry, boss. No can do." Adam indicated the fax. "That came in over the wires."

"What?"

"Don't look at me like that. It couldn't be helped. This iceberg is so huge, LANDSAT got it. My contact sent word as soon as the pictures came in, but in a few hours the wire services will pick it up, and the whole world will know."

"For crying out loud." Ben dragged a hand over his head. It figured. He and his engineers had been waiting for months for a decent-sized iceberg to break loose; then when one finally did, it was so huge its existence immediately became public knowledge. That meant they were going to have to fight the Australians for it, and Gillette was *not* going to be happy about that.

In hindsight, Ben never should have consulted with Australia Telephone and Telegraph. But after two years of struggling, his engineers had hit a wall. The problem lay in the strength of the beam. Soldyne's satellites produced low-frequency radio communication level microwaves—not even remotely close to the ten-gigawatt output needed to melt ice. Their challenge was finding a way to boost each satellite's power and join them in a phased array. Richard Mawson was the genius behind the microwave telephone relay system crisscrossing Australia's outback, and a leading authority on focused microwave signals. With a reputation for making the impossible a reality, everyone Ben consulted agreed that Mawson was his man.

But instead of Ben learning Mawson's trade secrets, Mawson had discerned his, and Ben learned the hard way that industrial espionage didn't necessarily come in the form of furtive men dressed in black spandex; it could be as innocuous as a charming Aussie accent saying "G'day." His only consolation was that the scale of their operation was so large, it would have been impossible to shield it from prying eyes indefinitely anyway. Wherever there were profits to be made, the vultures were always waiting on the sidelines. Even so, knowing that the Australians had gotten free what had taken his team three years and $2 billion to produce still made Ben ill.

"So they know." Gillette spoke from the doorway, his bulky frame filling the opening like a cork in a bottle. He was scowling, and his arms were crossed over his chest.

Ben scrambled to his feet. "We have to assume that, yes," he said, hurrying out from behind his desk to pull up another chair. How had Donald gotten wind of the situation so quickly?

Gillette remained standing. "And what else are we assuming?"

"We have to assume they'll go for it," Ben admitted. "The Australians are just as eager to try out the technology as we are, and they've been waiting for a suitable iceberg just as long. But honestly, Donald, I'm confident this is not going to be a problem. This berg calved off the Larson, near the Antarctic Peninsula, just four hundred miles from Eugene's crew in Punta Arenas. The location couldn't have been more ideal if we'd planned it. The Australians have to come all the way around the continent; four, maybe five times as far. There's no way they'll get to it first. This baby is ours."

"I hope you're right," Gillette said, and Ben caught the unspoken implication: *for your sake.* "We can't carry this project indefinitely."

"I understand that."

"This project has to pay off *now*."

"It will."

"It better."

Or what? Ben wanted to retort. He was so weary of Gillette's threat-and-innuendo style. It wasn't hard to imagine the tyrant he must be at home: "Clean your room"; "Fix my dinner"; "Bring me my slippers." Ben sighed. All he'd ever wanted was to help make the world a better place. How had he ended up with a boss who could have been Hitler's sidekick and a project as doomed as the *Titanic*?

Chapter 8

The small group assembled in Elliot's office: Zo, Mac, Dr. Rodriguez, Elliot, and Ross stood in a silent circle around Elliot's desk, studying the objects Zo had laid out for them. Each person wore an expression fit for a funeral. And, in a way, Zo thought it was—the death of one era and the beginning of another, the new and *unimproved* version in which Antarctica's vast untapped resources were up for grabs, ready to be carved up by whoever could get to them first and sold to the highest bidder. The destruction of the Larson was going to go down in the annals as one of the most audacious eco-crimes ever committed—worse than the *Exxon Valdez* disaster, worse in some respects even than Chernobyl or Bhopal, because unlike the others, this incident was no accident.

"All right," Elliot began, "if you would be so good as to close the door, Dr. Roundtree . . . thank you, yes—we'll get started."

With his clean-shaven face, crisp white shirt, dark jeans,

and conservative tie, Elliot could have passed for an IT executive addressing a boardroom, except that his skin was brown and weathered, the past ten Antarctic summers written on his face. The others accorded him the commensurate respect, not just because he was station director, or because he was older than the rest of them by at least a decade, but because he was the most senior scientist present. Elliot had made his mark years ago as one of the group of scientists who published the original article in *Nature* alerting the world to the dangers of CFCs and the hole in the ozone layer. Currently he was investigating whether other chemicals might not also be contributing factors in order to ensure that whatever gases took the place of chlorofluorocarbons in the world's millions of air-conditioners and refrigerators didn't cause further depletion. As staunch an advocate of environmental protection as any, Zo didn't have to guess what her husband would think if he found out her role in the present debacle.

He indicated the detritus on the table. "All right. It's clear what we have here is explosives residue. It's equally obvious that the explosion Zo witnessed was responsible for the creation of yesterday's iceberg. But before we consider the implications, I'd like to know exactly what we're looking at. I don't suppose any of you know anything about explosives?"

"I worked highway construction in Montana," Mac offered. "We did a lot of blasting in the Badlands."

Zo wasn't surprised Mac was able to come through for them. He'd worked a broad enough range of jobs before becoming an ornithologist to have learned a little something about everything. Rail thin, horse-faced, Thaddeus "Mac" Everingham was a Woody Allen look-alike whose frizzy blond hair bore an uncanny resemblance to the yellow tufts on his precious Macaroni penguins. Ever since his chicks had hatched, Mac had been working nonstop; taking the Zodiac inflatable to Torgeson Island early each morning and staying late, the endless days allowing him to work as long as he liked. There were six hundred breeding pairs on the island, and he needed a blood sample from every chick to resolve questions about cuckolding and parentage. He spent his days on his hands and knees, snatching chicks from their parents' brood patches and enduring bites and beatings from the adults' powerful flippers in order to steal the tiniest bit of blood for DNA testing. His arms and legs were covered with bruises, and the smell he brought back was indescribable. Once the weather warmed up, the island swam with what looked like slimy brown mud, which was actually penguin guano.

Zo felt her stomach contents rising at the thought. She swayed, suddenly dizzy, and leaned against the desk. Two trips across the peninsula in less than twenty-four hours with very little sleep, hardly anything to eat, to say nothing of her near-death experience were more than enough to send her blood sugar off the charts. She'd have to go shoot up as soon as the meeting was over. Meanwhile, it was a wonder she was still standing. She moved a stack of papers off the extra chair and sat down.

"This sack held ammonium nitrate," Mac indicated an empty burlap bag, "which means the drums in Zo's pictures likely contained fuel oil. Ammonium nitrate mixed with fuel oil makes ANFO, the logical weapon of choice, since ANFO has excellent cold weather blasting properties. This is detonating cord, and this," he picked up a cylindrical object, "is a cast booster. Cast boosters are primed with a mixture of PETN and TNT and are used to initiate the boreholes." He hefted the cylinder, then tossed it to

Dr. Rodriguez. "It's not live," he added, after the physician managed a deft, white-faced catch.

"Are you sure about the boreholes?" Dr. Rodriguez asked as he returned the cylinder gingerly to the table. "Drilling sounds like a great deal of unnecessary work. The ice shelves are riddled with cracks; no doubt some of them go almost to the bottom. If the blast zone were set up along a pre-existing fault line, breaking the ice shelf in two wouldn't have taken much more effort than a blow from a hammer."

"Well yeah, they could have done it that way. Except the evidence says otherwise." Mac waved his hand over the table. "And remember, this is only a fraction of what Zo found. This garbage went on for miles."

"I followed the trail for at least ten before I turned back," she said. "The Larson is—*was*—approximately thirty miles wide at that point. The blast zone probably stretched all the way across. An air reconnaissance could confirm that."

It felt strange to be speaking of the ice shelf in the past tense. She still couldn't wrap her mind around the idea that it was over. Never mind that when her hut was swept away, all of her research had been lost; the whole project was a bust now that the object of her study had been reduced to a free-floating, one-thousand-square-mile iceberg named Larson D according to the satellite images and news wire reports. Separated from the continent by a stretch of open water perhaps half a mile wide by her direct observation, the Larson Ice Shelf was now a giant blue ice cube two hundred feet high, its sides as straight and as sheer as if it had been sliced from the continent with a knife.

"So who swung the hammer?" Dr. Rodriguez asked.

"That's the million-dollar question," Mac said. "Followed closely by 'Why?'"

Zo, of course, knew the answer to both. "Who" was the Soldyne Corporation, and "why" was because they were greedy self-serving bastards who couldn't wait for nature to take its course. To think she'd actually believed Adam when he told her Soldyne's water-producing scheme was going to benefit the environment. "Think of all that fresh water melting into the sea," her former college dorm mate turned Soldyne engineer turned traitor had said. "The consequences to salinity levels would be horrific. Not only would the immediate ecosystem be ruined, but the influx of all that fresh water could permanently alter the oceans' currents. Imagine what would happen to the world's weather if the Gulf Stream shifted course. We could be looking at a climate change as disastrous as the last Ice Age. Now think of all the people who *need* that water," he'd continued, knowing exactly which aspect would tug at her heartstrings most. "African women who walk twenty miles every day to draw water from a contaminated well; their crops withering; their cattle dying; their children going hungry—even starving, to say nothing of suffering from disease. Just send us copies of the scans, and we'll do the rest. Help us monitor the ice shelves, and everybody wins." *Right*. As long as everybody was named Soldyne, that is. She turned her attention back to the meeting.

"Well, if you're right about them using ANFO," Ross was saying, "then this operation didn't originate in the States. Ever since Oklahoma City, no one can purchase large quantities without sending up red flags. There's no way anyone could have pulled this off without alerting authorities."

"Someone from the Middle East?" Dr. Rodriguez offered. "Or perhaps one of the 'stans?"

"I don't get the sense that this was an act of terrorism. It doesn't feel politically motivated. Figure out who has the most to gain, and you'll find out who's responsible."

"A logical approach," Elliot said, "and one we'll have time to pursue later. Right now, we need to decide what we're going to do with this information."

"What's to decide?" Ross said. "We report what we know, and the sooner the better. Whoever destroyed the ice shelf has to be punished."

"Report it to whom?" Mac asked. "Which agency? Which authority? Don't get me wrong, Ross, I'm as outraged as you are. But you seem to have forgotten there *is* no law in Antarctica. Even our own dear United States government is so ineffective they can't collect income tax from the people who work here. What makes you think another government will do any better?"

"I was referring to an appeal made under the Antarctic Treaty," Ross said, and Zo's hackles rose. It wasn't so much what he said, as the way he said it that made his pronouncements so hard to swallow. Ross's attitude had rubbed her the wrong way ever since their first conversation after her orientation meeting. All she'd done was ask in all innocence what he was researching, and Ross had responded with a ten-minute lecture on the wonders of extremophiles that began with the high-minded presumption that she'd never even heard of the things. While she hadn't known that jeans manufacturers used extremophiles in their stone-washing process ("The bacteria that live in acidic environments produce an enzyme that prevents the acids the manufacturers use in the bleaching process from destroying the cloth. Oh, come now, Dr. Zelinski. You didn't *really* think they used stones, did you?"), she was certainly aware that Antarctica's sealed underground lakes were prime locales for discovering new ones. That she'd subsequently learned he treated everyone as if their IQs were twenty points beneath his didn't make his arrogance any easier to bear.

"The treaty's protocol on environmental protection designates Antarctica a conservation area dedicated to peace and science," Ross continued. "Surely destroying the ice shelf violates the spirit of the treaty."

"The Antarctic Treaty's nothing but a piece of paper," Mac said. "Forty-three member nations agreeing to a bunch of lofty principles. But without an enforcement agency, the treaty is meaningless. I would think you of all people should understand that."

"I refuse to believe there's nothing we can do. What about environmental organizations? Greenpeace would love to sink their teeth into this. They'll take pictures, bring in journalists, get the public involved. Don't underestimate them; they're a very powerful organization."

"Which is exactly why they *shouldn't* find out," Mac countered. "I don't want people coming here and disrupting our research. TV reporters, news crews, government officials, scientists, protesters—What a disaster. Think tour ship times ten. My penguin chicks won't wait while we deal with the fallout. Call me selfish, but I'm not willing to sacrifice my research for a pile of ice. I say we sit on this information until after Raney shuts down for the season; then you can announce it on CNN for all I care."

"I agree with Mac," Dr. Rodriguez said, and Zo turned to him in surprise. She'd always had him pegged as more altruist than pragmatist.

"Raney can't handle an influx of the size he predicts,"

he continued. "Too many people crammed too tightly together is asking for an outbreak of disease. We're over-
crowded as it is. The iceberg isn't going anywhere, and
neither are the facts surrounding its creation. Better to wait
until everyone goes home before revealing what we know,
and then let the chips fall where they may."

"I don't believe this." Ross shook his head. "The deliberate destruction of the ice shelf is despicable. *Despicable*.
An act of environmental vandalism of the worst degree.
But there's a greater sin. *Condoning* the act is worse than
committing it. When I think of all the atrocities committed
down through history that could have been prevented if
decent, ordinary people hadn't looked the other way—"

He drew himself up to his full height. All eyes turned to
the imposing figure in denim shirt and faded jeans. Zo
noted that in addition to his usual silver crescent earrings,
he wore a turquoise-silver bracelet and a bear-tooth amulet
on a leather cord around his neck. Two small feathers
dangled from the end of his long braid. How was it that
Native American men could wear so much jewelry and
still look so *masculine*?

"Man is ruining the earth, and she can't do anything to
stop it. Antarctica can't speak for herself. If we keep silent,
we've sold her out."

For a moment, the room was quiet. Then, "Thank you,
Dr. Roundtree," Elliot said. He turned to Zo. "What about
you? You're most affected by this. What do you think?
Should we tell the world now, or break the news to them
later?"

She bit her lip. It was a tough call. In principle, she
agreed with Ross: The destruction of the ice shelf was a
terrible crime for which the guilty party should be called
to account. Unfortunately, that included her. There was no

way she could keep her complicity hidden indefinitely, but if the vote swung toward keeping silent for the next few weeks, she'd gladly take the reprieve.

"Later." She glanced at Ross, then looked away.

"I don't believe this. What is this? Decision by committee?"

"No," Elliot said. "It's my decision. I appreciate everyone's input, but as station director, this is my call, and I accept responsibility. You've argued eloquently and well, Dr. Roundtree, but Drs. Everingham and Rodriguez's concerns are equally valid. Your fellow scientists—not just those in this room, but the fifteen others working at Raney, have come at great personal sacrifice and expense. I won't negate their efforts. Whoever destroyed the ice shelf will be brought to account *after* Raney shuts down for the season. Meanwhile, nothing leaves this room."

He looked pointedly at Ross, then at the others in turn, finally finishing his gaze on Zo. "I trust you all can keep a secret."

Chapter 9

"So you're telling me we lost the berg." Gillette's expression was neutral, but that didn't mean Ben didn't know exactly what he was thinking. Donald had never approved of Ben's microwave method, and he never let an opportunity to denigrate it pass. No doubt he was already scheming how he could use the unfortunate turn of events—events that were completely and utterly beyond Ben's or anyone else's control (not that anyone seemed willing to acknowledge that or even cared)—to have another go at convincing the executive board that his technology was superior. Never mind that environmentally speaking, the High Frequency Active Auroral Research Program was arguably the worst idea mankind had ever come up with. Radiotelescopes transmitting megawatts of focused electromagnetic radiation onto the ionosphere, heating it, and physically lifting it higher before reflecting the EM beam back to earth *could* improve communications and enable the military to replace its echolocation frequency submarine and over-the-horizon radar with more accurate systems. H.A.A.R.P. technology could act as a wide-area earth-penetrating tomography to probe for oil and gas and mineral deposits. More to the point, the reflected electromagnetic beam could conceivably turn ice into drinking water. Unfortunately, H.A.A.R.P.'s high power transfer rate also had the potential to permanently disrupt the ozone layer, irreparably alter the ionosphere, and induce catastrophic climate change. In contrast, Ben's plan to use microwaves from orbiting satellites to melt Antarctic icebergs into drinking water was positively benign.

"We don't know for sure that we've lost it," he said, "but at this point it seems likely. Eugene finally got through this morning on the satellite phone. He says the storm's not letting up. Winds are holding at sixty knots, expected to continue throughout the weekend. As soon as they drop to thirty he'll head out, but for now, our ship is still stuck in port."

"Whereas the Australians—"

"Are coming from the east. They don't have to come through the Drake Passage, so this storm doesn't factor for them."

"And you think they've already claimed the berg?"

"Maybe. Probably. It's been three days." Ben took off his glasses and ran a hand over his head. Unbelievable, to think that three years of planning and engineering brilliance could be negated by the ridiculously childish principle of first come, first served.

Gillette made a tent of his fingers and leaned back in his chair. He was a master at using silence like a weapon, drawing it out and turning it over lovingly in his hand; then holding it over his opponent's head until they cracked and said something foolish. Ben knew better than to bite.

"All right." He leaned forward with his hands on his desk, elbows out, fingers spread, like a gorilla spoiling for a fight. "Assume the Aussies have it. What's next? Help me out, Ben. Give me something for the investors."

Ben was ready. "One of the reasons we were so excited about this berg," he began, launching into the argument he and Adam had earlier prepared, "is because it's so big. Once we started making water, we could have continued for months, maybe even years, with very little additional cost or effort. Another is its location. It's so close to our base in Chile that our resupply costs would have been ridiculously low. What's more, our tankers could have shot straight up the Atlantic *or* the Pacific depending on which coast was buying.

"Both these pluses pose big problems for the Australians. Mawson is grossly underfunded. His equipment is dated and substandard and his crew is inexperienced. The Aussies may have our process, but they don't have our know-how, and they certainly don't have the resources to harvest a berg this size. Even if they manage to make a go of it, the transportation costs are going to kill them. Best case scenario: In a few days they'll realize how overextended they are and pull back; worst case: They work the berg for a few weeks, and then pull out. Either way, we'll be ready to step up to the plate."

"You're that sure they'll give up?"

"Positive. Mawson may be arrogant and stubborn, but he's not stupid."

Gillette smiled and leaned back in his chair. Ben did the same, though inside he was anything but relaxed. No telling what was coming next from a guy who could cycle between Hannibal Lecter and Mary Poppins in seconds.

"It's lame," Gillette finally said, drumming his sausage

fingers against the desktop, "but the board will probably buy it. They don't exactly have a history of making intelligent decisions."

And there it was. Gillette couldn't have spelled out his intentions more blatantly if he'd painted them on a billboard. If the Aussies washed out now, no matter the reason, Gillette was going to spin their failure into a condemnation of the entire microwave process. As Ben left the office, he reflected on how strange it was that fate had placed him in the curious position of having to root for the Australians.

Chapter 10

Weddell Sea, 68° S, 60° W

Richard Mawson studied the ancient Bell 47 as he strolled toward the helipad on the forward deck. The helicopter wasn't much to look at, but Mawson wasn't asking much of it, either—just a few dozen shuttles between the ship and the berg to off-load men and equipment. He climbed into the front passenger seat and signaled his landing party to follow. A ship on the ocean wasn't enough to establish possession; he wanted men and equipment on the berg at all times. He trusted the Americans as far as he could spit.

"Everybody in?" The pilot stubbed out his cigarette without waiting for their answers. "Righto. We're off."

The iceberg filled the side windows as he took them straight up. Mawson could feel the cold emanating off it, its colors and striations as handsome as Carrara marble. As they cleared the top, he shielded his eyes and let loose a grin. Despite a dearth of manpower and equipment and a budget that was tighter than a tutu on a hippopotamus, they'd done it: They'd beaten the Americans to the berg.

Nature may have helped by conjuring up a three-day blow over the Straits of Magellan, but if he hadn't sussed out what the Americans were up to and hidden the *Austral Sun* nearby off the South Sandwich Islands, he couldn't have taken advantage. It wasn't what you had, he often preached, but what you did with it that mattered.

And what he had done with the knowledge that the Americans were secretly planning to blow the ice shelf to bits now had *him* flying over the berg instead of Ben Maki. Below, his prize stretched a hundred kilometers into the distance according to the satellite imagery sent over that morning from the mainland. More precise measurements would be taken in the days ahead; lakes and crevasses would be mapped and innumerable other calculations made before the location for their own lake would be selected. The decision was crucial. Set up in the wrong place and the stresses caused by a microwave beam ten times more powerful than sunlight could split the iceberg apart. Set up too close to the edge and their water could run off into the sea like butter on a pile of mashed potatoes. Too far inland and the cost differential between three kilometers of hose and thirty would eat them alive. The whole operation was a balancing act, and like a tightrope walker without a net, Mawson couldn't afford a single mistake.

He tapped the pilot on the shoulder. Off to the right along what had once been the ice shelf's leading edge, wave action had carved out an amphitheater-shaped section that stepped down to the water in a series of short plateaus, forming a natural harbor. The pilot set the helicopter down a hundred meters back from the top of the staircase and powered down the engine. Mawson climbed out, followed by his crew: Hank Owen, chief systems engineer, Colin Goldfinch, master mechanic, and Simon

Beaudry, Mawson's seventeen-year-old nephew on holiday from England.

Colin ducked into the cargo bay and began handing off supplies. Mawson turned to his nephew. "You sure you want to do this?" Thus far his sister's boy had demonstrated a remarkably level head, but in view of the tedium of the past two weeks, Mawson feared the lad was only trading one misery for another.

"Of course. I've been cold-weather camping before—two Christmases ago, when my mates and I went on a skiing trip to Finland."

"Because I promised your mother I'd look after you."

"I'll be fine, Uncle. Really. I wouldn't miss this for the world."

"All right then. The helicopter will be back in the morning once we relocate the ship. You know how to work the two-way?"

"Abso-bloody-lutely."

Mawson smiled. "Then I'm off. Have a good time. Meanwhile, Hank's in charge." He climbed into the helicopter as the pilot powered up the rotors. Simon ducked and ran. Mawson sent his pilot a look and shut the door.

Chapter 11

After the helicopter had gone, a silence settled over the camp that was thick and absolute. Simon lifted his binoculars to study the landmass looming across a narrow band of open water. *Antarctica*. He could hardly believe he was really here. He pictured his boyhood heroes, Scott, Shackleton, and Byrd, scaling those very cliffs, their dogsleds packed with a year's worth of supplies as they pushed off for the interior and parts unknown and shivered, not from the cold, but from excitement.

He unzipped the tent's windflap and poked his head inside. Colin was sitting cross-legged on a doubled-over sleeping bag, rubbing his hands to warm them while Hank worked the stove.

"Hey, fellows," Simon said. "Let's go exploring."

"Shut the door." Colin turned his collar up over his ears and hunched his shoulders. "It's bloody cold."

"Best way to get warm is by moving about. Besides, there's nothing else to do."

Hank adjusted the flame and stood up. "I'll go with ya."

Colin eyed the stack of *Playboy*s waiting on an over-turned crate. "I'll mind the stove."

Hank pulled on his mitts as Simon wound his scarf around his neck and they set off, their boots punching holes through the thin crust of snow.

"Mind your feet," Simon warned over his shoulder. "Watch out for the blue lines. Might indicate a crevasse. Never know when one could open up." Hank fell in along-side him, watching his steps closely.

The wind blowing off the cliff face gathered up the snow and flung it in their faces like rice at a wedding. Simon pulled his scarf up over his cheeks and shielded his eyes with his coat sleeve, wishing he'd brought along the snow goggles from his bedroom closet back home. Then he grinned. How could he have known when he was packing for a holiday in *Australia* that he'd need them?

When they reached the amphitheater, they sat down to survey the view, dangling their legs over the edge. Hank pulled off his mitts and fumbled in his pocket for a smoke. Simon lifted his binoculars. Off in the distance, he could just make out the ship steaming toward the harbor—or was that an iceberg? From this height it was hard to tell. Not that it mattered. After two weeks of pitching and roll-ing, the last thing he wanted to do was reboard. It may have been cold as a hangman's heart on top of the iceberg, but at least the ground wasn't moving. He tucked the bin-oculars inside his jacket for safekeeping and jumped down to the next ledge.

"Hang on," Hank called after him. "Remember, what goes down, has to come up."

"I won't go far." Simon walked over to the edge, jumped down again, then crossed the second ledge. Four steps down, a mottled brown mass the size of a Volkswagen caught his eye. He waved to get Hank's attention and cupped his hands. "Look down there! Something's moving."

"What is it?"

"I dunno. Some sort of animal, I s'pose." He scrambled down to the next ledge.

"Hold up. I'll come with ya." Hank stubbed out his cigarette.

Simon waited for Hank to join him, then led the way around a jumble of ice blocks. "Brilliant!" he exclaimed once they had a clear view of the ledge two steps below. "It's a walrus!"

Hank laughed. "Wrong pole, mate. That's an elephant seal. Look at its snout. Did you ever see such an ugly mug?"

Simon flushed. "It's huge. It must be fifteen feet long."

At the sound of their voices, the animal grunted and rolled over, exposing its pink underbelly to the sun. Its long nose flopped comically to one side.

"Bloody hell! That's a face only a mother could love."

"You're telling me."

The seal closed its eyes. After a few minutes, Hank sniffed and wiped his nose. "This is about as interesting as watching grass grow. Come along, mate. Let's go back to camp for a bite."

"Hang on. There's something else." Simon pointed to a half dozen small, dark creatures creeping toward the seal. "What *are* those things?"

"Damned if I know. They're too small for penguins. Gulls maybe, or skuas."

"They're not moving like birds."

"What else could they be?"

Simon took out his binoculars. "Bloody hell!"

"What is it?"

"They're rats."

"Rats!"

"See for yourself."

Hank looked to where Simon was pointing, then swept the binoculars over the rest of the ledge. "Bugger it. Look down there."

Simon peered through the glasses and sucked in his breath. Two levels down, directly below them, dozens of rats were pouring out of an opening in the cliff face. At first they milled about in confusion, blinded by the sun, but then they oriented themselves and began running toward the seal en masse. Simon covered his mouth. He'd seen enough television nature documentaries to know what was coming next.

What he wasn't prepared for was the violence of the attack, nor the speed. One minute the seal was blissfully sunning itself like an overweight matron at the beach, and the next, the ice ran red. Simon turned his head, but he could still hear the sounds: the rats' squeals and snarls and the doomed seal's bellows. And he could still smell the carnage: blood, and fecal matter, and raw meat.

Hank put a hand on his arm. "I've had a bellyful," he said in a low voice. "Let's get out of here."

"I don't get it," Simon said back at camp as he sipped a mugful of instant tomato soup. "Since when is Antarctica infested with rats? Nothing I've read ever mentioned it."

"It's a mystery, all right," Hank agreed. "If I hadn't seen it with my own eyes, I'd never have believed it."

"I'd a believed it," Colin muttered. "I'd believe anything about rats. Filthy creatures. I hate 'em. Once on a ship in

the Indian Ocean our cook found a nest in the kitchen. One nest. Next thing ya know, rats were everywhere. Some of 'em were so bold, they came right into the mess as we were eatin' and stole from the table."

"They hunted as a pack," Simon said. "I've never heard of rats doing that. They brought that elephant seal down as easily as hounds after a fox."

"Imagine what they'd do to a man," Colin added darkly.

"Belt up," Hank said. "We don't need talk like that."

"You think these walls would stop 'em if they decided ta make a meal of us? Rats'll chew through anything. Plastic, lead, cement . . . We had a garden shed back home where we stored seed and stuff. Cast block, it was. Those filthy mongrels chewed a hole right through ta get at the grain."

"Their teeth are like chisels," Simon agreed. "They bit through that seal's hide like it was butter."

Hank shuddered. "Anyway, fellas, I'm gettin' the shivers. Let's talk about something else."

Simon slept fitfully that night.

Not only because at two o'clock in the morning the weak austral sun persisted in shining through the orange tent walls like an unwelcome nightlight, but because Colin had insisted on regaling them with rat stories late into the night: grisly tales of rats chewing off a sailor's foot while he slept, or eating babies in their cribs.

He rolled onto his side and pulled the sleeping bag over his head. During the last hour, the wind had picked up, and every little noise—squeaking tent poles, ice crystals brushing against the tent walls—became the sound of rats. Scurrying, furtive, bloodthirsty rats.

"Simon," Hank whispered.

Simon grinned. Apparently he wasn't the only one having trouble sleeping.

"Over there. Look."

Simon sat up. Through the thin nylon fabric, backlit against the sky, he saw movement. It wasn't his imagination. Hank's expression said he saw it, too.

Rats. Hundreds of them.

Chapter 12

Los Angeles, California

Donald Gillette swung his Caddy into his six-car garage's number three bay and turned off the engine. He opened the door and climbed out, whistling as he ran his hand along the rear quarter panel before retrieving his briefcase from the backseat. He disarmed the door between the garage and the house, entered the foyer and reset the lock, then dropped his briefcase in the study and moved on, still whistling, to the kitchen. Carla was on the far side of a cooking island the size of Madagascar, stirring something simmering on the stove.

He kissed her a chaste hello. Donald's wife was no Emeril, but she took her culinary efforts seriously, and "Behave now, play later," was her unspoken rule. Considering that at thirty-five she was as trim and gorgeous as a supermodel, Donald was happy to comply. "Smells good," he said as he leaned over the pot. "What are we serving?"

"Chicken marsala, wild rice, and fresh green beans, with a Caesar salad for openers and lime gelato for dessert."

She glanced at the clock. "You'd better hurry. Sally and Quentin will be here any minute."

Donald retraced his path down the hallway, then climbed the right half of the double marble staircase to the master bedroom suite. He laid his watch on the dresser, hung his suit on a padded hanger, and headed for the bath, a glass-and-chrome construction worthy of a spread in *Architectural Digest*. Stepping out of his boxers, he dropped them in the hamper and headed for the shower.

The shower area was separated from the rest of the room by an S-shaped glass-block wall and offered a choice of three units. He eyed the beauty in the middle, a nine-thousand-dollar recirculating waterfall shower with twenty-seven jets capable of delivering a magnanimous forty gallons a minute; then conceded L.A.'s shortage by turning on the water-saving model instead. He closed his eyes as he lathered his chest and shoulders, imagining he was standing under the waterfall he and Carla had discovered during their honeymoon in Tahiti. Smiling, he added Carla to his fantasy and had just included the overture to *La Bohème* playing in the background when the automatic timer chimed a thirty-second warning. Quickly he rinsed his hair, then groped for an oversized Egyptian cotton towel.

He wrapped another around his waist and walked over to the bed to where Carla had laid out his black Armani. As he toweled off and dressed, he reflected on his good fortune in marrying a woman who understood that appearances mattered, even if their dinner guests tonight were only family. Especially because they were family.

When the doorbell chimed ten minutes later, Donald was waiting with his hair slicked back and a tray of drinks in hand: single-malt scotch for himself and Quentin, a highball for Carla, and a tall glass of iced orange juice for Sally.

Quentin's wife accepted her drink with a Mona Lisa smile. Patting her belly in the obnoxious way that pregnant women were wont to do, she went off with Carla to the kitchen. Donald frowned. If his sister-in-law's navy blue overblouse with white sailor collar and generous bow was supposed to make her look as innocent as a prepubescent girl, her waxing stomach proclaimed otherwise. If Carla ever had a child, he wouldn't hide her condition under yards of fabric; he'd take the Demi Moore approach and flaunt the consequences of her sexuality with sophistication and style.

At least Quentin was appropriately dressed. His Leveti was less expensive than Donald's Armani; a discerning choice, and just another example of his brother-in-law's impeccable judgment. Unfortunately, all the designer clothing in the world wouldn't help Quentin's appearance. Quentin was utterly hairless, a victim of inherited alopecia. Some men looked good without hair, but Quentin wasn't one of them. On seeing him for the first time, most people were taken aback by his ridged, knobby skull and nonexistent eyebrows and lashes, a reaction Quentin often used to his advantage. If his appearance unsettled his opponents, it also gave him a momentary edge. Donald liked that in a man: The ability to take what should have been a handicap and turn it into an asset. That talent was just one of the many reasons Donald had plucked Quentin out of Research and Development four years ago, married him off to Carla's younger sister, and groomed him until he was fit to serve as his number two man. Every king needed a prime minister, and Quentin served admirably as his.

Quentin lifted his glass and took an appreciative sip. "Glenfiddich?"

"Good guess."

"Then I take it we're celebrating tonight."

"Right again."

"And the occasion?"

Donald motioned him into the study and shut the door. He opened his briefcase and handed Quentin a telegram.

A slow smile creased Quentin's face. Donald grinned back. Quentin's smile more than made up for his lack of hair: a disarmingly open, boyish grin that even the most hard-hearted down-in-the-mouth never failed to return. No doubt his smile was a big part of the reason why Sally had married him. If Donald hadn't been straighter than the road to Reno, he might have succumbed himself.

"Congratulations." Quentin raised his glass. "This is incredible, Donald—even for you. I know you predicted the Aussies would pull out, but I never guessed it would happen so soon." He read the telegram again and laughed. " 'She's yours.' I'll give him this: Mawson's a man of few words. Why do you think they gave up so quickly?"

"Does it matter? The Australians were doomed from the start. I knew it; you knew it—even Maki knew it. Now Mawson knows it, too."

"Less than four days after they claimed the berg, they pulled out. That's got to be some kind of record."

Donald noted the mercenary gleam in his brother-in-law's eyes with approval, knowing it reflected the one in his own. "Now we'll show them how it's done. Eugene's back on standby. As soon as the storm quits, he'll get under way. If all goes well, we could be making water by the end of next week."

"Excellent. And he's approaching from the north, right? Because . . ." Quentin licked his lips.

Donald's smile broadened. He'd set Quentin up well.

Involve your underlings in your shady doings, let them think they were acting on their own initiative, and they covered for you better than you would yourself. "Of course. Eugene knows better than to land anywhere near the western edge. Your men are ready?"

"Our snowsuits have been packed for months."

"Great." Donald walked over to the wet bar and freshened their glasses. "Let's go tell the girls."

Chapter 13

Raney Station, Antarctic Peninsula

Zo stood on the beach looking out over the harbor, shielding her eyes with one hand and waving good-bye with the other, playing out her role as Official Station Hostess to the last. The new gig wasn't so bad. As the only unemployed researcher at the station, she was the logical draftee, and at least playing den mother to the tourists let her salvage something out of the season. Two boatloads had dropped anchor since she became a permanent Raney resident, and both times, Zo met the tourists at the shore, then shepherded them to the rec room for an orientation meeting spelling out the dangers (frostbite, snowblindness, and hypothermia) and the rules (don't touch the wildlife, don't touch the research, and don't take away any souvenirs except for the Raney Station paraphernalia for sale in the "gift shop"; an artful display of imprinted coffee mugs, T-shirts, postcards, and refrigerator magnets she and Mac set up in the rec room prior to each visit). After turning them loose, she hovered and clucked like a good mother hen until the Zodiacs ferried her chicks back to their ships once again.

Elliot hated the disruption. Zo couldn't really blame him. It wasn't easy balancing the needs of the scientists against the desire to be hospitable. She only wished he could bend enough to concede that the tourists didn't have an easy time, either. An expedition on even the most luxurious ship was an adventure. Berths in the bow came equipped with seat belts; in high seas, closet and bathroom doors turned into swinging projectiles, and the only safe place to store cameras and other breakables was on the floor. A vessel pushing through sheet ice was prone to sudden lurches severe enough to break an unwary passenger's arm or nose. Every ship had a doctor on board; the better ones included a helicopter for medical emergencies. A woman had shown Zo a snapshot she'd taken of her husband lounging on deck: wrapped in a blanket, wearing a fur hat and down jacket, he was covered with frost from his head to his toes.

At any rate, it wasn't as though Elliot exactly had a choice. Ever since the National Science Foundation had designated Raney an open station, welcoming tourists was an unavoidable part of station life.

Behind her came the crunch of footsteps on gravel. She turned around.

"Is that the last?" Mac nodded toward the receding Zodiac.

"That's it till Thursday."

"How'd we do?"

"I don't have the final tally, but it looks like we'll clear around forty-five dollars."

"That's great! I vote we use the money to buy a new VCR."

"What's wrong with the old one?"

"It keeps eating tapes. Last Sunday it ate *The Thing*."

"Not the John Carpenter version! That was my favorite. I love the special effects."

"So do I." Mac took a military stance and pretended to spray the beach with ordnance. "That flick has more flame-throwers per person than any research station *I've* ever worked at."

She laughed. "We'll definitely have to order a new player now. That, or convince the powers that be it's time to join the twenty-first century and switch to DVDs. I wonder if they have an extra copy at McMurdo?" The eighties Antarctic horror flick was a favorite at research stations across the continent.

"E-mail them and ask."

"I will—just as soon as I finish my paperwork." Zo made a face, but then the wind shifted, and her pained expression became real. She took a step back. Mac had changed out of his work clothes after he hit the station, but he hadn't showered, and the Hai Karate he'd doused himself with to cover the penguin smell definitely wasn't working. Not that the lack of hygiene was his fault. Antarctica was the driest place on earth, and water was a precious commodity, produced by a closed-loop system that passed the exhaust from the diesel engines that powered their generators through a heat exchanger to melt ice. The process was time-consuming and expensive, the open cistern in which their water was stored woefully undersized, making water rationing mandatory. Toilets were flushed only when necessary and showers limited to two minutes, two times a week.

"Are you okay?" Mac put his arm around her shoulders. "'Cause you look like you're gonna puke."

"I'm fine. Just tired, is all," Zo managed to reply.

He chucked her under her chin. "In that case, kiddo, a little supper will fix you right up. And you're in luck. Luis is fixing his specialty tonight: Tex-Mex chili."

Zo gagged.

When Zo heard shrieks coming from the dining room not long after the dinner announcement came over the PA that evening, she smiled and put down her pen. The dormitory-style living at Raney tended to foster an atmosphere reminiscent of summer camp, and with all of the scientists borderline if not outright geniuses, a certain amount of horseplay was inevitable. Every year as the season progressed, their stunts became more and more outrageous until Elliot had to intervene before things turned dangerous. Even so, last year one researcher suffered a bad case of frostbite when someone turned off the outdoor flood-lights as a joke, knowing their victim was outside following the flag line, and the season before that, Mac had smeared himself with ketchup and, brandishing a knife, grabbed a diminutive biologist and screamed "You're the last one!"—forgetting the researcher was also a martial arts instructor. Before he could explain, she had the knife, and he was on the floor with two broken fingers.

She pushed back her chair. Braving the odor of garlic and turmeric, she headed for the dining room and stopped just inside the doorway. Dr. Rodriguez was a popular cook, and the room was full. Whatever was up, the perpetrator had chosen their timing well.

The action was coming from the center of the room. "Eww," someone was saying. "That's gross! Get it out of here!"

"Geez, Mac. Don't be an idiot. We're trying to eat."

"What wrong with you guys?" Mac's voice carried over the clamor. "You're scientists, aren't you? I thought you'd be thrilled to see my wonderful new discovery. This little guy just made history. He's the first of his kind on the continent. Sam found him in the maintenance shed. Killed him with a wrench."

"I can tell." Shana, the Renée Zellweger look-alike who was Mac's confessed love interest this season, broke from the group, fanning her nose. As the crowd parted to let her pass, Zo caught a glimpse of Mac holding something on a plate.

"This settles it," Elliot said. "No more tourists for the rest of the season. I don't care what the NSF says; from now on, if anyone wants to visit, they can just go on to Rothera."

"There's no need to impose a ban," Ross said. "Dozens of ships stop every season, and nothing like this has ever happened."

"That's true," Dr. Rodriguez said. "Even if a whole horde of rats were to descend on us from off a tour ship, they wouldn't pose a threat. Rats proliferate under unsanitary conditions; they need garbage and filth. Raney's the cleanest place on earth. There's nothing here for them to eat."

"No kidding," Mac said. "This guy made a big mistake when he jumped ship. Poor little thing. Sam did you a favor when he smashed your head in. Otherwise, you'd have starved to death."

He caught Zo watching from the doorway and held out his trophy. "Hey, Zo! You hungry?"

She clapped a hand over her mouth. Mac had arranged the dead rat on a bed of crumpled green paper to simulate parsley, with a painted-red golf ball in its mouth in place of an apple. The haute cuisine accessories may have been fake, but the bulging eyeballs and the dried blood matting the rat's crushed-in skull were real.

Laughter followed as she ran down the hallway. Pushing past a pair of scientists blocking the exit, she sprinted for her ice cave—damning the rat that must have somehow stowed away with her in the Hägglunds, damning Mac's ridiculous, high-spirited antics, damning the pregnancy that made her so perpetually and inconveniently nauseous.

Reaching the entrance, she ducked inside and stopped short. Slowly, she backed away from the dozen sleek brown rats greedily devouring her vomit pile.

Chapter 14

Ben waited in the boardroom across the hall from Gillette's office, studying the reflections from the overhead lighting in the polished mahogany while the coffeemaker gurgled in the corner. Across the table, the pair of legal eagles appointed to prep him for his first-ever press conference crossed their legs and rearranged their papers as three minutes stretched to five and then ten. The room was hot, the drapes drawn to shut out the late afternoon sun, and smelled of Old Spice and sweat.

"Water is a RIGHT, not a NEED." The slogan wafted faintly through the glass. Ben canted back in his chair and parted the curtains. Across an acre of asphalt, the protesters surged against the chain link surrounding Soldyne's parking lot like a Pacific swell; blue LAPD uniforms and riot helmets made the occasional island in a sea of SAVE THE PLANET T-shirts and ICE SOLDYNE signs. Thankfully, there didn't seem to be any popguns in evidence, but that didn't mean the next vehicle to pull up wouldn't disgorge a

posse of Rebecca Sweet's protest-lovin', cardboard-totin' cowboys.

He let the curtain fall. The irony playing out in the mess six floors below was stunning. Not only did he used to be one of them, but even though he was now firmly ensconced on the side of the Evil Corporate Giant, he still understood the protesters' concerns, and even agreed. Their slogan wasn't a matter of semantics; it defined the entire issue as to whether water could be bought or sold. Human needs like food and clothing could be supplied in many ways, and no one objected to the supplier making a profit. But no one could sell a human *right*. Both the UN and the World Bank had ruled that water was a need, its distribution determined by the principles of profit, putting Soldyne firmly in the right. But the debate raised legitimate questions, and before he'd signed on for the Antarctic project, Ben had asked most of them himself. If Nature's lifeblood was simply a commodity to be bought and sold, who will buy it for Nature? What about the poor? Who owned the world's water sources in the first place? *Should* anyone own them?

The door opened and the room crackled to life. Gillette took his seat without apology or explanation, which was just as well. Ben's and Donald's exchanges had never been known for their affability or their scintillating wit, but ever since Eugene's team had claimed the berg and everything that could possibly go wrong had, the Maki-Gillette comedy act had deteriorated into a painfully tedious accusatory monologue.

Gillette nodded to the lawyers to begin. Trevor Johnston, Soldyne's chief legal counsel, gave his papers a final compulsive shuffle and settled his glasses on his nose. "Nervous?" he asked Ben.

"Not really," Ben said.

The lawyer raised his eyebrows as if to say, *You should be.* "Then let's get started. Some of this is going to feel like familiar ground, but remember, these are complicated, potentially explosive issues. How these topics are presented to the public is critical. First, let's look at the political ramifications. The iceberg comes from an area claimed by three nations: Britain, Argentina, and Chile. These nations have no intention of making water, but they're all claiming the right to decide what happens to ours by saying the iceberg falls under their jurisdiction. How do you answer?"

"The issue of ownership is complicated," Ben began, congratulating himself that he felt no compunction to look at his notes. The best cure for nervousness was preparedness, and he was so ready that not even Gillette's arctic stare blowing down the length of the table could uproot his oasis of calm. "In addition to the three you mention, Australia, France, New Zealand, and Norway have all made territorial claims. They use various means to establish their sovereignty: flagpoles, plaques, giant flags painted on the sides of buildings. The Argentineans take it the furthest, regularly sending women and children to their Esperanza Station at Hope Bay in an effort to strengthen their claims. In fact, back in '78, the wife of the station director there gave birth to the first native-born Antarctican, and since then several other Argentinean women have done the same. But these efforts are just window dressing. Because there *are* no native Antarctic peoples, land claims are tenuous at best."

"Good. Clear, concise, with a couple of nice sound bites. Just don't forget to smile."

Ben obediently bared his teeth as Johnston's second, a

red-faced, bulbous man who was clearly suffering in the stuffy room, took over. "Let's talk now about safety," James Everett said as he mopped his brow. "Microwaves shooting down out of the sky sound dangerous. Should the public be concerned?"

"Not at all. The earth is bombarded by microwaves every day—from the sun, from broadcasting satellites, and from radar, though most people never give them a second thought. Cell phones, and wireless devices like that Black-Berry in your pocket utilize microwaves, too. Microwaves aren't just confined to our kitchens; the technology is everywhere."

"Tell me about your technology."

"The core idea is simple. By itself, the sun's microwave output isn't sufficient to melt the ice at the poles—obviously, or the ice caps would have disintegrated long ago. So we've taken the natural power of the sun and enhanced it into a concentrated, targeted beam. Over the years, scientists have considered various means of melting ice; lasers and parabolic mirrors are two of the most popular. However, a concentrated microwave beam is far and away the most efficient method, because cloud cover doesn't factor; the satellites are up there collecting microwaves around the clock. Soldyne has three orbiting satellites—we're in the business of harnessing sunlight, you know—which puts us in the unique position of being one of the few entities able to actually implement the microwave method. Our beam originates from a hundred-square-kilometer, ten-gigawatt solar array that has a combined output of ten gigahertz radiating from a one-kilometer phased array, giving us a spot size of one kilometer and a power density of one watt per square centimeter. Taking into account the high-latitude obliquity factor—"

"Whoa—hold on." Everett held up his hand. "Remember, you're talking to laypeople."

"Right. Sorry. Well then, in laymen's terms, we're talking about a targeted microwave beam aimed at the iceberg that's about ten times more powerful than sunlight—strong enough to melt ice, but posing no danger to anyone on the ground."

"What if an aircraft gets in the way?"

"Airplanes are made of metal. Anyone who's used a microwave for cooking knows microwaves can't penetrate. Our beam poses absolutely no danger to passengers or the craft. Even so, we've taken precautions. Once we've calculated the trajectory, we'll notify the FAA so they can set up what's called a 'prohibited area': a ten-mile radius around the beam with an identifying name and number warning pilots to stay away. In addition, we have a dedicated radar satellite covering the beam area to act as a kill switch. If an aircraft *were* to mistakenly fly into the prohibited zone, our radar will detect it and shut down transmission before the plane gets close. There's no way anyone's going to get hurt."

"What about danger to the environment? Those protesters out there are only the tip of the iceberg, if you'll forgive the pun. For every one of them, there are hundreds, even thousands more at home."

"I would never do *anything* to hurt the environment." Ben clenched his fists, then caught himself and forced his hands to relax. It wasn't his integrity that was under question, it was his process. "We're not depleting existing water systems or diverting Great Lakes water to Japan, or harming the earth in any other way," he said, working hard to keep his tone light and remembering to cap his remarks with a smile. "We're melting icebergs. Turning them into water; something that was going to occur naturally on its own, I might add. While we're producing water, we'll set up what amounts to a small factory on the iceberg, but we're taking Greenpeace's Cape Evans station as our model. When Greenpeace dismantled the station in '92, every scrap was removed. When we leave the iceberg, we'll do the same. No one will ever know we'd been there."

"Yes, yes, we know all about your fondness for the environment," Gillette interrupted. He tipped his head toward the street. "What about the company?"

"What— Are you saying *I'm* responsible for this?"

"I'm just asking where your sympathies lie."

"I would *never* do anything to hurt the company," Ben said through gritted teeth. The whole reason the board had chosen him as Soldyne's spokesperson was because of his pro-environment views. Now Gillette wanted him to sign a loyalty oath? "Believe me, I know who writes my paycheck. I'm behind this project one hundred percent. All I want to do is make water."

"So do I." Abruptly, Gillette pushed back his chair and left the room. Ben and the lawyers exchanged puzzled looks. It wasn't until Ben heard the urinal in the executive washroom flush that he realized Donald had just made a joke.

Chapter 15

Ben pointed the remote at the television in his office credenza the next morning and pressed "rewind," then counted off the seconds and hit "play." After a moment he saw it again: a woman in the crowd, seen from behind, wearing a black velvet skirt and white blouse with an embroidered shawl over one shoulder and two thick black braids. He felt the same brief intuit of recognition he'd experienced the previous six times he'd watched the tape before his own face filled the screen and the footage cut back to the news conference.

He replayed the segment twice more before giving up. Short of tracking down the cameraman and examining everything that had landed on the cutting room floor, there was no way to know for certain if the woman he'd spotted was her. Yet just the possibility that she *might* be was enough to do a number on his gut. And if indeed that *was* Rebecca mingling with the crowd and urging the protesters toward God only knew what, then Soldyne was in serious trouble. Once Rebecca locked on to her target, she became a heat-seeking missile, and all the words in the world couldn't get her to alter course. That much hadn't changed since their UCLA days. He sighed. Being chosen as Soldyne's poster boy was beginning to feel less like an honor and more like he'd been set up.

The intercom buzzed. "It's Eugene," his secretary said. "It's a good connection this time, but don't forget the three-second delay."

He put down the remote and picked up the receiver. "Hey, Eugene."

"Hey, yourself," Eugene's basso profundo replied. Eugene O'Connor's voice matched his looks: a linebacker-sized Irishman with enough curly red hair covering his body for two average men.

Ben counted slowly to three. "How's it going?" he asked, ever hopeful that today's would be the call that ended Eugene's daily litany of disaster.

"Same old, same old," Eugene replied after three more seconds had passed. "Remember I told you yesterday we thought Toshi had a handle on the uplink code? Well, turns out, that's a no-go. He's rewritten it twice now, and the satellites still aren't responding. It's not his fault," he continued before Ben could comment. "The cold does weird things to the equipment. I wish I could give you a better idea of what it's like down here. It's a struggle to keep even the most basic stuff running. But that's not why I'm calling. We got a new problem. Last night, a rat got into the biodome. Scared the guys so much, Phil—"

"What?" Ben sat up straight. "Hold on. Our connection must be messed up. I could swear you said 'rat.'"

"—did, John. The berg is crawling with them. They're—"

"Rats!"

"—the air lines and chewing the hoses. Today we had to replace the ones on the generator twice, but they still—"

"They're *eating* the hoses?"

"—what to do."

Ben drew a deep breath. "I'm sorry," he said after counting slowly to three. "I missed most of that. Tell me again, and I promise I'll be quiet and listen."

"The iceberg is swarming with rats," Eugene said, and this time, there was no mistaking what he was saying. "They're chewing up the equipment and running around all over the place. They haven't gotten inside the control center yet, but they're everywhere else. Man, it's disgusting! It's like they came out of nowhere: Yesterday there was nothing, and now today it's a regular plague. I'm telling you, I've seen some big rats in Punta Arenas, but these are something else. And the worst thing is, they're absolutely fearless. I guess it's because they've never seen humans before."

"Now hold on. You're implying the rats were already on the berg when you got there? That's crazy. They had to have come off your supply ship."

"That's what we thought, too, but there's too many of 'em. Don't you think we'd have noticed? But here's what really worries me. It's not just the rats—it's their droppings. Quentin thinks the water's going to be contaminated, and for once, I think he might be right. What do you want us to do?"

"Hang on a sec." Ben let Eugene's anti-Quentin dig pass for the moment while he logged on to the Internet. He had a feeling the rivalry that had manifested itself between the two men only *after* they'd been sequestered for two weeks on the berg was quickly becoming the least of his problems.

A search on "rats+Antarctica" brought up dozens of

hits. Rats had invaded the Galapagos and were eating the wildlife and disrupting the food chain . . . South Georgia Island was particularly hard hit . . . Thanks to aerial eradication, Campbell Island had only recently ended a two-hundred-year plague dating back to the great whaling days. Rats had even been spotted on the continent itself.

A second search on "rats+water+disease" turned up more information, and none of it good. Cryptosporidiosis, *E. coli*, schistosomiasis, giardiasis—all parasitic diseases, all potentially deadly, and all easily transmittable through a feces-contaminated water supply.

"You still there?"

"I'm here. Listen, Eugene, I'm going to have to get back with you on this. Meanwhile, tell Toshi to debug that damn uplink."

"So I've decided to go there myself," Ben said later that afternoon after filling Adam in on the latest.

"Isn't that a little drastic?"

"I don't think so. This long-distance problem solving is too difficult. We'll never move forward as long as I have to work through Eugene. I'll bring the necessary water-testing equipment with me, and that's another reason for going in person. If word got out that our water might be contaminated, there'd be hell to pay."

"You got that right. It'd be just the thing the iceberg-huggers would use to shut us down. But what if the water tests positive?"

"We deal with it. L.A.'s so desperate, I'm sure the city will give our water whatever extra treatment it needs. It will add to the costs, but that's something Gillette and the investors will have to accept."

"Yeah, Gillette. You sure you aren't going in order to get away from him?" Adam drew a finger across his neck.

Ben smiled. "Can't say the thought didn't cross my mind. Anyway, there's no point in arguing; Janice has already booked my flight. Eugene's sending the supply ship to Punta Arenas to meet me; then it's on to the iceberg."

Adam shuddered. "Better you than me. I wouldn't trade L.A. sunshine for snow and ice any day."

"You forget I grew up in northern Michigan. I'm no stranger to cold. It'll be fun."

"What about the rats?"

"Don't worry, I'm packing a suitcase full of rat poison. I'll get rid of *that* problem in a hurry."

"Better pack a couple of twenty-twos as well. If these rats are as big as Eugene says they are, you're going to need them."

Ben laughed, but Adam wasn't smiling.

PART TWO

A scientist can discover a new star, but he cannot make one. He would have to ask an engineer to do that.

—GORDON L. GLEGG,
AMERICAN ENGINEER, 1969

Chapter 16

The blue-and-white Sikorsky circled the iceberg, dipping and banking like an oversized albatross looking for a place to land. Sunlight flashed off the windshield each time it turned, shooting the rays back into the infinity of a sky so blue it hurt to look at it. Inside the helicopter, Ben raised a hand against the glare.

"You're lucky," the pilot remarked as he angled for another pass. "Last time I brought someone up, the winds were so bad, it took four tries to land."

Ben acknowledged his good fortune by gripping the armrests and clamping his mouth shut. After three days at sea, his equilibrium couldn't take much more abuse. As a youth, he'd navigated Lake Superior in all kinds of weather, but nothing the meanest of the Big Five had thrown at him had prepared him for the rigors of the Southern Ocean. When the *Polar Sea* wasn't battling waves the size of small mountains, she was dodging icebergs almost as large. Punching through pack ice up to twenty feet thick required a terrifying combination of inertia and gravity, the ship's bow pointing impossibly skyward as they rode right up onto the ice until her weight tipped the balance and they came crashing down. While the Chilean cooks served the Norwegian crew a volatile mix of hot salsa and lutefisk, Ben fed the fishes.

When the helicopter settled inside a nest of orange flags, he pulled on his mitts and climbed out, steadying himself against the door frame while he waited to see if his stomach contents were going to accompany him. In every direction, the iceberg spread out as flat and as featureless as a wheat field in winter, giving the winds plenty of room to build into the kind of breath-sucking gusts he hadn't experienced since he was a child. Ice pellets stung his cheeks, making his eyes water. He shielded his face. Off to his right, six silver biodomes clustered behind a Quonset bristling with solar panels and a satellite dish. Six *tiny* silver huts. The sudden comprehension of the puniness of the earthly half of their operation and their complete and utter isolation made his knees weak. It was one thing to tout the glories of their water-making scheme at a press conference in Los Angeles; another to experience the reality firsthand. Ben couldn't decide if the men who had volunteered to pioneer their process were incredibly brave, or astonishingly foolish.

His my-God-what-have-I-done, I-must-be-out-of-my-freaking-mind moment ended when the door to the largest hut opened and Eugene came running toward him, bare-headed, and minus an overcoat even though the temperature couldn't have been above zero.

"You made it!" he boomed and scooped Ben up in an enormous man-hug. "It's great to see you here, buddy!" He slapped Ben on the back and slipped an arm around his shoulders to march him toward the Quonset.

After a ten-hour red-eye to Punta Arenas, Chile, three days in a city where few people spoke English and the idea of public order seemed to be a soldier with an automatic on every corner, topped off by a voyage on the icebreaker from hell, the absolute ordinariness of a roomful of metal office furniture and computers made Ben blink. He shook it off and exchanged greetings with the crew: Philip Patecki, thermal engineer; Susan Hunter, systems engineer, and of course Toshi and Quentin. The latter Ben knew quite well, the others only peripherally, but as he looked around the crowded room he conceded he was no doubt going to get to know them all *very* well before long. No wonder Eugene and Quentin were at each other's throats.

Quentin crossed the room to shake Ben's hand, his knobby skull tinged Frankenstein green from the overhead fluorescents. "Good to see you again, Ben. How was the trip?"

How was the trip? "Let's just say it was an experience."

Eugene laughed and reached for Ben's coat. "Let me take that for you, buddy. These wimps keep it so hot in here, you must be sweating like a pig."

Ben handed it over, then shivered and turned up his shirt collar. Quentin caught Ben's eye. He pointed to himself, and then to the others. The rest were wearing jackets, and Susan had on earmuffs and a scarf. Ben noted the dark circles under Eugene's armpits, the face shiny with sweat, and shook his head. Eugene was definitely an original, though Ben supposed that on the iceberg, it could be argued that eccentricity was practically a job requirement.

He pulled out the chair next to Toshi and sat down. Tomishi "Toshi" Kenjo was Soldyne's MIT wunderkind, the twenty-two-year-old who'd written the software program that controlled the satellites' direction and output—a program that had worked flawlessly every time they'd tested it in L.A. With his slender build, straight black bangs, oversized glasses, and anime baseball cap, Toshi looked every bit of sixteen.

"How's it going?" Ben asked.

"Great," Toshi answered. "In fact, I think I found the problem. You see this line of code here?" He pointed to the screen, then rolled his chair out of the way so Ben could have a look. "That ampersand should have been a semicolon."

"Good man!" Eugene muscled his way in and clapped Toshi on the shoulder. "I knew if you stuck with it long enough, you'd figure it out." He turned to Ben. "I've been telling this kid for weeks his code's wanky, but would he believe me?" He jabbed Toshi with his finger. "Maybe now you'll listen to your old Uncle Eugene, hey? As for this . . ." He pulled out a handkerchief and wiped Toshi's monitor. "If you'd just keep your workstation clean, maybe you wouldn't have so many problems. You got enough cobwebs here to knit a sweater."

"There aren't any—" Toshi began, but Quentin shook his head.

"Why don't you lend Toshi your handkerchief," he said to Eugene. "That way he can keep those cobwebs under control." He picked up a snowmobile helmet from a pile near the door and tossed it to Ben. "Up for a ride? Come on, I'll give you the grand tour." Under his breath he added, "We need to talk."

The snowmobiles were Arctic Cat Thundercats, with double wishbone front suspensions, hydraulic disc brakes, a low center of gravity, and 999 cubic centimeters of pure, unadulterated horsepower. A good trail machine would have served their transportation purposes just as well, but Ben had always subscribed to the adage that happy workers were productive ones, and now as he raced along next to Quentin, he reaped the rewards of his own philosophy. With a heated helmet, hand and thumb warmers, a borrowed snowmobile suit, and massive Sorel boots, he couldn't have been more comfortable as he sped across the ice, watching the speedometer attain speeds he'd never dared on Michigan's trails.

When Quentin came to a stop, Ben pulled up alongside him and lifted his visor. "Man, that was great!"

"You handle that machine like a pro."

"I haven't ridden in years."

"We have races on Sundays. You should enter."

"Maybe I will." Ben pulled off his helmet to admire the view. The 360-degree panorama was far and away the most dramatic he had ever seen. Thick, gunmetal clouds formed a low ceiling overhead while out over the ocean, the sun had punched a single hole and was shining through like a spotlight, turning the swells a luminous aquamarine. This far inland the winds were diminished, the air relatively balmy. Ben propped up his feet and leaned back against the seat. "Okay. I assume you brought me out here to talk about Eugene. Spill."

Quentin nodded. "Eugene's sick."

Ben cocked an eyebrow. He had anticipated a laundry list of complaints, not this. "What do you mean he's sick? He looked fine to me."

"I mean he's sick in the head. Stressed out. Out of it. You saw his performance back there."

"You mean all that yukking and backslapping? That's just Eugene being Eugene."

"No, it's not. I've known Eugene as long as you have, and trust me, that happy act was all show. He's lost it. He can't follow the simplest instructions, and half the time his orders are contradictory. I wouldn't be surprised if he planted the bug in Toshi's program himself."

"That's crazy. Why would he do that?"

"Because he's *sick*. Because he's not thinking straight. He's also seeing things. You know as well as I do there weren't any cobwebs on Toshi's monitor. Come on. *Spiders?* In Antarctica? Please."

"Then what about the rats? Don't tell me he's imagining them, too."

"Oh no, the rats are real, all right, but they're not the problem Eugene's led you to believe. Tell me, how many have you seen since you've been here?"

"I haven't seen any."

"Exactly. I've seen a couple, is all, and Phil's seen one or two. Eugene's the only one who claims to have seen rats by the dozen. Listen, it's tough down here; I won't pretend otherwise, and the pressure we're getting from Gillette is unbelievable. It's obvious Eugene's cracked because of the stress. He's even drinking the water."

"*What?* No one's supposed to melt ice for drinking anymore until I've had a chance to test it. Eugene knows that. Why would he do that?"

Quentin shrugged. "Because I told him not to. Listen, I know he's your friend, but if you want to turn this berg into water, you have to get rid of him."

Ben had a sudden image of Quentin pushing Eugene off a cliff. "How am I supposed to get rid of my chief engineer? Go back and give him a pink slip?"

"His wife just had a baby. He misses her, and she wants

him to come home. Tell him you'll take over so he can go look after the wife and kid."

"You think he'll buy it?"

"Trust me. Eugene's so out of it, he'll believe anything."

Chapter 17

Back at the operations hut, Ben parked his machine alongside Quentin's and killed the engine. Still following Quentin's lead, he pulled off his helmet and hung it over the handlebars, but that was as far as his subordinate role went. He was top dog on the ice; he was the one charged with getting water production up and running, and he wasn't about to accept Quentin's diagnosis and send Eugene packing without making his own assessment first. During the return trip, he'd had plenty of time to consider the information Quentin had handed him, and given what he had thus far, he could see it playing out equally both ways. Either Quentin was so set against their chief engineer he was willing to sabotage the entire operation in order to get rid of him (in which case the tables could well end up being turned), or their project was dead in the water as long as Eugene remained on the berg. As for which scenario was the correct one, time and Ben's own observations would tell. No way was he going to make such a critical decision based on secondhand information. Truth was, he could ill afford to lose either man.

Quentin pointed. "Middle dome is the mess hall. Walk over with me and we'll grab a bite. Our cook makes a mean rat stew. Joking," he added as Ben's head whipped around. "We're not having stew today. It's meat loaf." He smiled. "Beef, of course. One hundred percent Argentinean."

Ben returned the grin. Quentin had one stellar smile. Too bad the rest of his appearance didn't measure up. "I'll be along in a bit. I want to get the testing started first. The cultures are going to take time to grow."

"Okay. Join me whenever you're ready. I had Phil stash your stuff in the op center. If you need anything else, you can raise me on the intercom."

"Will do." As Quentin headed for the mess hall, Ben knelt down and picked up a fist-sized chunk of ice. He planned to run several dozen samples from both the melt zone and from random places, but first he wanted to get a feel for the process, and for that, any old piece of ice would do.

He opened the door to the Quonset, stomped his feet in the vestibule, and opened the second door. Toshi and Eugene looked up as he entered. The other chairs were empty; Patecki and Hunter presumably gone to lunch.

Ben hefted his sample. "Got my first victim. Any suggestions on where should I set up?"

"How much space do you need?" Toshi asked.

"Not much. Just enough for an incubator, a hot plate, and a little elbow room."

Eugene drained the bottle of water he'd been drinking, stuck a marker in the novel he'd been reading, and walked over to a utility table, where a swipe of his arm condensed several neat stacks of papers into one. He picked up Ben's suitcase and slung it onto the table.

Ben pursed his lips. If Eugene was as sick as Quentin claimed, it certainly wasn't physical. Ben had been lugging the case through airports for the better part of a week and could barely lift it off the luggage carousel. He clicked open the latches and took out the incubator.

Eugene leaned over his shoulder. "How does this thing work?"

"I'm doing a simplified version of the EPA's test for total coliform bacteria," Ben said as he traced the various electrical cords across the floor and plugged the incubator into an empty wall outlet. One advantage of working for a solar energy company, there was never any shortage of power. "Coliform is the name of a group of bacteria found throughout the environment. The full EPA test calls for some fairly sophisticated lab techniques, but we can get away with using the *Dummies* version because we don't need to know what kind of coliform might be present, or even the degree of concentration; we only need to know if they're there. This test checks specifically for fecal coliform, which are found exactly where it sounds: in the digestive tracts of warm-blooded animals. They aren't dangerous to work with, but their presence in a water sample is considered a reliable indicator of more serious bacteria."

"Such as?" Toshi asked.

"*E. coli* and a bunch of unpronounceables that are responsible for some of the world's nastier waterborne diseases. You probably don't remember the cryptosporidium outbreak in Milwaukee back in the nineties—heck, you probably weren't even born then—but I do, because I was living in Michigan's Upper Peninsula at the time. It was pretty bad. Half the city's population—four hundred thousand people—got sick, and a hundred died from that particular parasitic infection, all because the city's system failed to filter out animal waste."

"Wow."

"No kidding. Most people think contaminated water is a Third World problem. They have no idea that fifty million Americans are drinking from substandard systems."

"What do we do if our water turns out to be contaminated? Pack everything up and go home?"

"No way. If the tests come up positive, we'll notify Gillette, and he'll pass the word on to L.A.'s water department. There are any number of disinfection methods that can treat our water before it's absorbed into the city's system: liquid chlorine, gas chlorination, iodine—even simple filtration goes a long way toward getting rid of the potential for disease. Believe me, it will take more than a handful of renegade rats to shut us down."

Assuming they ever got started in the first place. Ben dropped his sample in a sterile glass dish and set the dish on the hot plate to melt. While he waited, he wrote the date, the time, and the source of the sample on two test tubes. Once a sufficient quantity of water had melted, he filled both tubes and placed them in the incubator. "And now we wait."

"For how long?" Toshi asked.

"Forty-eight hours. Meanwhile, I'm counting on you to get that uplink fixed. We don't need the test results in order to move forward."

"With pleasure. You have no idea how frustrating this has been. I get everything working, and the system fails. I fix it, and it fails again. I don't know—I'm starting to think this whole thing is jinxed. This is the buggiest program

I've ever worked with, and that's saying something, considering I'm the guy who wrote it."

"So how does this thing work?" Eugene asked.

"How does what work?" Ben said.

Eugene pointed to Ben's equipment. "Your water tests. What's the procedure?"

He can't understand the simplest instructions. Ben frowned. Was Eugene's repetition evidence of confusion, or merely a request for more information? He decided to presume the latter. "It's pretty simple, really. If the sample's contaminated, the purple liquid in these tubes turns yellow."

Toshi laughed. "This really *is* the *Dummies* version."

Ben smiled. In fact, he'd ordered the kits off the Internet.

"I wasn't asking *how long* it's going to take," Eugene said. "I want to know how it *works.*"

"I just told you," Ben said. "There really isn't any simpler way to explain it."

"Damn it, Ben." Eugene smacked his fist on the table. The box of test tubes rattled. "Don't be so obtuse. Just tell me—" He blinked and rubbed his neck. A line of sweat broke out on his forehead as his cheeks bloomed red.

"Are you okay?"

"I'm fine. My eyes are kinda blurry, is all. And I'm gettin' a killer headache. Stomach hurts, too, like I'm gonna puke."

"Sounds like a migraine."

"If it is, it'll be the first."

"My mom gets migraines," Toshi offered. "Sometimes she can't get out of bed for days. Maybe you should go lie down."

"Maybe I will," Eugene said. "Read a little. Sleep it off."

He got to his feet, gripping the edge of the table for support, and reached for his novel. *Sleeper Cell*, Ben read on the cover, by a Dr. Jeffrey Anderson. He looked at Eugene, sweating and breathing as heavily as if he'd just run a marathon, and wished they had a doctor right about now.

"I'll go with you," he said. He stood up to take Eugene's elbow.

"It's only a headache." Eugene shrugged him off and stepped away from the table, then swayed and put out a hand to catch himself, knocking the open box of test tubes to the floor.

"Oh my God! I'm sorry. I'm so sorry," he said to the sound of shattering glass. He grabbed a pair of file folders off the table and began shoveling up the mess. "I don't know what's wrong with me. I'm not usually so clumsy." He looked up. "I sure hope you have some more."

Chapter 18

The storage room next to Raney's water cistern had been called the biolab ever since Fernando Montoya, their Brazilian ichthyologist, set up a cold-water aquarium in one corner. Someone—not Fernando, but one of his many female admirers (who all agreed that Fernando was as cute as the proverbial button)—had made a sign to that effect and taped it to the door, a painstakingly calligraphied masterpiece decorated with butterflies and kittens and puppies that proclaimed *Ferdie's Biolab*, the domain of *All Creatures Great and Small*.

The aquarium was home to his rather uninspiring collection of limpets, starfish, and krill, along with several very impressive Antarctic cod: three-foot-long, one-hundred-pound monsters with leonine mouths and razor-sharp teeth—the same kind of fish Luis had caught on a long line and baked for their Thanksgiving dinner. Last season, Fernando isolated an antifreeze protein from his cod that had already been tested by an ice cream manufacturer in hopes the protein would prevent his product from developing ice crystals when it sat too long in the freezer. The experiment worked, except for one unfortunate problem: The ice cream tasted like fish.

Zo's specimen cage waited in the opposite corner. Science didn't often get the chance to observe what happened from the outset of the introduction of a nonnative species, and while rodentology wasn't exactly her area of expertise, she knew enough about basic research methods to lay an adequate foundation. Next season, if someone wanted, they could pick up her study where she left off. She actually didn't mind her new avocation. There was something about the rats' naïve, unmitigated fearlessness that appealed to her. She envied the way nature had conspired the circumstances that allowed them to do whatever they wanted. More to the point, now that Elliot had canceled the next three tour ship visits (even though he knew full well the rats had followed her across the peninsula after the destruction of the ice shelf disrupted their food supply, though he didn't know about the vomit piles she'd dropped like bread crumbs along the way), she had absolutely nothing else to do. Fernando had donated an old, cracked aquarium to her cause, and Mac had fashioned a piece of galvanized hardware cloth into a lid. Newspaper bedding and an empty tuna can water dish completed the habitat. All she needed now was a rat.

"Hey, Sam," she called as she stepped inside the maintenance shed and quickly shut the door. "Can I borrow a bucket? I'll bring it right back."

A hand appeared from beneath the Hägglunds and pointed in the direction of the worktable. "Over there."

"Thanks." Zo circumnavigated a disassembled engine block and stepped carefully over the arc welder's hoses. Sam's feet were always poking out from under one vehicle or another. For all practical purposes, he lived in the maintenance shed, taking his meals there, and often spending the night on a cot. Shortly after she'd arrived at Raney, Zo had been advised to give Sam as much space as possible with the promise that in return, he'd keep the Hägglunds running for her, and thus far the bargain seemed to be working. It didn't take a genius to figure out that a Class A mechanic with zero social skills and an empty continent that was murder on equipment were a good fit.

His workbench was littered with the usual mechanic's assortment: hammers, wrenches, grease guns; coils of wire, scraps of metal, balls of string; empty coffee cups, dirty rags, a roll of toilet paper, and jars filled with washers, nuts and bolts, and other unidentifiable but potentially useful objects. She found the bucket behind an open jar of peanut butter alongside a half-eaten loaf of bread. She was tempted to repeat Elliot's warning about not leaving food out in the open, but Sam was an adult, and a crotchety one at that.

"Can I use this piece of sheet metal?" she called over her shoulder instead. "And I need some tin snips, and some string."

"Why don't you just take the whole damn toolbox."

"That's okay. This'll do." She added a short length of pipe to her rat-catching paraphernalia and went outside.

Think like a rat, she told herself as she hiked away from the station. What did a rat need besides food and shelter? Food, they had in abundance: Raney's unsuspecting shorebird colonies formed a virtual rat smorgasbord. Two penguin carcasses had been found on the beach in the past two days, their bones picked as clean as museum specimens.

So the question was, after the rats bellied up to the bar, where did they go to sleep it off?

Working on the presumption that the simplest answer was the correct one, Zo shone a flashlight into each likely-looking crevice in the jumble of ice and rocks where the glacier met the shore. She felt like the host of one of those hands-on television nature shows. *Crikey, wot've we got here? [sticks arm into hole in the ground; pulls out something dark and wriggling] It's a banded gecko! Isn't she a beauty? And just look at those teeth! Ow!! Crikey, did ya see that? [laughs] She bit me finger!*

Finally, she found what she was looking for beside a crack six inches wide. *Ah, look here, mates. Ya see these brown pellets? Ya know wot these aar? [winks at camera] This is* rodent spoor. *You know what that means! Stay with me now, and maybe we'll see something!*

She tied one end of the string around the pipe, propped up the bucket, and placed a chunk of Velveeta underneath. After unspooling twenty feet of string, she sat down cross-legged on the gravel to wait. The whole setup looked suspiciously like something out of a Roadrunner cartoon, but it was the best she could do.

She sat as still as possible and tried to ignore her dripping nose. Realistically, the odds of catching a rat with her makeshift arrangement were ridiculously small. Ross's students had been sending him rat facts ever since he told them about the *rattus norvegicus* invasion, and according to the kids, rats were like miniature superheroes. They could climb, jump, fall fifty feet without injury, and fit through an opening the size of a quarter. And if they couldn't go around or over an object, they went through it, gnawing through materials as diverse as lead sheathing, cinder block, aluminum siding, and glass, to say nothing of cardboard and paper. Rats were excellent swimmers and could cross half a mile of open water, swim through sewer lines against the current, and tread water for three days. She frowned at Torgeson Island across the bay. She hated to think what would happen to Mac's penguin colonies if Raney's rats decided to go for a swim.

After ten torturous minutes that gave new meaning to the phrase "frozen as a statue," she saw movement. A black nose appeared, followed by a set of twitching whiskers, a slender brown head, furry body, and leathery tail. Zo held her pose. The rat studied her for a long moment, sniffed, then darted beneath the bucket to take the bait. She yanked on the string, and the bucket fell with a clatter. Inside, the rat scrabbled and hissed.

She grinned. Apparently the coyote knew a thing or two about catching critters after all. She hurried over to claim her prize, keeping an eye out to make sure that none of its pals were going to play the hero. Carefully, she worked the sheet metal between the bucket and the ice. With one hand pressing on the bucket's bottom, she slid the other underneath and flipped the contraption upright.

Suddenly the rat leapt at the lid, knocking the sheet metal to the side. The bucket tipped, and the rat tumbled out. For a moment the rat was as stunned as Zo was. She recovered first, grabbing the rat and flinging it back into the bucket before she could consider the consequences. She threw the sheet metal on top and sat down on it to hold it in place. Quickly she pulled the tin snips from her pocket, cut the excess metal into strips, and, using the snips as a hammer, bent the tabs down and sealed the bucket shut.

Breathing heavily, she stood up. Her knuckles were scraped, her back muscles ached, and her lip sported a snot mustache that would have done a Canadian lumberjack proud, but she had her rat. *And crikey! Isn't he a beauty!*

As she started back to the station, she decided that while Antarctic rat-catching would undoubtedly never become an Olympic event, it *should* be.

Chapter 19

Two days later, the winds gusted at sixty as Raney got socked by the first official blizzard of the season. Great, crescent-shaped mounds of snow curled around each corner of the buildings like sleeping guard dogs; by morning, the regulars predicted they'd be the size of small elephants. Zo took note of the drifts as she headed for the shore, gripping her hood about her face as the snow stung like BBs and her goggles fogged with every breath. The wind worked its way inside her clothes despite multiple layers, so cold against her skin it burned.

Ten minutes, she promised herself. If she couldn't finish the job by then, she'd hoof it back to the station and the Zodiac would have to take its chances. She'd helped Mac tie it off earlier when he got in from Torgeson, but she was no Girl Scout, and with the way the winds had picked up, she wasn't at all sure her knots were going to hold. She peeled back the cuff of one glove, exposing her wrist long enough to check the time, and continued toward the beach, shuffling her feet like a blind man. Inside her gloves, she curled her fingers into fists and stuck her hands under her armpits. After treating three cases of frostbite, Dr. Rodriguez had laid down the law: One more, and they'd all be confined to the station for the duration. Zo wasn't afraid of a little frostbite, but she wasn't about to be the one responsible for a lockdown. The atmosphere inside was frigid enough.

One week, one lousy week since the rats had invaded the station, and she was well on her way to taking home the award for Raney's Most Despised Person. The climatologists griped because the rats' body heat skewed their microclimate recorder calibrations—as if rodents could be expected to respect a roped-off research area. Dr. Rodriguez was concerned about disease, Shana was freaked because a rat had stolen her sandwich after she'd foolishly laid it on the ground, and so it went. Every time Zo spotted another rat skulking about the station, the cumulative guilt trip the others were laying on made her feel like the Pied Piper's evil twin.

Finally, she spotted the Zodiac. She hurried forward and crouched in the lee for a respite from the wind. Beside her, the inflatable tugged at its moorings like a balloon in a hurricane. She ran her hands along the rope, following the line into the snowbank to locate the knot. Halfway down, she touched something soft. She lifted her hand, and saw that her glove was smeared with red.

"Another one?" Fernando looked up from his evisceration as Zo came into the biolab carrying her bundle.

"Uh-huh. Found it by the Zodiac." She dumped the carcass on the worktable next to Fernando's cod and stripped off her gloves. "Third one this week," she said through stiffened lips. "Another chinstrap, I think." She sniffed and dragged her hand under her nose. "Hard to tell with so much meat gone."

"You're *louco, ne,* going outside in weather like this." Fernando lifted her chin and turned her face toward the light. "Just as I thought, *querida.* You better have Luis look at that. Your right cheek is pretty white."

She touched her fingers to her face. "It's okay. I haven't lost feeling yet."

"Gonna sting like hell later."

"Don't I know."

She shook the snow off her coat and hung it over the back of a chair. Using one of Fernando's scalpels, she sliced off a chunk of penguin meat, weighed it, noted the figure in her ledger, and dropped the meat inside the cage. The rat tore into its meal with a ferocity that belied its size. Quickly she replaced the cement block that secured the lid. Collecting penguin carcasses and comparing the amount of meat her specimen rat ate with how much meat was missing helped determine the total rat population, but every time she fed the rat, she couldn't help envisioning the victim's final moments as the rats tore into it like a pack of rabid hyenas. She estimated the count at 30 to 50 animals, though she wasn't about to tell the others that—or that the rats' numbers seemed to be increasing as more found their way across the peninsula every day.

Fernando shook his head. "I do not know how you can stand taking care of him. I hate that guy."

"Everything's got to eat. Besides, I think Pinky's kind of cute, in a penguin-eating, rat gang-member sort of way. All he needs is a little motorcycle helmet and boots."

Fernando laughed. "Why do I get the feeling you were

the strange little *menina* who kept tarantulas and scorpions as pets?"

"How'd you know? Besides, I—oh." She put her hands to her cheeks.

"Told you. You really should let Luis look at that."

"I'll be fine." Zo closed her eyes while she waited for her brain to convince her nerve endings this was an acceptable level of pain, then stuffed the penguin inside a garbage bag and stuck the carcass in the fridge. She cracked open a bottle of Dr Pepper and guzzled half, belched, then downed the rest, smiling at the confirmation that after three tortuous months, her nonstop morning sickness was finally gone.

"I'm going to hang out in the rec room for a while," she said. "Want to come?"

"Definitely. Just as soon as I wash up. Mac talked Elliot into doing his Frank Sinatra imitation."

"Really." Elliot only did Sinatra when he was feeling particularly happy. She wondered what had happened to put him in such a good mood—and why he hadn't told her.

"You think this is something?" Mac was saying as Zo entered the room. He and Shana were cozied up on one of the ratty orange vinyl sofas Zo was convinced were older than the station itself. She often wondered how they came to be here; who had donated them, and why they thought the scientists didn't deserve better than castoffs. Due to the wear and tear of decades, the couches were upholstered now with more duct tape than vinyl.

She scanned the room. Nearly all of Raney's residents were present, whiling away the blizzard playing Foosball or Ping-Pong, talking and reading. Elliot and Ross occupied

a love seat in the far corner. Elliot was gesturing anima-
tedly while Ross smiled and nodded. A few glanced her
way, but no one acknowledged her, or invited her to join
them. She leaned against the doorjamb, feeling as welcome as a leper in a bathhouse, while the conversation
swirled around her like the snow outside the windows.

"You should try spending a winter at the Pole," Mac
went on. "Six months of darkness; temps of ninety below.
It's so cold, your breath freezes. Suck the air through your
teeth, and it'll crack your enamel."

"Really?" Shana snuggled closer and looked up at Mac
with ingenue eyes. Zo shook her head. Shana's come-on
was so blatant, she may as well have batted her eyelashes.
Zo was surprised Mac couldn't see it. Then again, maybe
he had.

"Oh, yeah," he said, puffing out his chest and slipping a
macho arm around Shana's shoulders. "You have to wear a
respirator when you go outside to prevent lung damage or
mouth frostbite. But when it's that cold, your breath con-
denses, and the respirator clogs with ice. So then you've
got a choice: keep the respirator on and suffocate, or take it
off and let your tongue freeze." He put his free hand over
her face and pretended to smother her while she giggled
and pretended to struggle.

"And you'd better remember to keep your hand on the
flag line," Kevin, a three-year veteran said.

Mac shot him a look.

Zo grinned. So much for Mac's intimate little tête-à-
tête.

"One time the winds were quiet, so I thought I didn't
need to," Kevin continued. "Technically, I didn't get lost,
but I came back at a part of the station I wasn't expecting.
Believe me, I always follow the flag line now."

"I think the isolation is the worst," another station regular said. "You can cope with the snow and the cold, but being cut off from the rest of the planet isn't so easy to deal with. NASA actually studies the people who winter over at the Pole to determine the effects of long-term isolation."

"And you may have noticed," Mac said, manfully attempting to wrest control of the conversation again, "it's been a long time since—"

There was a tap on Zo's arm. She turned around. "We have trouble," Fernando whispered.

"What kind of trouble?" she whispered back.

"Your rat. He is gone."

"*Gone?* Good grief. Please tell me you're joking."

"Most definitely, I am not."

"I don't believe it. How could it happen? That lid was held down with bricks!"

"That sneaky *doida* chewed a hole in the screen."

"What's going on over there?" Mac called.

"Nothing," Zo replied.

"Zo's rat has escaped," Fernando announced to the room. "He chewed a hole in the lid."

"Pinky's loose?" Shana gasped and clutched Mac's sleeve.

"Good one, Zo," Kevin said. "Not only do you bring the rats to the station, you give them the run of the place as well. Why don't you just set up a feeding trough in the dining room and be done with it?"

"It's no big deal," she said, thinking of the myriad places a rat could hide. "I caught him once; I'll catch him again. I'll set up my trap in the kitchen; that's the most likely place he'll head. In the meantime, you might want to keep the junk food out of your rooms. That is," she added, looking pointedly at Shana, "unless you don't mind the idea of acquiring a new bunk mate." She left Mac to console his squealing girlfriend and headed for the mudroom.

"Where are you going?" Ross asked as she borrowed a dry coat off the rack.

"To the maintenance shed. I need to get a bucket." She dug through the communal hatbox for a scarf and gloves.

"I'll come with you."

"You don't have to."

"*Au contraire, ma chérie,* I do. Or rather, someone does. I presume you're familiar with a principle called the buddy system?" He tapped the wind gauge mounted alongside the exterior door. "Station rules: Anytime the winds are over forty, no one goes outside alone."

"Suit yourself."

"I always do."

He held the door for her and they went out. The wind whipped between the buildings, sweeping the ground clear in places and piling the snow higher than their heads in others. The sun shone weakly through the blowing snow, coloring the landscape a diffused, surreal yellow. High above, the sky was pocked with blue.

Zo broke trail while Ross gripped the back of her parka like an uninvited Siamese twin.

"So what's it stand for?" he asked, leaning over her shoulder to speak his question in her ear.

She got a whiff of Obsession for Men—the same cologne Elliot wore—and shivered. She hadn't been this close to a man in months. "What's what stand for?"

"Your name. Is it short for Zoe?"

"No, it's a nickname."

"Then what's your real name?"

She shook her head. "You'll laugh."

"No, I won't."

"Yes, you will."

"I won't."

"You will. Everyone does."

"Oh, come on, how bad can it be? Anyway, the door's open; may as well walk through it."

Indeed. Zo had been through this routine so many times before, she couldn't believe she'd gotten sucked in again. She turned around.

"Amazonia."

"You're joking." Ross's mouth twitched. He looked down at her—something not many men could do ever since a teenaged Zo had topped out at five ten. A part of her wanted to wipe the smirk off his face, even as another part had to concede he looked good wearing it. With his thick black braid, chiseled nose, and swept-back forehead he could have been the model for the Indian-head penny. God, or the Great Spirit, had blessed Dr. Roundtree with looks *and* brains. Trouble was, he knew it.

She lifted her chin. "Told you you'd laugh."

"I'm not laughing."

"Yes, you are."

"No, I'm not. I—oh, what the hell. So what if I am? You have to admit it's a bit—unusual. What's the deal? Were your parents hippies?"

She shook her head. "Environmentalists."

He slapped his thigh. "Perfect! And so the girl named after the largest rain forest ecosystem in the world goes off to work in Antarctica. Wouldn't Freud have fun with *that*?"

She didn't answer. It wasn't until they'd resumed their conjoined trek that she smiled. She'd often had the same thought herself.

Suddenly, her foot caught on something and she tripped, falling face-forward in the snow. Ross landed on top of her.

"Whoa," he said as he rolled quickly to the side. "Are you okay? I didn't . . . you know, hurt the baby?"

She searched his face for signs of sarcasm, but either Ross was a consummate actor, or his concern was genuine. "I'm fine. I'm only three and a half months. The baby's not much bigger than a pea. Plenty of room in there for it to bounce around." She brushed the snow off her knees and pointed. "Something's down there."

He knelt and dug through the snow. *"My God,"* he said and stood up, his expression grim. He grabbed her arm. "Come on. We've got to get back to the station."

"Wait. What is it? Let me see." She tried to twist free.

He tightened his grip. "Believe me, you don't want to."

"Oh, good grief, Ross." She felt like slapping him. She hated when men played their stupid chauvinistic games. "I'm not Shana. I'm not going to fall apart at the sight of a little blood. If it's another penguin carcass, I need to bring it into the sta— *Jesus*!"

Her hand flew to her mouth as Ross stepped to the side. It was another rat kill, all right, a bloodied, masticated mess. Only this time, it wasn't a penguin carcass.

It was Sam.

Chapter 20

Forty-eight hours after Eugene dispatched Ben's entire supply of water testing kits with a single blow, Ben opened the incubator door. As he took out the two surviving samples, he felt like a fool. By themselves, the results were worse than useless; all they said was that two days ago, the ice outside the Quonset hadn't been tainted. But Eugene was so appalled by what he had done, and so contrite, hanging around Ben's heels like a scolded puppy, that Ben didn't have the heart to punish him further. And so as he held up the purple liquid for everyone to see, he made a great show of being pleased before he tossed the test tubes in the trash.

That done, he symbolically wiped his hands of the mess. The water would have to be tested after the tanker arrived in Los Angeles. Gillette was going to be furious, and rightfully so—the whole point of the tests had been to keep the possibility of contamination from an interested public. Ben had delegated Quentin the job of breaking the bad news. May as well get some use out of Quentin's much-vaunted status as Gillette's number two.

Announcing the Big News, however, was a privilege Ben had reserved for himself, and if all went according to schedule, as soon as the next communications window opened, he would be making that momentous call. Toshi's latest fix seemed to be holding; everyone else was as ready as he; and so barring any unforeseen last-minute developments, Ben had declared today D-day. Or "B-day," as Phil jokingly put it: the long-awaited auspicious day in which the cosmos would give birth to a brand-spanking-new microwave beam.

"How do we look?" Ben asked Toshi.

"Great," Toshi said. "Still holding steady. No sign of satellite drift."

"Susan?"

Their systems engineer raised both thumbs. "All systems go." Susan had come to them straight out of four years at NASA, and it showed.

"Phil? You done there?"

"Almost." Phil typed a string of numbers into his computer, studied them for a long moment, and sat back. "Okay. Ready."

"You sure?" Eugene asked. "'Cause we sorta got a lot riding on this, you know."

Phil's face fell. "Of course I'm sure. Twenty-five joules per cubic centimeter melts water. The solar constant in space is 1.5 kilowatts per square meter. Our solar array spans 1.8 million square meters, and we want our target lake to be one meter deep, spread out over a one-kilometer area. That means we're looking at a total of 2E13 joules, or 20 trillion photons—5.5 million kilowatt hours." He checked his figures again. "I'm sure that's right."

"I know it is." Eugene punched Phil's arm. "Don't take everything so seriously, man. I was just messin' with you."

Phil glared.

"Okay guys," Ben said. "If we're done with the fun and games, let's get this show on the road. Everybody ready?" He glanced at Quentin. "Let's *do* it."

Toshi raised his index finger, held it dramatically over his keyboard while he made sure he had everyone's attention, then hit "enter" with a flourish.

Nothing happened.

Nothing visible, that is, which was exactly to be expected. If everything was working as it was supposed to, Toshi's keystroke had initiated a three-part pilot beam emanating from the center of the rectenna grid that had been constructed over the melt zone. The beam was shooting thirty-six thousand kilometers into space to Soldyne's three orbiting satellites. Circuits in each satellite's antenna subarray were comparing the pilot beam's phase front with their own internal clock phase, then following the pilot signal back to the ground. In theory, it was a fail-safe method of beam targeting, but in practice . . . well, the "practice" part of the equation simply hadn't been done yet.

Ben counted off the seconds. Exhaled after thirty. A minute crawled past; then two.

"How long is this supposed to take?" Eugene asked.

"How are we supposed to know?" Quentin snapped. "Why don't you shut up for once, and just wait like the rest of us."

"You shut up."

"You—" Quentin half rose from his chair, then shot Ben a *he's hopeless* look, and sat back down.

Another minute passed.

Then, "Temperature's rising," Phil said, his voice crackling with excitement. "Up point-oh-three degrees."

Ben hurried over. "Where? Which sector?"

"Right there." Phil tapped his screen. "Sector thirteen. Right smack dab in the middle of the melt zone. Sensors twenty-three and twenty-four are going up as well." He pushed back his chair and let out a whoop. "We did it! It's working! Just like it's supposed to."

The room broke out in cheers. Susan and Quentin embraced. Phil, Toshi, and Eugene traded high fives, then laughed as Eugene pretended to hike up his skirts and danced a jig.

Ben laid his glasses on his work surface and scrubbed his face. So many hours . . . so many dollars . . . the years of R&D, the months of waiting, the last-minute problem solving . . . all culminating in this historic moment at the bottom of the earth, ten thousand miles from home and family in a cramped Quonset littered with candy wrappers and soggy parkas. Finally, *finally*, the tanker that was costing a small fortune as it waited in the lee of the berg could be filled and sent on its way. The water would reach L.A. in three or four weeks, by which time Ben would be back in his office, ready to celebrate its arrival along with the rest of Soldyne's staff and the investors with all the hoopla of a ticker tape parade.

He closed his eyes and massaged his temples to ease the tension headache he hadn't even realized was there. *It worked*. It actually *worked*.

Eugene jostled Ben's shoulder. "Hey, boss. Wake up and join the party." He handed him a paper cup and cracked open a thermos. "Technically, it's not first water," he said as he poured, "but it's still water from the melt zone. Come on, everybody! Drink up! A toast!"

Ben looked from the cup to his team's expectant faces. He didn't want to drink. Then again, the odds of contamination were so low, and their spirits so high, he supposed it wouldn't kill him just this once to go along.

He raised his glass to their success and took a single, discreet sip as Eugene and the others guzzled theirs down.

Chapter 21

Ten minutes later, Quentin closed the door on the celebration and walked over to the bank of snowmobiles parked outside the maintenance hut. He brushed the snow off his favorite, pulled on his helmet, threw a leg over the seat, and turned the key. According to the manufacturer, the machines could do zero to sixty in 3.2 seconds, and every time he took one out, Quentin proved their claim. He was an expert rider who could handle a snowmobile on any terrain—even skip over open water in an emergency if the need arose. His father had taught the maneuver to both of his sons; Lake St. Clair near their home north of Detroit was notorious for ice-fishing conditions that could deteriorate without warning. Every spring, the Coast Guard had to rescue dozens of stranded anglers, and Quentin's dad wanted his boys to be able to handle themselves. Quentin's brother could barely work up the nerve to attempt crossing a six-inch crack, but as soon as the fifteen-year-old Quentin learned that a machine going seventy-five could power across three feet of open water, he'd gone looking for the chance to give it a try.

Here, the thin crust of snow over ice presented its own challenges. He eased back on the throttle when the machine started to skid, then accelerated once he found good cover again. A steady sixty would have him at the pump-house in less than five minutes. Another five to make his call, five more for the return, and with luck he would be back at the op center before he was missed. Not a bad pay-off: fifteen minutes in exchange for Ben Maki's career.

He laughed to think that Ben had actually charged him with reporting the testing fiasco. Ben was an idiot, and Eugene was toast. Once Quentin told his version, Eugene would be tossed off the berg like a lame contestant on a *Survivor* show, with Ben right behind him. It was too bad Ben had managed to get the satellites turned on—Donald was *not* going to be happy about that—but the day was young, and Quentin was an optimist. There were still plenty of things that could go wrong.

He gave the throttle a twist, and the machine leaped forward. That was one of the things he loved about snow-mobiling. Maintain your equipment, and it did exactly what you wanted. People were so much more difficult to maneuver. Still, he'd managed to best Ben back at the op center when he caught their fearless leader sipping his water like he thought it was poisoned. The others had seen it, too. Quentin had read the disappointment on their faces, and so he'd grabbed the moment by polishing off his own cupful and tossing back Ben's as well, then capped his victory by exchanging Eugene's watery toast for whiskey and beer.

A hundred yards to his left, a dark mass hugged the surface like a low-lying cloud. He slowed and lifted his visor. The mass seemed to undulate; shifting and changing shape as though it were alive. He lowered his visor and shivered. There was a malevolency emanating from the cloud, a vague sense of something evil that made his heart race.

He sped up. Inexplicably, the cloud-mass matched his speed. He slowed, and it did the same. *Enough,* he told himself, and opened the throttle wide. It was his imagination, a trick of the weather; a mirage, an illusion of distance and light. There was nothing to be afraid of; no reason for his heart to go into overdrive.

He powered forward, then glanced back. The cloud-mass was gone.

Two minutes later, he executed a neat bootlegger's reverse outside the pumphouse and killed the engine. He hung his helmet over the handlebars, tugged on a wool cap, and stood up. Immediately a wave of vertigo doubled him over as effectively as if he'd been punched in the gut. He sat down and counted off his heartbeats while he waited for the dizziness to pass. Then he got to his feet again, slowly, and hung on to the handlebars for support. He let go, took a tentative step, and then another, staggering toward the pumphouse with his arms out for balance like a drunk.

By the time he reached the door, his shirt was soaked with sweat. He put his shoulder to the door and pushed, then pushed again. Strange. He didn't remember the door being so heavy.

Then he looked down. *Of all the—* He hadn't even turned the handle. What was wrong with him? His eyes were all blurry, and his head felt like it was going to explode. He wondered if Eugene had spiked his water, maybe with that date-rape drug, PCB. No, that wasn't right. PBB. PCP?

He opened the door and stepped inside, groping for the light switch, and inventoried the room. *Chair. Table. Another chair. Wastebasket—*

Phone. That was what he was looking for. He needed to use the satellite phone. But who was he supposed to call?

He stumbled back outside, hoping the fresh air would clear his head. As he lurched toward the snowmobile, his feet tingled like he was walking on needles. He sat down on the seat and fumbled on his helmet, then reached for the key.

What next?

Turn the key. No, the other way. Okay, good.

Now what?

The throttle. Something about the throttle.

He twisted the throttle, and the machine took off. It smashed into the pumphouse and flipped.

He lay on his back and tried to figure out what had happened. He was on the snowmobile, and now he was looking at the sky. His helmet was gone, and the ice was cold. His legs hurt. Something was sitting on them, something heavy.

Think.

Get up.

Go back to the op center. Get help.

He raised himself on his elbows. He couldn't see his legs. The snowmobile was on top of them, and the headlight was shattered.

He was in for it now. John was gonna kill him for wrecking the machine. *John?* Why did he say John? *Ben* was gonna kill him. Who the hell was John?

He lay back down and looked up at the clouds. Something was moving. He squinted. It was Sally, sitting in a rocking chair, with a baby at her breast.

She'd had the baby! Why hadn't anyone told him? Was it a boy or a girl? He hoped it was a girl. Sally wanted a boy, but he wanted a daughter. Emily, they were going to call her, after Quentin's grandmother—that is, if Sally hadn't gone ahead and named her something else—

"Sally! Over here!" He smiled and waved. "Look down here! It's me!"

She stopped rocking and looked. Quentin's lip trembled as he lowered his hand.

Why was Sally crying?

Chapter 22

Ben clicked off the satellite phone and set it down carefully on Quentin's desk. He took off his glasses and folded the stems inward, then laid the glasses alongside the phone and rested his head in his hands. His stomach churned. Two calls to Donald in the span of as many hours, one conveying the best of all possible news, the other the absolute worst, left him feeling raw. Bad word choice, he corrected himself, considering the condition in which they'd found Quentin's body. He shuddered. Accidents happened; he knew that; the world was a dangerous place. Across the centuries, history had proved that undertakings of a magnitude such as theirs were not without risk. Still, he'd never expected death to make an appearance here.

Quentin was dead. Worse, he'd met his end in the most appalling way imaginable. Ben pictured the mutilated body wrapped in bedsheets and stored in an unheated shed and felt like throwing up.

"You didn't tell him about the rats." Behind him, Susan's voice was heavy with accusation.

He turned around. The others were clustered behind her in an anxious knot. Eugene's normally ruddy face was pale as powder, Phil's lower lip was bitten red from the effort not to cry, and Toshi's frenzied blinking said he was struggling against the same. Susan was holding up better than the rest, no doubt because of her NASA training, but Ben was willing to lay odds that inside, she, too, was a wreck. He ran his hand over his head. It was hard to believe this demoralized group was the same team that two hours earlier had pulled off the engineering coup of the decade.

He put his glasses back on and squared his shoulders. "No, I didn't tell him about the rats, and I expect you to do the same."

"Why?" she persisted. "I'm sorry, Ben. I don't like to question your authority, but Gillette's the boss. It's not right to withhold facts."

"I'm not withholding information. Donald will get a full report eventually, but now is not the time. Don't forget, Donald was Quentin's brother-in-law. It's bad enough to have to tell him Quentin's dead without including the details. Besides that, Quentin's widow is six months' pregnant. She just lost her husband. You want to be responsible for her maybe losing the baby as well?" He held out the phone.

Susan scowled and shook her head.

"All right, then." He turned to the others. "The supply ship is leaving within the hour to bring Quentin's body to Punta Arenas, and from there, the body will be flown home. Meanwhile, we have a tanker that needs filling."

"We're going ahead?" Phil blinked his surprise. "I thought . . . I mean . . . well, considering what just happened, I figured—"

"That we'd pack it all in? Believe me, I feel as badly about what happened as you do, but there are far too many dollars and man-hours invested to quit now. People *need* our water; quite literally millions of them. Besides, we just got the satellites turned on."

"But what about us? If the supply ship leaves, and then the tanker leaves—"

"We won't be stranded. The captain's giving us his pilot and helicopter. We're only a few miles from the Antarctic Peninsula. There are any number of research stations within range. If necessary, we could pile into the helicopter and hop over to Raney Station or McMurdo, but that's just a contingency. The supply ship will be back in a week." In truth, the captain had told Ben that with winter weather setting in, it would take "at least" a week to make the trip. He'd also cautioned that the helicopter would be useless in bad weather, but under the circumstances, a little judicious editing seemed prudent.

Eugene shook his head. "I don't like it. Not one bit. Phil's right: We should get off while we can."

Susan snorted. "Or what? You think the big, bad rats are going to hunt you down?"

Eugene turned on her. His eyes were slits. "They *ate* him, Susan. *The rats* ate *him.* You wanna be here when they decide it's time for another meal?"

"We don't know that the rats killed Quentin," she said. "Most likely they found his body after he was already dead. Rats are opportunists; scavengers, not predators. Given a choice, a scavenger will always take the easy way out."

"Exactly. Which do you think is easier: taking down an elephant seal, or dragging my buddy Phil here out of his bed?"

"Holy crap." Phil covered his mouth.

"Enough," Ben said. "We'll hold a memorial for Quentin on Sunday. If anyone wants to offer a few words, let me know. Meanwhile, I'll only say this once: Get back to work."

Chairs creaked as the team members swiveled around to their stations. Ben leaned back and exhaled. He felt like he'd just averted a mutiny.

He opened Quentin's desk drawer to look for names of people he should contact or personal effects that should go back with Quentin's body. Inside was Quentin's wallet. He picked it up. It opened to a picture of Quentin's wife. Ben frowned, then went through the contents: 200 American dollars, 10,000 Chilean pesos, a receipt for three bottles of whiskey from a duty-free store, a Visa card, and an American Express, with a dog-eared business card tucked behind it. He extracted the card, then tapped it thoughtfully against his lips.

Why was Quentin doing business with an explosives expert?

Chapter 23

"So you think plastique is the way to go."

"*Aoo*—yes. Definitely." Ramon Yellowhorse laced his fingers behind his head and leaned back against the park bench, stretching his legs in front of him and closing his eyes as if there were nothing more important on his mind than catching a few rays.

"It's completely stable," he went on in a low voice, his face still turned toward the sky. "You could use it as a baseball bat if you wanted. Plastique won't explode on impact—not even if it's exposed to flame. The only thing that'll set it off is a blasting cap."

"How much will you need?" Beside him, Rebecca Sweet mirrored his affectation with her shorts turned up to her thighs and her ICE SOLDYNE T-shirt knotted beneath her breasts.

"How much destruction you want?" Ramon smiled as he ticked off the possibilities. "A quarter pound of C4 rolled into a cigar shape and placed along a steel I-beam will cut it as easily as a torch. A pound of C4 at all four corners of a building will take it down. One hundred pounds will breach your ship's hull, and two or three will break its back."

"*Nizhóní.* Excellent. Let's go with door number three."

"In that case, four divers carrying twenty-five pounds each will do." He grinned. "Be sure to save yourself a ring-side seat. Water increases plastique's concussive effect."

"How will you set it off?"

"As long as it's waterproofed, any kind of remote-control electrical detonator will do."

"And detection?"

"Not a problem. Detection would have to be visual. Unless someone gets suspicious and jumps over the side, there's no way anyone will find it."

"And no one gets hurt, right?" Rebecca pointed her finger. "We're talking structural damage only. Just enough to blow a hole in the side and release some of the water."

"Of course."

"Because we don't want to destroy the ship; we only want to make a statement. I want to be sure we're absolutely clear on that. No matter what the FBI thinks, we're not terrorists."

"Understood."

"Radical times call for radical measures."

"I got it."

She pursed her lips. "Where will you get it?"

He shook his head. "Better you don't know."

He was right about that. Last August, when she and her crew had been caught down in Florida boarding a cargo ship carrying Brazilian wood, only the fact that she was pregnant had saved her from significant jail time. She looked at Pablo, asleep in his stroller, and as if sensing her concern, he began to cry.

"What's the matter, *K'aalógii*? Did you have a bad dream?" Rebecca fished between the baby's diaper and the stroller for his pacifier. "Listen," she said to Ramon as she wiped off the fuzz and stuck the pacifier in Pablo's mouth, "I've got to go pick up Jesse and Joshua at preschool. Meet me here same time next week. Tell your people to get ready. And *hazhóó ógo bidiní*—tell them to be careful."

Chapter 24

Elliot raised himself up on one elbow to watch as Zo lowered her jeans and sat down on her side of the bed. She took a bottle of insulin from the apartment-sized refrigerator that served as her nightstand, stuck in a syringe, and drew up half her usual dose. He frowned. Zo's blood-glucose levels had been fluctuating wildly over the past three days, no doubt because of all of the stress. The whole station was in an uproar over Sam's death, and who could blame them? Add in the fact that she was going to have a baby, and it was no wonder her diabetes was a mess.

She detached the needle from the plunger and dropped the needle in the wastebasket, then returned the insulin to the fridge and switched off the lamp. She slid under the covers, keeping her back turned toward him as usual. He rolled onto his and stared up at the ceiling, the creaking bedsprings masking his usual sigh. At least now, he understood why.

He'd figured it out three days ago. Zo's physical and

emotional distance, the way Roundtree was always hovering near—a blind man could have seen that the two shared a secret, and Elliot's vision was clear. He wasn't the only one who suspected an affair; he'd heard the whispers, seen the pitying looks.

Then he'd caught a glimpse of Zo's belly, and the answer appeared like the prognostication in a Magic 8 Ball. Roundtree confirmed his deduction when Elliot questioned him in the rec room the day Sam's body was discovered and Zo's rat disappeared. Elliot's stomach had been churning ever since. The betrayal he felt at Zo's months-long deception, combined with elation that at forty-seven he was going to become a father, mixed with fear for his family's—*his family's!*—health and safety, left him trembling and wet.

He pulled up a corner of the blanket to dry his face, then tucked it beneath his chin. A sliver of light from the hallway spilled under the door. He watched Zo's shoulders rise and fall evenly as she slept, and his eyes blurred. He understood how much her research meant to her, how hard she'd worked to get here, and why she'd lied rather than give it up, but if anything had happened— Just thinking about the possibilities made him feel ill. The women who came to Antarctica had to be tough—Jerri Nielsen's courage in the face of breast cancer, and Michelle Eileen Raney, the first woman to winter over at the Pole, were two of many who came to mind—but the risk Zo had assumed without consulting him was inexcusable.

Even so, he was going to miss her. Zo didn't know it, but as soon as the icebreaker arrived to pick up Sam's body, she'd be gone. He dreaded telling her; they rarely argued, and his decision was going to spark a terrible row. He'd make the same call for any of the women at the station, though he doubted she'd believe him. He sighed. He hated to think their last words would be angry ones. Then he reminded himself *he* was the one who had been wronged.

At any rate, with the near-winter weather upon them, God only knew when the ship would arrive. He listened to the wind roaring around the building, shaking the windows and rattling the doors like a demon trying to get in, and shivered. The very conditions that demanded she be sent home prevented it.

He rolled over with a long sigh and closed his eyes, then opened them again as a wave of dizziness made his head swim. He fumbled open the drawer to his nightstand and unwrapped a Werther's, savoring the buttery sweetness while he waited for the dizziness to pass.

It didn't. Instead, a spasm gripped his stomach. He moaned. *Hot.* He was so hot. He threw off the covers as the bile rose in his throat. Swallowed, then swallowed again.

As he leaned over the side of the bed and grabbed for the wastebasket, the light came on.

"Elliot!" he heard Zo exclaim. "What's the matter? Are you okay?"

Chapter 25

"Is he—"

Dr. Rodriguez put a finger to his lips and motioned Zo into the hallway, then shut the door and pointed down the corridor. Obediently, she trailed him to Elliot's office, the odor of vomit clinging to her hands and clothes.

Inside, Ross was leaning against Elliot's desk. Dr. Rodriguez waved her toward the extra chair. She remained standing, fight or flight response on high alert. Whatever was behind their impromptu powwow couldn't be good.

"Another one?" Ross asked Rodriguez.

Luis nodded. "Dr. Peterson."

Ross exhaled a low whistle. His eyes flicked to Zo, then looked away.

"What?" she asked. "He threw up, that's all. It's no big deal. Is it?"

"We're not sure," Dr. Rodriguez said.

Not sure? What was that *supposed to mean?*

"I asked Ross to meet us here after you told me Elliot

was ill," he continued. "With Elliot out of commission, I'm the station's acting director, and frankly, I'm struggling. I can use Ross's expertise."

"Elliot's not the first person to get sick," Ross told her, "in fact, he's the fifth. Fernando was first. He woke Mac up yelling crazy stuff about aliens and spaceships, then spewed right across the room."

"That's what happened to Elliot. He was fine when we went to bed, then all of a sudden, he threw up. Totally missed the wastebasket. He said he hasn't done that since he was a kid."

Ross nodded as if that was exactly what he had expected. "After Fernando threw up, Kevin started competing with him for bathroom time. Then Todd and Vikas started in. At this rate, we're going to run out of buckets."

"What did we have for dinner?"

"It's not food poisoning," Dr. Rodriguez said, "though I thought so, too, at first. The victims all have fever, chills, muscle aches, and abdominal pain, but then they progress to blurred vision and headaches—even mental confusion. That part doesn't fit."

"Some kind of flu?"

"More like gastroenteritis. Influenza is a respiratory infection. Worse, this looks infectious, and it's quite a bit more severe than your garden-variety GI infection."

"How do we treat it?" Ross asked.

"Well, there's the rub. Problem is there are thousands of bugs that cause gastrointestinal infections. Most aren't serious, but the ones that are generally have specific symptoms. Agents like shigella, salmonella, and *E. coli* 157 will cause diarrhea, usually with blood or mucous. I'm not seeing that here. It's too cold for giardia to survive, and this looks nothing like cholera. And there's something funny about this presentation."

Zo wanted to say there was nothing funny about the situation at all, but bit back the retort.

"In what way?"

"It's not unusual to see confusion and blurred vision and similar symptoms with infections in the elderly, but with the exception of Elliot, these are young, healthy victims. I don't know what to say except that it doesn't fit." He sighed, and Zo noted the dark circles under his eyes. His skin was sallow. If Luis got sick . . .

"However, I can tell you this," he went on. "Sometimes when a doctor sees a patient, they get an instinct. It's hard to identify just what it is about the patient that bothers you, but there's something unnerving that you can't dismiss. I'm getting that feeling here. Warning flags that things could go south quickly."

"My, God." She sank into a chair.

"I'm sorry, Zo," he said quickly. "I shouldn't have said that. It's totally unprofessional of me to be so alarmist. I know you're worried about Elliot, and it's true—he's thrown up once. Nothing worrisome about that. I just want to be cautious because some of these other patients are troubling me. It strikes me as an outbreak; one that's more serious than the usual GI illnesses I've seen, but that doesn't fit the symptom profile of any of the more aggressive ones I know. Plus, I'm having trouble figuring out how this infection would spring up out of nowhere. We haven't had a tour ship stop in weeks, and the incubation period is too long for an aggressive virus."

"Don't some GI and respiratory bugs have animal reservoirs?" Ross asked.

Dr. Rodriguez nodded. "Bird flu in poultry, campylobacter in dogs and cats, hantavirus in rats—"

"Oh no. No way." Zo shook her head. "This is *so* not my fault."

"We're not looking to assign blame," Ross said, "just for an explanation." He turned to Rodriguez. "You think this is hanta?"

"Hard to say. If it is, it's atypical. Hantavirus is predominantly a respiratory infection, though patients do suffer significant GI symptoms. After that first big outbreak in Four Corners, hantavirus became a recognized pan-American zoonosis. Outbreaks have occurred as close to us as Argentina and Chile. It's possible we're looking at one here. There are several varieties, each with a distinct rodent host. It may be that Zo's rats harbor a new strain."

"Hantavirus is transmitted by direct contact," Ross said. "Humans become infected when they handle diseased rodents, or their droppings." He looked at Zo.

"You're saying the virus was introduced though me? But I'm not sick."

"It's possible you have a natural immunity. It's also possible that sometime within the next few hours, you'll be sick as a dog."

"Thanks." She made a face.

"Hantavirus is nothing to joke about," Dr. Rodriguez said. "After the initial stage, the infected person feels somewhat better, but within a day or two they experience an increased respiratory rate caused by a seepage of fluid into the lungs, leading eventually to respiratory failure. Even with intensive therapy, over fifty percent of the diagnosed cases are fatal. Of course, we don't have those respiratory symptoms here, not yet at least, but still . . ."

"People are going to *die*?" Zo asked, shocked.

"Not if I can help it," Dr. Rodriguez said. "Not on my watch. Besides, I'm not at all convinced this is hanta. Some things fit, but a lot doesn't. For instance, hantavirus isn't passed between humans. In order to contract the disease, victims have to have direct contact with an infected rodent's feces. While it's possible that some of the personnel came in contact with the rats' feces, the number who are falling ill, and the rapidity with which the illness is spreading, make that highly unlikely. This strikes me as airborne or droplet spread."

"Perhaps instead of speculating about the virus's identity," Ross said, "we should be asking how we contain it."

"Unfortunately, we can't," Dr. Rodriguez said. "Infections like this tend to spread rapidly—especially under crowded conditions. We don't have the luxury of isolating our victims, and even such simple preventive measures as sterilizing infected dishes and bedding aren't practical. It's tough enough to produce the quantities of water we need under normal circumstances—I've been telling Elliot for years that our open cistern system is inadequate—even dangerous—and this extra load is going to make that impossible. And if the support staff gets sick—well, let's just say that the next few days are likely to be a challenge."

"Maybe we should evacuate," Zo said. "When the ship comes for Sam's body, maybe we should all be on it."

Ross burst out laughing. "I'm sorry, Zo," he said, "but have you *looked* outside lately?" He pointed toward the sleet-spattered window. "There's no way the ship will get here before the end of the week, and by then the virus will have run its course. Not even an Amazon Woman could conjure up a rescue before then."

"So we just wait it out? Twiddle our thumbs and do nothing?"

"Oh, we'll have plenty to do," Dr. Rodriguez said. "Those who aren't sick are going to have to look after those who are. I have a good stock of anti-inflammatory drugs to make folks comfortable, and we'll need to make sure those who are ill drink plenty of water. We can't stop the course of the infection, but we can make sure no one succumbs to dehydration."

There was a knock on the door. Mac came in, barefoot and dressed in sweats. His hair was as wild as the expression on his face. "Where's Rodriguez?"

"Right here." Dr. Rodriguez stepped forward. "What do you need? Are you sick?"

"I'm fine, Doc." Mac's voice cracked as his eyes filled with tears. "But Fernando is dead."

Chapter 26

Los Angeles, California

Sometime during the past twenty or thirty years, Donald mused, somehow—maybe because of their overpowering fragrance, or maybe it was simple collusion among the Canadian greenhouse growers—freesia had managed to supplant gladiolas and mums as the number one choice of funeral flower. Certainly the main viewing room at the Wujek-Calcaterra Funeral Home on downtown Wilshire Boulevard gave evidence; the noxious, spotted pink-and-white blooms were everywhere.

Donald had hated the flower since he was a child. The enmity began at his grandfather's funeral, when the five-year-old Donald had been sandwiched between his mother and his grandmother on a wooden folding chair in the front row while a dozen feet away, his powdered-pink grandpa ignored his favorite grandson by staring fixedly at the ceiling. Throughout the service, the young Donald had sniffed and rubbed his nose—not because of sorrow, but because of a stink strong enough to melt the paint off his

tricycle and an as-yet-undiagnosed allergy to all things
floral. The women had slipped their misunderstanding
arms around his shoulders, adding Dior and Calvin to the
mix. It was no wonder the grown-up Donald associated
sweetness with death.

Mercifully, today, protocol had him sitting in the second row, an additional three feet between him and the le-
thal sprays. That, combined with the double dose of
antihistamine he'd taken before he left the house, were doing a fine job of keeping the allergies at bay. Behind the
fresh-faced and obviously allergy-free minister, the flowers were positioned in descending order on either side according to the status of their giver. Donald's scentless roses
were in the middle. His offering was also the largest; an
extra hundred to the florist had seen to that.

Carla sat beside him, sans perfume as always, and Sally
sat in front of them, flanked by Quentin's parents and Donald's in-laws. Quentin was noticeably absent. Cremation
was the only option for a body so badly mutilated—though
Donald was the only one who knew about that. As executer,
Donald had offered to handle the arrangements, and Sally
had gratefully accepted. No doubt some would argue that it
was wrong of him to withhold the truth from her, but Donald had never shied away from making the hard decisions.
The higher your position, the higher your level of responsibility. Heads of households, heads of corporations, heads of
state—the difference was only a matter of degree. Let them
think Quentin had died of a heart attack; as far as Donald
was concerned, that may well have been true. If he'd been
attacked and eaten by rats, he'd have had one, too.

"Bless this thy servant, who has been taken unto our
Lord's bosom into heaven . . ."

Heaven. As the minister's drone wormed its way into Donald's consciousness, Donald looked up at the ceiling, feigning piety, while his imagination carried him far beyond; through the troposphere, past the stratosphere, beyond the mesosphere . . . 250 miles above the earth to that last, thin, precious layer separating mankind from deep space: the ionosphere. Next year, it would be his H.A.A.R.P. technology all the way. Ben's environmental scare tactics may have intimidated the board into choosing his microwave method over Donald's, but this season's imminent spectacular disaster would put an end to that.

He smiled. Donald had always been ahead of his time; a visionary who didn't just see the big picture, he drew it, forming and shaping it into a faithful representation of his own worldview and values. Nothing would stop him from churning out water at the rate Soldyne deserved—three times faster than Ben's microwave method, to be exact—not Quentin's untimely death, not Ben's pitiful pathological lies, not the bickering, positioning politicians, and most certainly not the protesters who rallied every day outside Soldyne's gates. It wasn't oil that greased the wheels of industry, it was water. Water that produced the goods in the quantities sufficient to keep America competitive in an increasingly complex global economy. And as head of Soldyne's water-producing division, Donald would be on top of it all.

An elbow in his side brought him back to earth. Carla glared and pointed. The mourners' heads were bowed as the minister began his final prayer. Donald lowered his head as well, taking advantage of the opportunity to purchase additional insurance by beseeching whichever gods might happen to be listening to grant him success.

Chapter 27

Don't look. Don't even think. It's only a blanket. Just pick it up.

Zo bent down, grasped her two corners, and straightened, bringing the corners up to form the back half of a sling. At the front of the blanket, Ross did the same. He shifted his grip to open the door and they went outside, walked six feet forward, and then stopped so Zo could kick it shut; a drill team whose coordination had been learned out of necessity and that had been formed under duress.

She kept her eyes on the back of his parka as they followed the flag line to the maintenance shed; noting the contrasting blue and yellow stitching, his neck burned an unhealthy red despite his genes, the long braid swinging against the sway of the blanket—*no, not the blanket . . . don't look down; don't think about what's in the blanket*—

She looked out over the bay. Giant ice pancakes jostled

the shore while above, the wind gathered the clouds into monstrous cumulonimbus billows. She hunched her shoulders as she and Ross cleared the building and a gust whipped past, taking her breath with it.

She glanced down. Dr. Rodriguez's eyes were closed. He was coatless, with one arm draped across his chest. Snow dusted his lips and his lashes, piling into drifts in the creases alongside his nose. His cheeks were stubbled, evidence of how hard he had worked during the past thirty-six hours. *His last thirty-six hours.* She noted the ring on his left hand and looked away.

When they came to the maintenance shed, they executed the same door-opening/door-closing routine and laid the blanket on the floor. Zo crossed to the worktable and cut two lengths of rope. She handed the ropes to Ross, who tied the blanket shut and laid Rodriguez alongside the others. Straightening, he bowed his head.

"Hozo-go nay-yeltay, a-na-oh bi-keh de-dlihn. Yeh-wol-ye hi-he a-din—"

She perched herself on a high stool to wait, right foot jiggling in irritation. What good were prayers for the dead? The living needed their help more than the dead did. The whole funeral scene—the flowers, the casket, the long-lost relatives' my-how-you've-growns had always rung false to her, a collection of rituals as predictable as a soap opera, and a rerun at that. She propped her elbow on the worktable to rest her chin in her hand and studied the lengthening row of bodies. Whatever the cause, the virus was virulent and unstoppable. It was hard to believe that less than two days had passed since the first person fell ill.

The really shocking thing about tragedy wasn't that it happened; it was how quickly one became inured to it. Sam's death had been appalling; *Friday the 13th*/Freddy

Krueger horrible; worse than anything Hollywood could dream up because *it was real*. Fernando's death so soon after hit like a sledgehammer in the gut, a never-saw-it-coming sucker punch that left her uncharacteristically weepy, dazed, and confused. But smash your thumb often enough, and after a while you didn't even feel it, and that was what had happened when within hours, Shana, then Kevin, then Todd, and finally Luis succumbed. Each time another friend or colleague died, the blanket surrounding her emotions wrapped itself tighter. Shock, grief, and denial were a predictable progression. Equally predictable was the certainty that she was going to collapse into a quivering pile of jelly once this was over (assuming she lived to tell the tale), but for now, she could hold it together. She had to. She and Ross were the only ones standing.

Finally, Ross lifted his head. She tugged on her gloves and slid down off the stool. Last count, there were two more bodies to be moved.

"We'll take care of the others later," Ross said once they were back inside the station. "I'm going to see if an answer came in from McMurdo; then I'm going to move some more stuff before the weather gets worse. We'll need a head count. Find out who can walk, and who will have to be carried."

Relocating to the emergency shelter was their Plan B. It was also Plans C through Z. With no doctor, no support staff to maintain essential systems, no rescue ship on the horizon, no communication with the outside world thanks to the storm, and no reply to their SOS e-mail to McMurdo because of the same, all they could do was retreat, and wait. The emergency shelter was located inland from the

station, constructed of cement block, three-quarters underground; a single, low-ceilinged room as spare as an army
barracks with a kerosene generator for heat and lights and
bunks along three walls. Previously she'd considered the
shelter a joke. Now she could appreciate the wisdom of
having redundant systems.

They split up and she moved off down the hall, ignoring
the pleas for help her footsteps engendered. "Zo? Is that
you? I need another blanket; this one's soiled." "My puke
bucket's full; can you empty it for me?" "I need a drink.
Please. I'm so thirsty." "Look out! He's got a gun!" This
from a staff member she knew only as Scott. She glanced
into the room. Scott was yelling and flailing as he fought a
losing battle with his blanket. In the other bed, his room-
mate lay ominously still.

She paused outside her bedroom door. *Please, God,* she
whispered—a prayer for the living—and went inside, re-
coiling at the odor of vomit and sweat. She crossed to the
bed. Elliot's face was pale and his breathing was shallow,
but at least he *was* breathing, she told herself fiercely. She
took off her outerwear and laid it on the bed, then bent to
pick up the pile of candy wrappers surrounding the wastebasket and refilled his water glass from the jug in the
fridge. She wet a cloth for his forehead and took a swig for
herself, then put the jug back, the insulin bottles reminding
her that it had been hours since she'd checked her glucose
level. Not that it mattered. For some reason, her insulin
needs had diminished dramatically in recent days. She presumed the reduction was because of the hormonal changes
associated with pregnancy, though right now, figuring out
why was the least of her concerns. She was just happy to have
one less thing to worry about.

She sat down on the edge of the bed. Elliot didn't stir.

She picked up his hand and laid it in her lap, absently tracing out the corded veins that twined between his liver spots like rivers. "We don't know how much longer we can keep going," she told him, though she wasn't at all sure that he could hear. "Once the heat fails, it won't be long before we'll be out of water as well. Ross says the cistern is already down by half." *"And believe me, you don't want to know what's at the bottom," he'd added, then told her anyway: "Twenty years' worth of flotsam and jetsam, including one very bloated, very dead rat."* She shuddered. At least Pinky wouldn't be giving them any more trouble.

"And when the heat goes, the lights will go, too." She sighed. "It's all a bit of a mess. So we're moving everyone to the shelter. Ross is stocking it with food and water. We're hoping once the storm quits, we can get a message through—" She stopped. She supposed she should be telling him that everything was fine and that help was on its way, but after all of the lies she'd told over the past weeks, she couldn't bear to tell another—especially considering these might be their last words. She blinked. Incredible, to think that after twenty years of operation during which Raney's personnel had overcome every conceivable challenge, the station should be brought low by a virus.

She kissed Elliot's hand, then tucked his arm under the blanket and stretched out beside him on the bed. She was so tired. If she'd slept during the last thirty-six hours, she couldn't remember.

She woke to a draft blowing across her cheek. Her first thought was that Elliot was hogging the covers again. She reached for her share, then remembered that she was on top and he was underneath. She sat up. The room was freezing.

Had the heat failed? She shrugged on her parka and scrounged another blanket from the closet, laid it over him, and took her gloves and wool cap from her jacket pocket and put them on him as well. As she went into the hallway and closed the door, she thanked God that the room was small. Elliot's body heat should be enough to maintain temperature for the next few hours.

In the hallway, the draft turned into a full-fledged gale. She followed it down the corridor and around a corner to its source.

Of all the idiotic— She shook her head in disgust. Unbelievable. She and Ross had been killing themselves for two days trying to hold everything together, and he goes and leaves the door standing open. She waded through the drift that was rapidly accumulating on the tiles and reached for the handle, then squinted. Outside, almost obscured by the blowing snow, a figure was running toward the shore.

What in the world? The shelter was the opposite direction. She went outside, making sure the door latched behind her, and hurried after, zipping her coat as she ran.

She cupped her hands. "Ross! Stop! What are you doing?"

The figure turned.

It wasn't Ross, it was Mac—she could tell by the frizzy blond hair whipping around his head. But that was all that was blowing, because except for a pair of boxers flapping around his skinny, pipestem legs, Mac was naked.

She caught up to him at the water's edge.

"Are you *crazy*?" She grabbed his arm and spun him around. His skin felt like frozen lunch meat. His lips were blue, and he was shaking so hard he could barely stand.

"I w-was h-hot."

"I guess you were." The twin red circles on his cheeks

spoke not of cold, but of fever. "Come on. We've got to get you inside."

"Nuh-uh. It's t-too hot in there."

"You have to. You'll freeze out here." She tugged on his arm.

"I have to ch-check on my ch-ch-chicks." He pulled free and took off in the direction of the Zodiac.

She sprinted after, ice and gravel crunching beneath her boots. How could he run so fast barefoot? His feet must be frozen. She hoped all he'd lose were his toes. Though with Rodriguez gone, who would perform the amputation was up for grabs. She pictured herself and Ross drawing straws. *Impossible.* Doctors in Antarctica had performed all manner of surgeries under extreme conditions—even operating on themselves—but she hadn't even had EMT training.

She put on a burst of speed. A pain shot through her gut. Gasping, she clutched her stomach. Stress. It was only stress. That, or she'd pulled a muscle. It wasn't a cramp. It couldn't be a cramp. *Please, God, don't let it be a cramp—*

She bent over with her hands on her knees and used the Lamaze breaths she'd been practicing in secret until the spasm eased. By the time she lifted her head, Mac had already reached the Zodiac and was fumbling with its moorings. She took off running again.

He looked up at the sound of her footsteps. "You c-can't c-c-catch me!" he laughed, and dashed out into the bay.

"No! Stop! Come back!"

He slogged on, not hearing or not caring, his movements slowing dramatically as the water deepened and the cold took hold. How long could he last? A minute? Two?

The answer came when his limbs stiffened abruptly and he pitched forward. She held her breath, hoping he was holding his, and waited for him to reappear.

Nothing.

She stripped off her parka and ran in after him, crying out as every blood vessel in her legs constricted and the pain shot straight up her chest. She pushed it back and floundered over to where Mac had vanished and felt about with her feet.

Still nothing.

She thought of her infant in its warm, watery womb; then grabbed a deep breath and plunged beneath the waves, swinging her arms in a wide arc, hoping to connect with something—anything; half-walking, half-swimming as she reached blindly into the void, the water so stupefyingly cold it barely registered.

She stood up, panting from shock and fear, and shook the water from her hair.*"Mac!"* she screamed as soon as she was able to draw breath. "Where *are* you?"

A shorebird screeched. She hugged herself to keep from shivering and scanned the surface. There was no movement anywhere, no telltale stream of silvery bubbles, no pale flesh bobbing beneath the waves—nothing but angry gray water reflecting an angrier sky, while the wind blew the tops off the waves and the gull mocked her distress in a rasping falsetto as it swooped effortlessly toward the shore.

Then Mac burst out of the water a dozen feet to her right.

She sloshed over and grabbed him as his eyes rolled back and his knees went limp. Slinging his arm over her shoulders, she started for the shore. His weight seemed to double with every step as they reached the shallows and he lost buoyancy. She shifted him higher onto her shoulders and staggered on: up the graveled headland, past her discarded jacket; one determined foot in front of the other, keeping her eyes fixed on the station door, teeth clenched against the burn in her shoulders and the paralyzing cold.

She traversed the final yards on sheer willpower and opened the door. Dropping him on the floor, she noted the trail of bloody footprints from the beach to the door.

"Ross! Come here! I need your help!"

Mac curled in the fetal position, his body racked with deep, shuddering shivers. She unfolded his limbs enough to grab him by the armpits and dragged him down the hall, thankful for the lubricating mix of blood and snow. Her jeans felt like cardboard and her whole body was on fire. Pain is good, she told herself. Pain is normal. Not being able to feel anything would mean trouble.

Mercifully, his room was the third door on the right. She dragged him inside and hefted him onto his bed. Mac's body was so battered, he looked like he'd just fought off a serial killer, or a surgeon gone berserk. She hoped his cuts were superficial; she couldn't stitch his wounds any more than she could tend to his poor, frozen feet. Shock; gangrene; the unknown virus—this week, Antarctica was offering specials on any number of ways to die.

She stripped off his boxers and toweled him dry with a blanket, then dressed him in thermals and sweats and piled all the blankets she could find on top.

Ten minutes later, dressed in dry clothes and with her hair in a wet ponytail, she was sitting at the kitchen table inhaling the steam from a cup of hot chocolate; too tired to pick it up; too tired to cry.

Chapter 28

Los Angeles, California

Adam drained his morning Starbucks and returned the travel mug to the cup holder as Soldyne's parking lot came into view. He gripped the wheel. So far, no one had thrown anything more damaging than a bucket of water, but there was always a first time, and given his rather unfortunate history of making the long odds, it was pretty much a given that when the protesters decided to up the ante, he'd be the one to cash in. An IRS audit three years in a row, the new love interest with a job offer in Australia—it seemed as though whenever the gods got together for an evening of unholy fun, Adam Washburn was their favorite target. Which was why he was driving a rental to work these days instead of his Miata.

He showed his ID to the security guard and pulled into the lot, keeping an eye on the rearview as the protesters closed in behind. He'd heard the rumors: POP was responsible for spiking trees in the Pacific Northwest, trashing research labs in Massachusetts, torching luxury homes in upstate New York, and given what he'd seen of this group, he believed them. He'd caught the Sweet woman enough times on the eleven o'clock news to know that she was anything but.

A woman broke from the crowd; not POP's fearless leader, but someone who could have been her soul sister: a zealous twenty-something in a white shirt and black pants and a Baja Fresh apron who'd stopped off for a few hours of protesting on her way to work; shaking her fist and shouting what Adam presumed were obscenities judging by the expression on her face. He shook his head and drove on. He didn't care how worthy the cause; 6:00 a.m. was too early to be that worked up.

He parked, grabbed yesterday's *L.A. Times* off the front seat, and crossed the lot to the lobby. After exchanging pleasantries with the new hire behind the information desk, he took the elevator to the third floor, topped off his mug from the never-ending pot in the break room, set both mug and paper on his desk, and fired up his computer. While he waited for the machine to boot, he put the phone on speaker and punched in the iceberg's number. After an interminable succession of clicks and pauses, the call went through.

"You're home," he said, and opened up a game of Minesweeper while he waited for Ben's reply. Patience had never been his long suit. Multitasking helped.

"Yeah, I was just about to head out to the donut shop for a latte and a croissant, but you caught me," Ben joked after three tedious seconds had passed. "I hope you're calling with good news."

"Good news" for Ben would have meant that the supply ship was on its way. Unfortunately, while the *Polar Sea* had made the crossing to Punta Arenas in record time, the storm that was delaying its return wasn't expected to end anytime soon.

"Sorry."

"Damn," Ben said after another long pause during which Adam managed to beat his best score by ten. "Paula's going to kill me if I don't get home soon. I just got off the phone with her. Sarah's still acting out."

"What's she done now?" Adam didn't have kids, but he could sympathize. Sarah's increasingly outrageous misbehavior culminated last week when she and her girlfriend were caught shoplifting at the mall. The store manager hadn't pressed charges, but security still held the girls long enough to give everyone a good scare. And for what? A freaking book—a picture book about Shackleton's Antarctic misadventure, no less. If that wasn't sending dear old dad a message, Adam had forgotten entirely what it was like to be thirteen.

"She hasn't done anything this time, thank God," Ben said. "It's what she wants me to do. You know that Internet classroom project her social studies teacher has going with a scientist over at Raney? Apparently the class got an e-mail from him yesterday saying everyone at the station is sick and dying and they need help. Now Sarah's begging me to go save her precious Iceman."

"Holy crap. What kind of thing is that to say to a bunch of kids?"

"Oh, it's not real. Who'd send an SOS to a classroom in the States? I'm sure it's just an exercise—you know, a what-if scenario to get the kids thinking. But just try convincing Sarah of that. Ever since Mr. McMurtry started this project, it's been 'the Iceman says this,' and 'the Iceman does that.' She's so nuts about this guy, she's totally bought into it. When I told her I couldn't fire up the old helicopter and take off in the middle of a snowstorm on her say-so, well—let's just say right now, I'm not exactly flavor of the month."

"Sorry to hear that. Though in a way," Adam said as he studied the newspaper spread open on his desk, "it's too bad the emergency isn't real. You could use the PR. It's hard to hate a hero."

"What are you talking about?"

"I'm gonna read you a headline from an article in yesterday's *Times*, okay? You sitting down? Here we go. It's a question: 'Was Engineer a Victim of His Own Technology?'" He paused to let the significance sink in, then added the kicker: "The article speculates that Quentin was killed by the microwave beam."

"*What?* That's crazy."

"Well yeah, I know that, and you know that. Unfortunately, there're about a million Los Angelinos right now who aren't quite so sure. You should see the article. The argument's pretty convincing."

"How'd the story end up in the paper? And why would anybody care?"

"Oh, I dunno. Maybe because Quentin died in an exotic location under mysterious circumstances? Or maybe because his body was cremated before his widow even had a chance to see it? Or how about this? Maybe somebody doesn't want your microwave method to succeed."

Ben sighed. "All right. I see where you're going."

"Damn straight. How did Quentin die, anyway? No one's ever said."

"You know I can't tell you. I signed a nondisclosure agreement before I came down. We all did. What happens on the berg, stays on the berg."

"Well now, you see, there's your problem. Looks a tad suspicious, wouldn't you say?"

Silence. While he waited for Ben's response, Adam's hand strayed to the mouse to start another game before he caught himself and called it back. He closed out the program.

"Okay," Ben said after a pause that lasted considerably longer than three seconds, "I can tell you this much. You know the microwave levels fall off rapidly as soon as you get outside the melt zone. Quentin's body was found at the pumphouse. That's a good half mile away. That proves he wasn't killed by the beam. Make sure the papers understand that."

"Won't do any good. First one out of the gate wins. Once an idea is out there, you can't call it back. People are going to believe what they want, no matter what you say. And you gotta admit, Gillette's version makes good copy."

"I guess you're right." Ben sighed again. "Okay. Gillette may have won this round, but I'll figure out a way to deal with this after I get back. Meanwhile, let me know if anything else comes up. And for God's sake—get me off this iceberg."

"Will do."

Adam clicked off and walked over to the window. As he stared down at the protesters, briefly, he envied them their conviction. If only the world really were that black and white. He thought about the storm brewing inside Soldyne's hallowed halls. It wasn't hard to tell which way the wind was blowing. The question was, was he going to keep the wind at his back, or was he going to let it knock him flat? If he had a choice, he'd pick Ben over Gillette any day, but this wasn't a popularity contest. Whichever way their tug-of-war ended, Adam needed to be on the winning team. Payments on the Miata weren't cheap.

Chapter 29

Iceberg, Weddell Sea, 68° S, 60° W

Ben handed the phone off to Toshi and grabbed his parka. As he shut the door, it was all he could do to keep from slamming it. *My method. Your method.* Gillette's never-ending rivalry made him feel like a two-year-old. *My ball. No, it's mine.* Bottom line: The world needed water desperately, and Soldyne was in a position to supply it. That should have been their focus. Instead, Donald had turned their entire water-making endeavor into one giant pissing contest.

He zipped up his coat and charged off to the mess hut. The sky as black as his mood. As long as Ben was stuck on the berg, Gillette held all the cards. Donald could disseminate all the misinformation he wanted, and there wasn't a thing Ben could do about it. Ben was beginning to suspect that even his coming was the result of a carefully contrived plot. What better way to gain the upper hand than to send your rival to the most isolated place on earth? Gillette was clever enough and powerful enough to have massaged events to a particular outcome. Not the rats, of course, but everything else: the chewed up hoses (or had they been cut?), the buggy uplink code (or was it sabotage?), and all of the myriad other "problems" *could* have been concocted with the sole objective of Ben's coming along as "problem solver." Since Quentin's death, everything had been running smooth as butter. Coincidence? Ben didn't think so. He wondered if there was a more sinister explanation behind the *Polar Sea*'s delay.

He was still fuming when he opened the double doors to the mess hut and stomped inside. Susan was standing at the counter eating a sandwich. She looked up, frowning. Too late, he composed his features.

"Everything okay?" she asked.

He offered the most innocuous explanation. "I just got off the phone with Adam. Looks like we're going to be here for a while."

"Ah." She looked at her sandwich. "Perhaps I should save this then."

"Maybe you should." He laughed, but even to his ears, the joke rang hollow. They both understood the situation. The team had enough food for several weeks, and thanks to the microwave process, they could always make more water, but Antarctica was a harsh mistress. Better men than he had died at her hands for lack of resources and supplies. Ben liked to think of himself as a leader, but he was no Shackleton. Sarah wanted him to rescue the Iceman, but if the supply ship didn't return, who would rescue them?

He rummaged through the cupboard for peanut butter and jelly—not his favorite choice of sandwich, but he wasn't complaining. Nothing like doing without to realize how spoiled you'd become. The iceberg was a microcosm of the entire globe. Here, their supplies were limited in a visible, tangible way, but Earth's resources were just as finite—except that when the earth ran out, there was no place to go for more.

"Ben!" Toshi's voice over the intercom interrupted. "We need you! Get back here quick! Something's come up."

Inside the operations hut, Toshi, Eugene, and the helicopter pilot, Cam Kessler, were huddled over a table. On the table, a radio was emitting bursts of static.

Ben hurried over. "What is it?"

"It's the radio," Eugene said.

Toshi rolled his eyes.

"I know it's the radio," Ben said. "What's going on?"

"Listen." Toshi held up his hand.

Ben leaned closer. Interspersed among the electronic pops and hisses was a man's voice, faint, and laced with static.

"—ation. ¡Aytación . . . resca—"

"Turn off your heaters," he said. "Quickly. Anything with a blower or a motor. They're causing interference."

Hands scrambled to yank the offending plugs.

"—ation. ¡Ayuda! Ésta es estación de Raney." Now the voice was clear. "¡Tenemos una emergencia médica y necesitamos rescate inmediato."

"That's Spanish," Susan said.

"What's he saying?"

"Sorry. I'm not fluent."

"Anyone?"

More shrugs. The speaker repeated his message, then switched to English:

"Help! This is Raney Station. We have a medical emergency and need immediate rescue—"

Raney? Sarah's SOS e-mail was *real*? "Answer it," Ben said, his heart thumping. *"Hurry."*

Toshi grabbed the mike. "Hello! Yes! We hear you! Can you hear me?"

"Help! *Ayuda!* This is Raney Station—"

Toshi looked helplessly at Ben.

"Keep trying." He signaled the pilot off to the side. Raney was fifty miles across the peninsula, within easy helicopter range. "What do you think?" he asked. "Can we help?"

Cam stroked his chin. The gesture would have looked weighty and thoughtful if he'd had the beard to go with it, or even a hint of five o'clock shadow. Instead, Cam looked like a boy pretending to be a man, his cheeks soft and full, with a face more suited to a Calvin Klein commercial than a Marlboro man. Ben touched his own stubble. When had he reached the age where the experts he relied on were younger than him?

"I don't see why not," Cam said. "I did three years search and rescue with the Coast Guard. Flown in all kinds of weather. I'd like to talk to someone on the other end first, though. Find out the wind speed, local weather conditions, what kind of terrain to expect. We could get over there and find out there's no place to land."

"I understand. We'll keep trying to raise them. And if we can't get a response?"

Cam grinned, a perfect orthodontic smile bursting with the confidence of the highly trained—or the very young. "I'm game if you are."

Ben considered. There was so much he didn't know. "Medical emergency" could mean almost anything. According to Sarah's class's e-mail, Raney's personnel were sick and dying, but from what? Was it contagious? Would effecting a rescue put his own people in danger? His primary responsibility was to his own crew—yet could he live with himself if he ignored the call for help?

"Help! *Ayuda!* This is Raney—"

"Okay. We're in." He shrugged on his jacket and walked back to Toshi. "We'll give it ten minutes. If we don't have an answer by then, Cam and I will take off regardless. Keep trying to raise them after we're gone. Let them know we're coming. Susan—you're in charge."

He began a mental checklist: blankets, whatever medicine they could scrounge, maybe some high-protein bars and a case of water. Not too much, since their helicopter was only a six-seater, but enough to make the victims comfortable while they were airlifted to McMurdo.

As the minutes counted down, Ben's crew watched him with a mix of admiration and awe. He noted their expressions and tried not to grin. Adam was right. It *was* hard to hate a hero.

Chapter 30

Raney Station, Antarctic Peninsula

"Someone's coming?" Zo shook her head in disbelief. "My God, Ross. *Who?*"

"I have no idea. The reception was terrible. All I could make out were the words 'helicopter,' and 'be right there.' That's good enough for me."

"Me, too." She laughed, a high, giddy giggle that sounded so out of place after the stress of the past days, it bordered on lunacy. "It has to be someone from McMurdo. You're a genius to have thought of the radio."

She shook her head again. In her heart, she truly hadn't expected to survive. Now in a few short hours, they'd be on their way to a station that, compared to Raney, was a regular city. McMurdo had over a hundred buildings, daily flights to Christchurch, New Zealand. Best of all, the station boasted a fully equipped (and by Antarctic standards, state-of-the-art) hospital.

"I wonder how big the helicopter will be. How many it can carry."

"McMurdo has a couple of ski-equipped Hercules. Those things are huge. We'll have to mark out a landing pad on top of the glacier. That's the only place big enough."

"*On top?* We can't get people up there. Half of them can't even walk." *And the other half are comatose.* She pictured the glacier's leading edge: a steeply sloped, hundred-foot-high cliff that served as backdrop to the station. Access to the top was by means of a set of stairs cut into the ice that were steep and narrow, with heavy-gauge wire handrails strung along both sides. The first time she saw them, she was reminded of the Golden Stairs that had been cut into the Chilkoot Pass in the Yukon during the Klondike gold rush days. Zo assumed the construction for their set had been justified by some crucial, planet-saving research being carried out on top. She got a better understanding of Antarctic priorities when she learned the stairs provided access to Raney's softball field.

"Don't worry," Ross said. "They'll send the necessary manpower and equipment. McMurdo's a major station. They know how to handle an emergency. These people are pros."

Professionals or not, Zo couldn't imagine any viable means of transporting their victims to the top. "We can't presume they'll send a Hercules. They could just as easily send something smaller. If they do, a landing site on the beach would be ideal. The winds are less erratic, and it would be far simpler to get our people on board."

"We don't have time to prep two sites. Whatever they're sending, it'll be here inside of an hour. Better to mark out one site that can accommodate any size craft. If they send a smaller helicopter, it can land on top, and hop on down to the beach."

"Okay." Ross's presuming the leadership role rankled. Zo wasn't a follower by nature, but he was right about one thing: The clock was ticking. Sometimes the most expedient thing to do was to give in and go along.

"What should we use to mark out the landing pad?" she asked. "Flares?"

He laughed. "Not unless you're planning to blow the thing up. You don't want open flame around a helicopter. Anything brightly colored and easily visible will do."

"Then how about survival suits? They're bright red. There are a few dozen in the storage room. We could use lengths of pipe as stakes to fasten them down."

"Works for me. You get the coats, and I'll get the rest of the stuff and meet you on top. Be sure to wear your snow goggles. The helicopter's going to kick up a lot of debris. And dress warmly. In cold weather, the downdraft from a craft that size can cause a drop in temperature severe enough to give you instant hypothermia or frostbite. And while we're talking safety, don't go running up to the helicopter as soon as it lands. This won't be like the movies. In real life, you never approach a helicopter until the pilot gives the okay. Stand at two o'clock where he can see you, then wait for his signal."

"Got it. I suppose you're going to tell me you learned all this from your three tours of duty in Iraq, where among other things, you picked up a Purple Heart, and a Silver Star, and a Medal of Honor."

"No." He flushed.

Ross was *blushing*? This was going to be good.

"Actually, I learned that from reading Tom Clancy."

She burst out laughing. Ross didn't join in.

Zo was long past laughing as she bundled the last of the survival suits together forty-five minutes later and slipped her arms through the ropes. Three contiguous trips to the top of the glacier and back were enough to kill anyone's good mood. She shifted the bundle higher onto her shoulders like a peasant carrying a load of straw and turned sideways to fit through the door, then trudged past the emergency shelter, past her old ice cave, and on to the Stairs of Affliction. She was out of breath by the tenth step, but kept climbing, gripping the guide wires with both hands as the winds tore at her from above and below, ignoring her leg muscles that twitched in refusal.

When at last she cleared the top, she kept her profile low until she was well away from the edge. Straightening, she staggered over to Ross and dropped her bundle.

"You okay?" He had to shout to be heard. Zo judged the gusts to be topping out at forty to fifty.

"I'm fine," she shouted back. "Just a little winded." She smiled wryly.

Ross nodded absently and went back to hammering a section of pipe through the chest of a suit as though it were a vampire.

She cocked an ear. "Do you hear that?"

He stopped to listen, then shoved the hammer into the back of his jeans. "Come on," he said, pulling her to her feet. "It's showtime."

Together, they carried the last bundle to what Clancy presumably deemed a safe distance and scanned the sky. The air reverberated with increasingly concussive thumps. At last the helicopter appeared, a blue-and-white dot against the gray ceiling.

"It's so small," she said as it came closer.

"That's no Hercules," he agreed. "Must be a reconnaissance flight. Looks like they're going to scope out the situation first. Find out what we need, and then come back for us."

A chink in his Clancy-armor. What else had he gotten wrong?

The helicopter circled the airfield and began its descent, hovering like a dragonfly coming to water. Then it was lost in a wall of snow that welled up from the rotor wash. She turned her head as the pressure wave engulfed them. The thumps diminished, buried by the sound-deadening blanket.

When at last the air cleared, she wiped the snow from her face and lifted her goggles. The ballfield was empty.

"Where—?"

"Too windy. They'll have to come in from a different angle."

The minutes dragged past. As the sky remained empty, she shivered, not only because of the wind, but because she'd never warmed up from her earlier swim. Ross slipped his arm around her shoulders. She tensed, then decided he was offering body heat and nothing more, and leaned in.

At last, the helicopter reappeared. It flew around to the far side of the ballfield just as Ross had predicted. Zo held her breath as it descended, rocking from side to side. Then abruptly, it stopped pitching and rose straight up into the air as if yanked by a string—twenty feet . . . fifty feet— She gasped.

It stopped, and for a long, hopeful moment she thought it was going to recover. Then the craft tipped sideways and flipped. She screamed as the helicopter plummeted toward the earth and slammed into the ice. The rotors shattered. Chunks of metal flew out in every direction.

Ross threw her to the ground and threw himself on top. She raised her head, watching in horror as the helicopter bounced across the ice, the stumps of its rotors still turning. Then it came to the edge of the cliff and disappeared.

Chapter 31

Cold.

Quiet.

Ben opened his eyes.

White.

And dizzy. His shoulders burned, his head throbbed, and his arms were dangling over his head.

He turned his head to the side. Pinpricks of light filled his vision. He closed his eyes until the spots retreated, then tried again.

Cam was sitting in the seat beside him, but strangely, his arms, too, hung over his head. His eyes were closed, and his face was covered with blood. A wave of nausea welled in Ben's gut as he remembered everything: Cam cursing and yelling as he fought to control the stick; screaming for Ben to take the crash position when they flipped; shoving his head between his legs as he braced for impact. Contrary to popular expectation, his life hadn't flashed before his eyes; all he had seen were the bungee cords and white foam cups and dirty Kleenexes beneath his seat.

He remembered the impact; the screaming, the bouncing, the not-knowing, and then inexplicably, the screaming and falling again until at last, the helicopter crashed to a stop.

The helicopter had crashed.

Dear God.

The helicopter had crashed, *but he had survived.*

His face was wet. He reached up and touched his forehead. His hand didn't come away red. Snow. The helicopter was packed with it, like the engine compartment of a car that had plowed into a ditch. The snow had saved him.

Or maybe it was jet fuel. He touched his fingers to his face again and sniffed. The air smelled of fuel and something else—a sharp, pungent odor he'd experienced once when he was a teenager and he'd spun out his Camaro on an icy road. Fear.

Beside him, Cam groaned. He opened his eyes, then closed them again.

Ben blinked. *They were both alive.*

The fuel smell made him nervous. They had to get out. Cam's helmet was gone, but Ben still had his. He'd have to unbuckle and drop. He twisted around in his harness, trying to see what was beneath him. He wasn't about to fall on something sharp and end up skewered.

"Are you all right?" a man's voice asked.

Ben looked to the side. Two faces were looking in, a man's and a woman's.

The man reached through the shattered window and touched Ben's shoulder. "Hey, there. Talk to me. Are you okay?"

"I think so," Ben said. It came out, "Eh sin sa."

"He's in shock," the man said to the woman. "We've got to get them out of there. Smell that jet fuel? This thing could blow any second. I'll hold him up while you unfasten his seat belt. Tuck your head in, pal," he said to Ben. "This might hurt."

Hands lifted him, held him, fumbled with the latch.

Then his head smacked the ceiling and everything went black.

He woke up on the ground. He lay still and looked up at the darkening sky while he did an assessment: He wasn't knocked out; he knew who he was; he knew where it hurt. He raised himself onto his elbows, then sat up.

Cam was stretched out beside him. The man and the woman were bent over his leg.

"It's broke." It was Cam's voice, matter-of-fact, almost cheerful. Was he in shock? Ben's medical knowledge was next to nonexistent. He and his had been disgustingly healthy, accident-free, until now.

Behind them, the helicopter lay against a massive ice boulder at the base of a cliff. It looked like a crumpled ball of tinfoil. Had they really rolled all the way down? Ben could see the scarring on the slope where the helicopter had cut a path. It was the boulder that had saved them from rolling straight on into the sea. He shuddered to think what would have happened if it hadn't been there. He and Cam were both wearing life vests—standard operating procedure when flying over water, Cam had explained when he gave Ben his—but the water was barely above the freezing point; he doubted the vests would have saved them.

"We'll have to carry him into the station," the man said to the woman. He was talking about Cam.

"I'll get a blanket," the woman replied. "What about him?" She pointed at Ben.

"He'll be all right. Probably just a concussion and some bruising. If he can't walk, we'll carry him, too."

"I'm okay," Ben said.

"He's mumbling again," the woman said.

"Don't worry. His head will clear in a bit. This guy's the one in trouble. We have to stop this bleeding."

There *was* a lot of blood. Something white was poking through Cam's jeans. Ben looked away as nausea threatened again, and noticed something moving along the base of the cliff. He squinted. The man said Ben wasn't thinking clearly, but as he watched the thing come closer, he was pretty sure of what he was seeing . . .

"Behind you," he said to the woman, just in case. He tapped her arm and pointed. "Over there. I think that's a rat."

The woman followed his finger. She yelled and jumped to her feet.

"It's okay," Ben said, even though he had a feeling it wasn't.

She picked up a rock and threw it. The rat ran off. Then another one darted up. Ben flinched as the second rat leaped onto Cam's leg and bit down hard. Cam screamed. The man and the woman beat at the rat with their fists, and the rat retreated.

"Look out!" Ben yelled. Rats were streaming out of an opening at the base of the cliff like ants from a nest. He scrambled to his feet.

"This way! It's closer!" The woman grabbed his hand and hurried him toward a cement block building.

He stumbled. She put her arm around his shoulders and

fast-walked him to the door, then dumped him inside and ran back out.

He crawled to the door. The man was dragging Cam by his life vest. Cam screamed as the rats nipped his heels. The woman ran over to them, kicking and yelling, and the rats scattered. She picked up Cam's feet, and she and the man ran to the shelter. Once they were inside, Ben shut the door.

Chapter 32

Gakona, Alaska

The High Frequency Active Auroral Research Program observatory eight miles north of Gakona was open to the public only once a year. Not because the project was classified—it wasn't, though because it was managed jointly by the Air Force Research Laboratory and the Office of Naval Research, the uninitiated could be forgiven for thinking that it would be. In actuality, there was nothing secret about the H.A.A.R.P. observatory at all. The research it produced was published regularly in peer-review journals. The faculty sponsored an annual Ionospheric Interactions Workshop to showcase projects and report advances. Photos, construction stats—even laymen's explanations of the science involved were posted freely to the Web. The reason the university physicists, their students, and the government and commercial scientists who worked there welcomed visitors only once a year was the same reason research institutions everywhere limited access: Visitors were a nuisance.

These restrictions didn't apply to Gillette. He had come to the facility on business. He'd left L.A. early to fly 2,687.8 air miles in Soldyne's private jet, then driven a rented SUV seventeen miles up the Tok Highway to Milepost 11.3 to make what was for all intents and purposes a courtesy call. A good-faith gesture. Dr. Steven Headrick, H.A.A.R.P.'s project overseer and the man Donald had come to see, needed to understand without ifs ands or buts that when Donald promised Soldyne would be using H.A.A.R.P.'s resources next season, it was as good as done. When the board voted in favor of Ben's microwave method three years earlier, Donald's credibility had taken a serious hit. Now he was prepared to do whatever was necessary to assure, reassure, and otherwise ensure that this time, the outcome would be different.

The two men admired the HF transmitter array as they stood on a planked deck outside Headrick's office. The 180 interconnected finned antennas spread out over 33 acres reminded Donald of something he'd once built out of Tinkertoys. The day was sunny and bright; cold, but that was to be expected. This was Alaska in February.

The outdoor location wasn't Donald's idea. But if standing on a porch in subzero weather with a man whose conversation could have put Rip Van Winkle to sleep advanced Soldyne's interests, he'd do it. And because he was Donald Kershaw Gillette, executive vice president of the largest and most successful solar energy corporation in the world, he did it better: Chuckling at Headrick's inane jokes, listening attentively to the scientist's obvious and predictable concerns, offering a thoughtful comment or a leading question at appropriate moments, never letting slip that what he was really thinking of was the half-finished bottle of Scotch on the Gulfstream's teakwood table.

Headrick detailed the improvements since Donald's previous visit. The facility had upgraded from 960 kilowatts of power to their projected 3.6 million watts—on schedule and on budget, he made a point of saying (the implications of which were not lost on Donald), adding that they'd attained the maximum size and power level that could be constructed in accordance with the Environmental Impact Process (as if Donald cared).

Mercifully, his cell vibrated. He checked the number. "Sorry," he said to Headrick with his best what-are-ya-gonna-do good-old-boy shrug. "I need to take this."

"Not a problem," Headrick said. "Join me inside when you're finished. I'll have the coffee on."

Donald flipped open the phone. "This better be important," he growled after the scientist was out of earshot.

On the other end of the line, Adam said soberly, "It is."

As Adam related how Ben's team had learned of a medical emergency at Raney Station, and how Ben had gallantly helicoptered over to save them, but the rescue attempt appeared to have gone bad because it had been twenty-four hours with no word and everyone was worried about what might have happened, Donald's tension evaporated like ice cream on a summer sidewalk. He tsked the appropriate noises, told Adam to keep him posted, and went inside.

"Problem?" Headrick asked as he held out a steaming white foam cup.

Donald smiled. "Not at all. Everything is just fine."

Chapter 33

"Zo. Wake up. We have a problem."

A hand jostled her shoulder. She forced open one eye. Ross squatted beside her bunk. His shirt was open, and his hair hung loose around his shoulders. She noted his developing beard with disapproval. Granted, after a day in the shelter following two days of medical madness, she probably didn't look her best, either, but she was pretty sure she didn't smell.

She rolled over and faced the wall—not an easy thing to do since the bunks were narrow and her legs were long. They had a problem, all right, but not in the way he thought. She was furious with him; as angry as she had ever been. Every aspect of their present predicament—every single part—went straight back to him. The helicopter had crashed because Ross insisted on marking out the landing pad on top of the glacier. They'd been forced to retreat to the emergency shelter because the crash stirred up the rats when the helicopter dropped into their nest. They were stuck in the shelter because of the rats, and because of the storm, which wasn't Ross's fault, but the fact that the crash had taken out the flag line was. The pilot had a broken leg they couldn't set and a level of pain the Tylenol 3 in the medical kit couldn't touch—again, because of the crash.

And as if all of that weren't enough, snoring away in the next bunk was the man who was responsible for the destruction of the ice shelf. *A man who also happened to be Ross's friend.* In one of those small-world coincidences that weren't as rare as people liked to think, it turned out that Ross and the guy from the iceberg (and not McMurdo Station as Ross had mistakenly presumed—another error) had gone to school together. After they took off their helmets and hoods and realized they knew each other, the two had a great time playing old home week, but who cared how many kids Maki had, or who Ross's sister had married, or which of their old pals was working where? Maki worked for Soldyne. Soldyne destroyed the ice shelf. End of story. Maki insisted he didn't know anything about the explosion, and repeated the same tired pro-environment justifications Adam had used to coerce her cooperation, but claiming that melting icebergs into drinking water was good for the environment was a non sequitur after your company took steps to hurry things along.

But more than anything, she was furious because she was frantic to get back to the station. The others didn't have days or even hours; their life prospects were measured in minutes. Elliot was as good as dead, if he wasn't already, and she had no way to reach him, even though they were less than a football field apart—and it was all Ross's fault.

He shook her shoulder again. "Come on, Zo. Get up."

She swung her legs over the side of the bed. If she made a show of listening, maybe he'd go away.

"Here." He handed her a glass of water. "Drink this."

She accepted the glass not because she was taking orders from him—she was done with that forever—but because she *was* thirsty, and downed it in one long pull. She set the empty on the floor next to her boots. Boots stained with blood, thanks to Ross.

He leaned close and cupped a hand over her ear. "Bad news," he whispered, and pointed toward Cam's bed.

As if the news could have been good.

Chapter 34

The whispering woke him. Ben opened his eyes, then immediately closed them again. His head throbbed. Every bone and muscle ached. He felt drained, as though someone had siphoned out his blood while he was sleeping and replaced it with water. As he fumbled for his eyeglasses, his eyes burned and his hands shook.

He threaded the stems over his ears and blinked to clear his vision. Across the room, Ross and Zo were huddled on her bed, whispering. They looked like they were sharing a kiss, but Ben knew better. Zo hated Ross; ten minutes had made that abundantly clear. He didn't know their history, and he didn't care. Whatever her issues, they were her problems, not his.

Right now, nothing was more important than getting Cam medical help. He looked toward Cam's bed. Thankfully, Cam was quiet. The meds must have kicked in. Cam had suffered horribly during the first few hours, thrashing and moaning—literally out of his mind with pain. (That is, unless the shelter really *was* populated with green and purple snakes packaged like ramen noodles.)

He rubbed his eyes again. There was a brief period while Ross was administering first aid and Zo was checking the window every five minutes to see if the rats had retreated when Ben blamed Cam for their troubles. After all, he was the one who had claimed to be such a hotshot rescue pilot. But in the end, Ben had to admit responsibility. He'd wanted to play the hero, now he had to accept the consequences. They were stuck in an emergency shelter with only the barest of medical supplies while outside, man-eating rats lurked and the mother of all storms raged. All he could do was wait, and pray.

He reached for the glass someone had left beside his bed and drained it. Moments later, he clutched his stomach.

He stood up. Inexplicably, the room grew dark. The whispering stopped. He gripped the edge of the bunk rail and waited for his vision to clear. He felt muddle-headed. Disconnected. Light and floaty, like an angel.

Like an angel.

Maybe, he thought, as a realization struck him that was so overwhelming in its significance it made his knees buckle, maybe he really *was* an angel. Maybe he *hadn't* survived the crash, and Ross and Zo and the emergency shelter and Cam's broken leg and the storm and the rats were just a weird, afterlife illusion.

As he crumpled to the floor, he wondered: Could you die without knowing it?

Chapter 35

The guy just melted. One minute Ben was standing up, clutching his gut like he needed to go to the bathroom, and the next, his eyes rolled back and his knees quit. Ross broke off in midsentence.

"What's wrong?" Zo craned her neck to look past him. "Holy cow! Is he—"

"Nah. He just fainted." Ross clenched his teeth. He was so sick of her questions. Zo was as excitable as a little kid, always ready to presume the worst, her emotions ruled by a hair trigger that was forever shooting her in the wrong direction. He was tired of having to rein her in.

He crossed the room and pressed two fingers against Ben's neck. "Pulse seems fine. Has he been drinking?"

"What, you mean alcohol? We don't have any. At least, none that I know of."

His jaw worked. "I meant water. He could have fainted because he's dehydrated."

"Oh. Well." She pointed to the empty glass. "That was full last night. I topped it off before we went to sleep."

Ross hadn't slept, but he didn't correct her. Zo would only interpret his watchfulness as chauvinism, when what had really kept him awake was the normal care and concern that any decent human being would extend toward another. He honestly didn't know what Elliot saw in her. Sure, she was smart; tall and blondly good-looking if you were attracted to that sort of thing, and her childlike naïveté along with her earnest idealism could be mildly appealing on occasion. But most of the time she was far too prickly for his taste. Women like her were a stacked deck. Do something for yourself, and you were an insensitive boor; do something for her, and you became a macho pig. You couldn't win.

He turned his attention to the person who wasn't likely to give him an argument, and who would appreciate his help—or would have if he'd been conscious. Ben was still out cold, sweating, though his color was good. Ross nodded toward Ben's feet. "Help me get him into bed."

She flushed an angry pink, but did as he asked. He sighed. Did she have to take offense at everything? He was only trying to get the job done as expediently as possible. He supposed in her mind, he should have phrased his statement as a question, "Heads, or tails?" or at a minimum added a "please," but it was just too tedious to have to give consideration to every sentence. Ross was a patient man, but patience had its limits, and she had no idea how close he was to reaching his. Zo didn't like him; well, guess what—he didn't much care for her.

She went over to the door and stood on her tiptoes to look out the window. "Still storming," she said in a petulant voice, and went off to sulk in the area they had designated the kitchen: one big crate for a table, three smaller crates for chairs. She filled a glass from one of the jugs he'd brought over from the station, popped the top off a can of mandarin oranges, poured the syrup into a small dish and set it aside, then dipped in a spoon.

He left her to her breakfast and tucked the blanket around Ben's shoulders. It was strange, seeing Ben again after so many years. He seemed little changed from when they'd gone to school. Funny, how one of the guys who had come to rescue them was someone he knew. Back at UCLA, he and Ben hadn't been close; Ben was more like the friend of a friend of a friend; members of the same environmental protest group, was all. Ben hadn't been part of the inner circle, which was why Ross was surprised yesterday when Ben confessed to a crush he'd had all those years ago on Ross's sister. He wondered what Ben would think if he told him what his sister was planning to do to Ben's ship.

His stomach growled. He stood up and stretched, then went over to the kitchen and dug through the food boxes until he found a low-calorie protein bar and a packet of freeze-dried coffee. He filled a mug and started it heating in the ancient microwave, then joined Zo at the table.

"I should be sick, you know," she said.

So she was speaking again? And just when he was beginning to enjoy the peace and quiet. "I thought we decided you're a carrier."

"I'm not talking about the virus. I'm talking about my diabetes. I've been stuck in here for over a day without any insulin. I should be dizzy, thirsty, confused—all the lovely stuff that goes with hypoglycemia, and yet look." She held out her hands. "Steady as a rock. If you knew anything about diabetes, you'd understand how strange that is. What's really weird is that over the past few days, I've been needing less insulin. At first I thought it was because I was pregnant—you know, that maybe the hormone changes had thrown my blood glucose level out of whack. There's something called gestational diabetes, where a woman without diabetes develops the symptoms during pregnancy, and I thought maybe my case was the opposite. But everything I've read says that pregnancy is more likely to exacerbate diabetes than not. I know diabetes doesn't go away—yet this is the first time since I was ten that I haven't had to take shots. It must be because of the stress."

"Stress can affect blood sugar levels, but it wouldn't reduce your insulin need. If anything, it would increase it. And I do know more about diabetes than you give me credit for. I'm diabetic, too."

"You're kidding. I had no idea."

"It's not as though we wear signs on our foreheads. I told you there's a high incidence of diabetes among Native Americans."

"Then you should be sick, too."

"Exactly. But what you're describing has been my experience as well. You say this has been going on for several days. When did it start?" He had an idea, but wanted her to confirm it.

"I guess I first noticed around the time everyone started getting sick. After Mac pulled his death-by-drowning stunt and I got back to the station, I remember thinking I should check my glucose level, but I was so cold and tired, I just didn't feel like it. I remember thinking it wasn't all that urgent anyway, so I guess by then it was already happening enough that I'd noticed it. The last time I can clearly remember taking a full dose was the day we found Sam."

"It's been the same for me. There has to be an explanation. Let me think."

He took the mug from the microwave and stirred in the coffee as he mulled the mystery. Their decreased insulin needs coincided with the day Sam died, but beyond that, it was hard to see the connection. Sam stayed so exclusively apart from everyone else at the station there was nothing linking them other than they all lived at Raney. Yet something had initiated the change.

After a moment's reflection, he found it: Sam had died the same day Zo's rat disappeared. The rat that was later found in the cistern. The cistern that held the station's water supply. He looked at Zo's water glass on the table, at the empty beside Ben's bed, and at the mug in his hand.

"Ross," she said.

"Be quiet. I'm almost there."

"It's the water." She held up her glass. "The water is contaminated with insulin. That's got to be it. When people drink the water, they get sick because they're getting too much insulin. All of their symptoms, the shakiness, the drowsiness, the sweating and dizziness and blurred vision and headaches—even their personality changes and hallucinations—are all symptoms of hyperglycemia. Elliot can't get enough candy because he's self-medicating to compensate for the insulin in the water he's drinking, though he doesn't know it. I'll bet anything the others have been doing the same. That's why some people are sicker than others; the amount of insulin overdose they're getting depends on how much water they drink and how much sugar they eat to counteract it. The extra insulin doesn't bother me because I watch my glucose levels and compensate by taking smaller doses." She put down her glass and sat back satisfied. "That's it. I'm sure of it. Everything fits."

He rubbed his chin. Talk about losing a horse race by a nose. Aside from a few small differences, the scenario Zo had just laid out was exactly the one he'd been about to outline.

"Close," he said. "Remember, the insulin molecule is water soluble. A diabetic can drink all the insulin-laced water they want, and it won't have any effect on them because the insulin molecule gets broken down in the gastro-intestinal tract and becomes inactive. But a compound with insulin-like properties that acts on human insulin receptors would behave as you've described."

"Okay, so it's a compound with *insulin-like functions*. I still say it's in the water."

"And I agree. How do you think the water got contaminated?" He was curious to see if she'd discerned the answer to that, too.

"Pinky drowned in the cistern. I think there must have been something in his body that was producing insulin—the insulin-like compound. Maybe a bacteria in his feces. As Pinky decomposed, the compound was released into the water. You're the microbiologist. What do you think?"

"I think you're probably very close to being right. Though most likely a virus is involved, and not a bacteria, for a whole lot of reasons I won't go into now. The virus would have been created purely by chance, selected for like all of the other useful substances found in microorganisms. A harsh environment makes the development of novel survival strategies more likely."

"A viral infection explains some of the other symptoms people are experiencing, like throwing up and upset stomachs. Besides suffering from hypoglycemia, the victims are just plain sick. No wonder Luis couldn't figure it out. Too many vague and overlapping symptoms." Her expression sobered. No doubt she was thinking of the bodies stacked like cordwood in the maintenance shed.

"Here's how I think this works," he said. "Nothing happens in nature without a reason, so the virus has to get a survival advantage somehow. Viruses that produce proteins tend to wear them on their sleeve, incorporating their products by displaying bits on their outer membrane as something of an emblem. These bits of protein are called epitopes, and they have good and bad functions—they allow our immune system to recognize viruses, and they often give the virus uniquely helpful properties. In this case, displaying something analogous to insulin would trick our immune systems into thinking the virus was a natural part of our bodies, so our bodies wouldn't attack the virus and destroy it."

"Score one for the virus."

"Exactly. Epitopes allow the virus to stick to the cells with insulin receptors for periods of time, facilitating their entry into target tissues like muscle, fat, liver, and brain. It's a cruel world for microbes, and anything that doesn't contribute to their survival advantage will kill them— especially if it's something that requires energy to produce."

"Okay, but if the virus produces a compound that sticks to insulin receptors, and it tricks the body into thinking it *is* insulin, and the virus lives in the rats' intestines, how come the rats don't get sick?"

"Drugs act differently on different species. It's entirely plausible that the compound has a much more limited effect on rat receptors than human. If you don't believe me, try giving a sleeping pill to a cat." Ross was speaking from experience. When he was a teen, one of the family cats needed to be put down, and Ross had volunteered to do the deed. Out of kindness to the cat (and to make the job easier on himself), he'd wanted the cat unconscious first. But after shoving three Sominex tablets down its throat, instead of going to sleep like a good, little victim, the cat was completely wired, flying around the house like a Tasmanian devil on speed. Later, when Ross researched the experience on the Internet and confirmed that sleeping pills have the opposite effect on cats, he got his first lesson in pharmacology.

He smiled faintly at the memory. "There have to be advantages to the rats for harboring the virus. Our rats are on a severe carbohydrate restrictive diet. Some scientists believe that increased basal insulin function helps process glucose more efficiently."

"Sorry. You lost me now."

"Remember back when Oprah and others were promoting all those low-carbohydrate fad diets? The thought is that somehow, high carbs cause high insulin, and that makes people gain weight. Gaining weight is generally considered a bad thing in our society, but it's a terrific idea if you're a rat without a lot of food."

"So somewhere between the time the first rats jumped ship and now, this virus/compound/rat symbiosis developed. It's been working fine for decades. Everybody gets a survival advantage; nobody's hurt; everybody's happy. Then humans enter the picture, and everything goes to hell. And we'd never have figured it out if the helicopter hadn't crashed and the rats hadn't chased us in here."

"That's about the gist of it." He shrugged. "Other major discoveries have been just as serendipitous."

She shook her head in amazement. "Do you realize what we've done? We've just discovered a cure for diabetes."

"Not a cure. The compound couldn't be used to regulate blood sugar because the pulsatile flow would be all over the map. But it certainly represents an entirely new class of pharmaceutical agent. Most of our current drug strategies use similar techniques—finding something that works on a receptor of a related hormone or drug. In the drug world, a tiny selective advantage means you capture all of the market share until your patent runs out. If this drug were studied, maybe modified slightly, it could yield a whole new class of diabetes medications. It could be worth billions."

"I can't believe the solution is so simple." She picked up the dish of discarded syrup and hurried over to Ben. Ross held him by the shoulders while Zo parted his lips and dribbled the syrup in.

Ben coughed, then groaned. After a moment his eyes fluttered and he sat up. "What happened?"

"You fainted," Ross said. He caught Zo's eye and shook his head. She was positively glowing and he knew that given half a chance, she'd start blabbing all the details. Their discovery *was* amazing and marvelous and all of the splendid and magnificent things she was no doubt thinking and feeling, but it was far too early to say anything about it—particularly to the latest victim.

"Huh," Ben said. "I've never fainted before. First time for everything, I guess."

"We've *got* to get back to the others," Zo said. "We can cure them. *We can save them.*" She ran to the door and peered out. "Our luck's finally changed. Look! You can see the moon."

Chapter 36

She turned around. Ross was already digging through the food boxes.

"We need something sweet," he said. "Something liquid or semiliquid that'll be easy to dispense and carry."

She crossed the room and tore through the boxes. Now that they knew what to do, there had to be survivors. They'd only been gone twenty-four hours. Some had to be hanging on, self-medicating by eating sweets, or unconscious and unable to drink and reinfect themselves. *Please, God. Let one of them be Elliot.*

She found a box of condiments—*condiments* in an emergency shelter—and took out a teddy bear–shaped plastic squeeze bottle. "What do you think?"

"Perfect," Ross said. "Are there more? We should each have a bottle."

She looked through the box again. "Just one."

"That's okay. Ben and I will work the men's rooms together, while you check the women's. Give everyone at least two teaspoons. If they're not conscious, squeeze a little through their lips; then give them the rest as soon as they're able to swallow. We want people to recover, not choke them to death."

She stuck the bottle in her pocket and bit back a retort. What was it with men and control issues anyway? She thought Ross had softened, and was ready to treat her as an equal. Instead, he'd gone right back to taking charge and issuing orders. So much for old dogs making changes.

Ben was sitting on the edge of the bed with his head in his hands. He looked surprised when she put her hand on his shoulder. She knew how he was feeling. Coming out of an episode of insulin shock entailed an emotional collapse that was hard to describe to someone who hadn't experienced it: A vague, vulnerable sensation as though you'd been peeled open and the layers whittled down until your very soul was exposed. It was a feeling she had experienced only twice, and hopefully never would again.

"Can you walk?" she asked. "We're going back to the station. The storm's quit."

Using the top rail for balance, he got to his feet, then let go and took several tentative steps. He swayed, but stayed standing. "I can walk."

"Good. Put this on." She handed him his coat. "And be sure to zip up. The wind is down, but it's still plenty cold." She started for the door.

"Wait a minute. What about Cam?"

She turned around. "I'm sorry. Your friend didn't make it."

Ben studied the lump beneath the covers. He sighed, then squared his shoulders. "I didn't think he would."

Zo noted the set of his jaw with approval. Thank God he hadn't started blubbering like a baby. She wasn't ready to take him off her enemies list, but he'd definitely moved up a notch.

"We'll come back for his body as soon as we can. Right now, it's critical that we get back to the others. We found some . . . medicine . . . while you were sleeping—a treatment that we're sure will help." She wasn't about to tell him the particulars. The new microbe was so potentially valuable, the last thing she wanted was for Soldyne to get its hands on the information. Hopefully Ben was still enough out of it that he wouldn't ask questions.

He nodded. "Then let's go."

The moon was a small, white circle in an expanse of sky bluer than her darkest jeans, a rich, deep indigo magnified by the reflection in ice and snow. As she stepped outside, Zo felt like she was walking underwater. The cold made her cough, but she breathed it in, grateful to escape the claustrophobic shelter.

The moon was a reminder of how far along they were in the season. Even if Elliot hadn't canceled the remaining tour ships, they wouldn't have had visits from more than another one or two. The sea ice was already moving in. After mid-February, any ship entering Antarctic waters risked getting stuck for the next eight months.

Ahead of them, the station was obscured by shadow; a square, black box barely discernible against the blue horizon. She wanted to run, but forced herself to hold back. Ben would never be able to keep up. Ross was helping him along as it was. More important, running might draw the rats' attention. Presumably, they'd gone back to their shelter, but now that the storm was over, who knew how long they'd stay there—or how long it had been since they had eaten. She scanned the sides of the path like a driver watching for deer.

To the left, the helicopter glowed a soft silver. Near it was what looked like a boulder where previously there had been none. A piece of wreckage, or another body? Someone from the station who, like Mac, went outside to cool off? A picture of Sam's body came to mind, and she shuddered, remembering how the soft meat of his cheeks and both of his eyes had been gone.

Enough. Yes, the rats were out there, perhaps stalking them this very minute, but she refused to let herself be cowed. The world was full of danger. All that mattered was that Elliot was sick, and she had the means to save him. She walked faster. She couldn't help it. She was a horse who'd scented the barn, a runner at the finish line, a mountain climber within feet of the top. A few more yards, a few more minutes, and all would be well.

Then she stopped. There were no lights at the station. No lights meant no heat.

She ran. Surely the building still held enough heat to keep people from freezing. They hadn't been gone that long. Elliot had to be safe and warm in their bed—

She reached the building and darted into the shadows, then stopped again. She looked at the main door, and it was all she could do to keep from crying.

The door was open.

Chapter 37

Ben watched Ross and Zo intently as they looked from the door to each other. They didn't say a word to him, but they didn't need to. Ben's poor, conked-on-the-head brain might be operating on three-quarters power, but he could still add two and two.

He waited for them to acknowledge the obvious. Maybe they thought they were protecting him, the way parents shielded their kids from the seamier side of life, or doctors held back bad news. What they didn't realize was that as far as the rats were concerned, he'd already earned the T-shirt. He'd seen Quentin's body; watched the rats go after Cam's leg like it was a ten-foot sub at a frat party. If the rats were inside the building, and the residents were as sick as Ross and Zo claimed, he knew as well as they did what they'd find.

"Okay," Ross said. "Change of plan. I'm going over to the maintenance shed to restore power. You two will have to take care of things here on your own."

Still nothing about the rats.

He turned to Ben. "When you get inside, take the corridor to the right. The men's dorm rooms are all on the outside wall. As long as you keep hanging right, you won't get lost. When you find someone sick, give them two teaspoons of this."

He handed Ben a plastic squeeze bottle. The shape felt familiar. Ben stepped out of the shadow and held the bottle up to the light.

What the—? This was their miracle cure? The stuff he used to spread on his toast when he was a kid?

"Some of them might be unconscious," Ross was saying as matter-of-factly as if he went around dispensing bottles of honey as medicine every day. "If they are, go easy with them. Not everyone's necessarily going to be in their right mind, so some of them might fight you because they won't understand you're trying to help. But no matter what, you have to get two teaspoons in them. Got it?"

"No," Ben said. "I don't." He felt like he'd landed in the middle of someone else's nightmare. What they were asking was beyond bizarre. "You expect me to go into a building with no lights that's most likely swarming with rats, find people who are sick, and then, even if they don't want me to, I'm supposed to squirt *honey* down their throats? You're out of your freaking minds." And they thought *he* had cognitive problems.

"We have to tell him," Zo said.

"You got that right." He'd already risked life and limb (and poor Cam had given his). No way was he going in without full disclosure. "Follow me! Come on! Walk this way!" they had burbled like purple dinosaurs. Well, this kid had had enough. Give him informed consent over blind obedience any day.

"There's no time," Ross said.

"Make time." Ben crossed his arms over his chest.

"All right. You want to hold us hostage until you get your way, then fine. Short version: The station's water is contaminated with insulin. The people inside aren't sick, they're suffering from insulin overdose. Eating something sweet will cure them. If they don't get it, they'll die."

"Some of them already have," Zo said. "Please. We don't have much time."

Ross's Cliff Notes explanation raised more questions than it answered. Ben remembered now why he and Ross had never been close. You'd think someone with an IQ that was three times anyone else's on the planet would have learned how to make his point without being rude. Still, Zo seemed sincere, and if they were right . . .

"Do I get a flashlight?"

"Sorry, Zo said. "I didn't think we'd need them."

"Don't worry. I'll have the power back in a few minutes. Now if you're done wringing your hands like a little old lady, can we *please* stop yakking and go save some lives?"

Inside, it wasn't completely dark, but it was close enough to pitch black. Down the length of the hallway, indistinct pools of light hinted at open doorways. The squares weren't enough to see by, but at least they gave a sense of space and place.

As Zo's footsteps dopplered down the corridor, Ben headed right, keeping one hand on the wall while he swung the other in a wide arc, not really expecting to connect with anything, not sure what he'd do if he did. He wasn't afraid. The situation was so far beyond the norm that any terror he should have felt was tempered by an overwhelming sense of unreality. He wasn't here. Not really. He couldn't be. He wasn't an adventurer. He was a desk man. His world was phones and faxes, not rats and dead bodies.

He groped his way down the hall. Ross's bombshell reverberated in his head. "The water is contaminated with insulin." "Survivors might be unconscious." Drink the glass of water someone had oh-so-thoughtfully left beside your bed, and the next thing you knew, you were on your way to dead. "You fainted," Ross had said when Ben woke up with the taste of syrup on his lips. Right. And somewhere in Brooklyn was a bridge with his name on it. He clenched his fists. Not fifteen minutes earlier, he'd nearly died from insulin overdose. Ross and Zo both knew it, but wouldn't admit it. Their omission was as obvious as it was intentional. He wondered if they'd given him the water on purpose as a test. Once someone lied to you, all bets were off.

And now the three of them were supposed to be allies: Ross, Zo, and The Human Guinea Pig.

He came to the first doorway and felt his way in. The light from the single window was mirrored by an identical square on the tiles. Asbestos, by the look of it, the same green-and-white marbled kind his parents had in their basement. Not a particularly useful detail, but Ben filed it away since it was the only thing he could see.

The rest of the room lay in deep shadow. Ben strained to hear signs of life—creaking bedsprings, rustling bedcovers, a cough, breathing that wasn't his own—then laughed. This wasn't a morgue. If he was looking for living bodies, all he had to do was ask.

"Hello! Anyone here?"

No answer. He shuffled to the right and immediately bumped something solid. A dresser, he concluded after patting it down. He edged around the perimeter taking stock: clothes on hooks (a nylon windbreaker and the ubiquitous flannel), a low dresser with a lamp he almost knocked to the floor, a set of bunk beds.

He ran his hands over the bottom bunk. The covers were rumpled as though the bed had been slept in, but the bed was empty. Ditto for the one on the top. Ten steps farther, he found a third bed, also empty. If everyone was as sick as Ross and Zo claimed, where were they? Unless these were the beds of those who were already dead—

Shuddering, he continued on. He was almost to the door when his foot nudged something soft. A body. Naked, or nearly so, with skin as cold as the room. He lifted one wrist, not expecting to feel a pulse, but checking anyway, then muscled the body onto the bed, covered it with a blanket, and went back into the hall.

After the scant light in the bedroom, the corridor seemed even darker than before. He strained to hear voices: Ross's, Zo's, anyone's—

Instead, there was a rustling sound, the barest whisper of movement, followed by a series of tiny clicks.

Toenails on tails?

He broke out in a sweat. God, this was awful. Where was Ross? What was taking him so long? Why couldn't he get the lights back on? He leaned against the wall and fought his rising panic. Sarah wouldn't think him so heroic if she could see him now. And Paula—if Paula ever found out, she'd never let him out of her sight again.

He took a deep breath. For some reason, thinking about his family made him feel better. After all, these people had families, too.

He stepped confidently into the next room and turned to the right. Immediately he slammed into a dresser. The dresser tipped. *Cheap dorm-room furniture* was Ben's thought as he went down. Then he was back in the helicopter again, falling, falling, falling, his heart racing like a rabbit's as yesterday's terror came flooding back. He lay on the floor amid the wreckage until his heart rate slowed.

The room reeked of spilled aftershave. He put out a hand to get to his feet, mindful of the broken glass, and bumped something cylindrical, which rolled away with a metallic clatter. He grinned, thanking God for scientists who were afraid of the dark.

He switched the flashlight on and swept the beam over the room. Two beds, two bodies. After confirming that they were dead, he moved on.

The next door was closed. Ben opened it and went in. Beneath a travel poster of Rio de Janeiro, one bed was completely stripped of blankets. The other was piled high. He hurried over and pulled back the covers.

A man lay underneath, pale, trembling, *alive*. The man's lips were cracked and quivering as though he were dreaming.

Ben sat down beside him and put the bottle to his mouth. The man sucked greedily as if his body knew by instinct what was needed. After he'd slurped down what Ben guessed was the appropriate dose, Ben took the bottle away.

A hand grabbed his wrist. "More." The voice was weak and thick.

"I don't have any more." The bottle was full, but the rest was for the others. Judging by his own experience, the man would feel fine in a few minutes. Incredible, to think that a spoonful of sugar was all it took to bring someone back from the dead.

"Thirsty." The man reached for a glass on his nightstand. Ben beat him to it and grabbed it away.

"Hey! That's mine. Give it to me."

"It's empty," Ben lied. "Hang tight. I'll go get you some more."

He looked at the glass, and felt like pitching it against the wall. Instead, he dumped the contents into a wastebasket, dropped the glass in after, and continued on.

Chapter 38

Ross could hardly keep from laughing as he double-timed over to the maintenance shed. Ben probably wanted to deck him for calling him a little old lady. In a way, Ross wished he had. Not that he was a fan of physical violence; he just wished the guy would show more backbone. Provoking him into action was the same trick coaches and drill sergeants used to fire up their men. Get their adrenaline raging, and the fools rushed in. He was actually sorry that Ben had fallen for such an obvious ploy. The backbone thing again.

He was even sorrier that he had to tell Ben about the insulin compound. God only knew what Soldyne would do with it. Ben's boss was responsible for one of the worst acts of environmental vandalism of all time. What else would he be willing to do in the name of profit? Ross would have loved to give the Diabetes Foundation a flask of tainted water as a gift, but that wasn't how the pharmaceutical industry worked. The new treatment could never be brought to market without significant backing and big bucks; a massive investment that would yield even greater results. Still, he hated that a corporation that had shown such gross disrespect for the planet would benefit.

He also hated the way Ben had forced his hand, but there wasn't much he could do about that. With the three of them standing outside arguing while inside, people were dying, he didn't exactly have a choice. Ben's self-righteous, "I'm not going in until someone tells me what's going on" pose was as disgusting as it was dishonest. He wasn't taking a stand; he was only doing what was best for Ben. Bottom line: The guy was afraid to go in.

Well, he was inside now—hopefully, doing his job.

The moon lit the way, sparkling the ice on the graveled path and making the metal shed glow. As Ross came near, the moonlight revealed something else. The entry door alongside the two giant overheads was open.

He pursed his lips. One thing he and Zo hadn't discussed when they discovered the door to the main building open was why. Neither was the kind that could blow open by accident. Both doors had a windproof double-latching system that prevented it. Only a human could open the doors. Only a human could forget to shut them.

He stuck his head inside. There was a shuffling sound from the back.

"Hello!" he called. "Who's there?"

He moved toward Sam's worktable in search of a flashlight. As he passed beyond the faint circle of light the open door afforded, he continued with his arms outstretched, side-stepping obstacles both real and imagined like a quarterback in slow motion—a careful dodge here, a cautious feint there. He stumbled once and swore as he fell over what turned out to be an engine block, banging both shins.

At last he came to the worktable. Ross explored the tabletop by feel, mindful of knives and saw blades and nails. He found a flashlight on a high shelf. The beam threw up shadows like the lodge fires that had accompanied his grandmother's ghost stories when he was a child. The legends were as real to her as the science he had learned from books; stories of the ancestral dead, not properly buried, who roamed the earth until they found a home in a skeleton uncovered by erosion, or a corpse buried too close to the surface—or in a young boy foolish enough to touch the handprints on the ancestral cave walls. He detoured around the Hägglunds, avoiding the morgue he and Zo had set up in one corner.

The emergency generators were in a storage room at the rear. When he found the door, he discovered it was padlocked.

He sighed. Doors that should be closed were open; doors he needed open were closed. Coyote was up to his tricks again.

He retraced his path back to Sam's worktable and returned with a sledgehammer and a crowbar. Hinges broken, he entered a room piled with cardboard boxes and garbage bags. He shook his head. Generators needed regular maintenance. If theirs were somewhere beneath, the prospects didn't look good.

He started tossing boxes and finally found a NorthStar nine-horsepower. He unscrewed the fuel tank cap, shined the light inside, and swore. You were supposed to put just enough fuel in the tank to run it for thirty minutes, not go off and leave the tank half full. The spark plugs had been left in place, and with the piston at the top of the stroke, not the bottom, he'd bet the farm the cylinder walls were coated with rust.

He went through the motions anyway, but after three tries, he gave up. Zo and Ben needed him back at the station. He'd already been gone too long.

Shining the light on the floor, he picked his way to the far side of the Hägglunds, then stopped. A body lay beside the track. Sam's assistant, the kid from Iowa, Scott Bergstrom. There was just enough of his face left to tell.

He blew out his cheeks. It wasn't hard to guess what had happened. When the electricity failed, Scott must have come out to start the generators. But because he was suffering from hypoglycemia, he wasn't thinking clearly, and he'd left both the station door and the door to the maintenance shed open. He'd collapsed out here and died, and the rats had discovered his body. That is, unless the rats had gotten to him first . . .

He tucked the flashlight under one arm and bent down to pick up Scott's body. It was warm. He couldn't have been dead for more than a few minutes. Probably came in right before Ross, in which case Ross had a good idea what the sounds he'd heard when he first came in meant.

As he approached the temporary morgue, six pairs of eyes looked up. Six mouths stopped chewing. Ross tensed. Moving forward, he laid Scott on Sam's worktable. Free of his burden, he swept the flashlight around the room. The beam picked out at least a dozen more. The rats stared back, unblinking, unafraid, and for one crazy moment, Ross felt as if they knew they commanded the only path to the door.

He looked around. There was a fire extinguisher hanging on the wall. He pulled the pin, took aim, and depressed the lever.

The rats squealed and scattered. He fired the extinguisher

in short bursts, sweeping it from side to side as if herding cattle and yelling until he was hoarse; struggling to keep his footing in the foam as he drove the rats toward the door.

The extinguisher quit as the last rat ran out. He tossed the cylinder aside. Leaning against the building, he asked the souls of the desecrated for forgiveness. Breathing heavily, he shut the door.

Chapter 39

Zo ran down the hallway like a blind woman in her apartment: Left, right, another left until she came to her bedroom door. The door was closed. Was that a good sign, or a bad one? She had no idea.

"Elliot!" she called out as she felt her way to his side of the bed. No answer. She patted the covers, climbed up onto the bed and felt toward the middle, then crawled over to her side.

Nothing. The bed was empty. Elliot was gone.

She blinked her disappointment. For twenty-four hours she'd been desperate to get back; to be with him, take care of him, stroke his forehead or hold his hand. *To find out if he was still alive.* Now that the moment was here—and not only that, she had a cure for him in her pocket—he was gone.

She slid off the bed and dropped to her knees, thinking he might have fallen off and rolled underneath. She lay down on her stomach and stretched. There was a pile of candy wrappers beneath the bed, but that was all.

Still, she was encouraged. If Elliot had been eating candy, the effects of the insulin compound would have been mitigated. He'd probably just gotten up to use the bathroom. Or maybe he was feeling so much better he'd gone to the kitchen for something to eat. She ran her hands over his bedside rug. Sure enough, his slippers were gone.

On the other hand, if he was hallucinating or confused, he could be anywhere. She bit her lip and hurried back into the hallway. Access to the kitchen was through the rec room at the end of the corridor—not the most logical or convenient arrangement, but then nothing at Raney was.

She ran down the hall. If anything happened before she could tell him that he was going to be a father— Funny, how the lie that had once seemed innocent and convenient had turned into something evil. One deception had led to another and then another until there was no digging out. Now that she was ready to confess all and beg his forgiveness, it would be too horrible if she were too late.

As she doglegged around the last turn, she smashed into something solid. Her head whiplashed and she flew back with a yelp. She landed on her back. Moaning, she watched the stars circle and held her nose. Of all the idiotic— Her nose was broken, she was sure.

She blinked away tears. Nose throbbing, she sat up. It was no big deal, she told herself. Lots of people broke their noses. Happened to football players all the time. She'd probably end up with a black eye or two, but a crooked nose gave a face character.

As she started to get to her feet, her hand touched something soft.

A body.

She shuddered, patted it down. A flannel shirt, and a pair of jeans. The kind of clothing that Elliot wore, but then, so did 90 percent of the men at the station. She squeezed the arms. Too thin. And the nose was beaky, hooked, like hers was going to be, and the hair felt frizzy. Mac? Someone else? It was impossible to tell.

Whoever it was, they were definitely dead. Shivering, she stood up. The movement triggered an explosion in her face. Gasping, she bit her lip. Physical pain, she could handle. Emotional pain, not knowing what had become of Elliot or what was going to happen next, that was worse.

She groped her way into the rec room. The two small windows on the opposite wall let in just enough moonlight for her to make out vague outlines.

"Elliot? Are you in here?"

A shuffling sound. Then a rustling, followed by a series of quiet clicks. She kept her hand on the doorknob and cocked an ear, ready to slam the door and bolt it if she had to, but the noise didn't repeat.

If only she could see. What was keeping Ross?

She skirted the Ping-Pong table in the middle of the room and patted down each couch and chair. Elliot might have gotten this far and collapsed, or if he wasn't thinking clearly, he might have simply gotten tired and decided the rec room was a good place to take a nap. But the room was empty.

She paused in the kitchen doorway. The windowless room was as dark as a cave. From somewhere inside, the rustling sound came again.

"Elliot? Is that you?"

A moan, or a groan.

"Elliot?"

She edged around the doorway. There was life in the room, she could feel it. Not that she could hear breathing or see movement—not even a sound or a smell. Instinct told her she was not alone.

The hairs on her neck crinkled. Human, or rodent?

She moved into the room. There was an ancient, gas-burning cookstove on the opposite wall that predated automatic pilots. The burners had to be lit with a match. There was always a box on the counter.

Something crunched and collapsed under her weight. She stopped. A cardboard box? Another step, and she kicked what sounded like a tin can. Strange. The kitchen was always spotless. She pictured the layout: the stove on the far side of a butcher-block-topped prep island in the middle. Shuffling her feet, she crossed the room.

Six steps, and she bumped against the work island. Running her hands along the edge, she moved around to the opposite site.

The stove should be directly opposite. She took two steps into the void. Her right hand touched the stainless steel sink.

Close enough. She fumbled for the box of wooden matches, opened it, and struck a match. It fizzled and went out. She tried again. This time, the match flared. She moved it off to the side. Too fast. The flame blew out.

She struck a third, waited until the flame was burning steadily, then slowly lifted it above her head.

A rat was sitting on its haunches on the cookstove, gnawing a piece of bread.

The match scorched her fingers. She dropped it into the sink.

Jesus, she didn't need this. Heart hammering, she turned to leave. Then the moaning sound came again.

Hands shaking, she struck another match.

The rat was still sitting on the stove. Zo took a step to the side. The rat opened its mouth and hissed. Startled, she dropped the match. It sputtered out, and all was darkness again.

This was insane. If she was going to do this, she needed better equipment. There was a roll of paper towels on the counter. She reached for it, expecting the rat to latch on to her hand at any second, found it, and tore off the towels until she was down to the core. She twisted the cardboard tightly and set it on fire. As the light grew steady and strong, she held the torch high.

And screamed.

Rats were *everywhere*.

Chapter 40

She screamed again. She couldn't help it. Rats on the counter, on the table, in the cupboards, on the shelf above the stove, eyes looking at her, tails twitching, mouths agape and glittering with teeth that belonged to creatures she knew would eat you as soon as look at you.

She turned a slow circle. Rats in front of her, rats behind, feasting on spilled pancake mix and instant oatmeal and shredded loaves of bread, heads lifted, eyes alert, watching.

Waiting.

She took a step backward. The rats didn't move. She took another and then another and bumped against the work island. Rats skittered across the butcher block and jumped to the floor.

She edged around the table, keeping her eyes on the rats that were watching her just as intently, rats that could easily span the distance with a single leap. Edgy, poised to spring. Choking down the urge to run, she took another slow step backward. Another, and another. Glanced over her shoulder to gauge the remaining distance and stopped.

The rats had closed ranks behind.

She paused, considered. Rats were intelligent; well, so was she—certainly smarter than they. If she made a dash for the rec room, she could slam the door and seal the rats in the kitchen before they even realized what she'd done. She wasn't facing down lions. They were only rodents. Some might make it through with her, but she could deal with a few . . .

She bent her knees and tensed. The rats wouldn't attack; their instincts would prevent it. It would take too much energy to bring her down. Animals always took the easy way; it was how nature made them. Rats were scavengers, not predators. That they were in the kitchen scarfing down cereal instead of chomping on dead bodies proved it.

She focused on the doorway and psyched herself to run the distance.

A rat darted from the pack. It leaped onto her foot. She stomped, and the rat fell off and ran back to its fellows.

Her chest tightened as her breath came in small, panicked gasps. She wasn't hurt, but the attack left her with the unnerving impression that it was a feint, meant to induce terror in the rat's prey—in *her*—to incite her to panic, to run.

She took a slow step toward the door.

As she did, another rat dashed toward her. It leaped onto her calf and scrabbled up her leg, its claws digging in, and bit down hard.

She screamed as the rat's teeth cut through her jeans and tore a chunk from her thigh. She hit it away. Stumbling backward, she blinked back tears. The pack moved toward her, snarling and hissing, scenting weakness—*scenting blood*. She retreated another step as the pack drove her against the counter.

My God. She'd postulated the rats hunted as a pack. Now she was the proof.

She crouched and thrust her torch out. The front rank squealed and fell back. She smelled singed hair and burnt flesh and thrust again, jabbing like a boxer, swinging the torch in a manic arc, the flame flaring brighter as she cleared a path to the door. Bits of glowing paper dropped like stars. She was Saint George battling the dragon, Hercules versus the Hydra, Perseus slaying Medusa. An Amazon Woman.

A rat leaped onto her back. Its claws dug in like needles. Teeth sliced into her shoulder. Another rat leaped onto her head and clamped onto her ear. She whirled around. Dropping the torch, she grabbed the rat with both hands and squeezed until it hurt.

At last, the rat let go. With a triumphant yell, she flung it into the fire.

The fire.

At her feet, a cereal box burned brightly.

She was an idiot; she should have been more careful; Antarctica was a desert; one of the driest places on earth. Fire was the worst thing that could happen. She looked around. There had to be a fire extinguisher nearby.

A piece of glowing cardboard blew onto the pile of paper towels. They ignited with a *fwummp*. Flames shot to her knees, scorched her shins. The rats scattered.

She ran to the stove, grabbed a stock pot, and ran it to the sink. Turned on both taps and filled it, dumped it on the flames, filled and dumped again.

The work island was burning. Thick, black smoke rolled out from the doors and drawers. Flames spread across the floor, licked the walls, wicked up the plywood paneling, touched the ceiling.

She looked at the wall of flame separating her from the doorway and poured the last potful on herself. The water ran down her jacket, soaked her jeans, turned to steam. She wet a dish towel and held it over her mouth and nose, then dropped to her knees. Down. You were supposed to stay low in a fire. It wasn't the flames that got you. It was the smoke.

There was an exterior door next to the walk-in cooler at the far end of the room. She crawled toward it. A rat ran over her hand. More rats scrambled over her head and back, but they didn't bite. They only wanted to escape, as terrified as she.

The air smelled of burnt plastic and rubber. Her eyes stung. She coughed, tried not to breathe.

At last, her head bumped the wall. She groped for the doorknob, one arm shielding her face. The door was hot. Metal. She found the handle, grabbed it, burned her hand. Draped the cloth over the handle and pulled again.

Wrong door.

She glimpsed metal shelving and rows of boxes before the cool air from the walk-in refrigerator mixed with the hot air in the room. A white fog engulfed her, then dissipated quickly as the fire won out.

When the fog cleared, a man was standing in the doorway. His hair was frosted white, his eyes wide, his skin tinged blue as death. He looked at her, opened his mouth, tried to speak.

For a moment, she was as speechless as he.

Elliot.

Chapter 41

"This way!" She grabbed his hand and pulled him toward the exit as he gagged and coughed. She gave him the dish towel, now nearly dry. "Put this over your mouth! Hold on to my jacket! Don't let go!"

She ran her hands over the wall, found the exterior doorknob, turned it. Sweet, oxygen-rich air flooded the room. She breathed in deeply and pulled her husband into the night.

Behind them, the fire exploded with a *whoomp* that knocked them flat. Too late, she realized what she had done. She scrambled to her feet and slammed the door. The kitchen had no windows, but she didn't need any. She could see the fireball rolling through the rec room, down the hallways, into the labs and offices and bedrooms, consuming everything it touched.

Everything.

She shuddered, gagged, threw up. Straightened, then threw up again. *My God . . . my God—* What she'd done was too horrible to contemplate, too enormous to comprehend. She could roast in hell forever, and it wouldn't be enough.

"We've got to get inside!" She grabbed Elliot's hand and took off for the front door.

Elliot. My God. *He was alive.* She glanced at him as they ran. He was in his pajamas, slippers flapping, running strongly. Why was he in the freezer? How come he wasn't ill?

They skirted the building, every window they passed a throbbing yellow. *No . . . no . . . please, God . . . don't let it spread so fast . . . There was still time to get people out . . . There had to be time . . .*

They rounded the corner and stopped. The main door was open. Rats poured out into the night as though chased by a demon.

Elliot grabbed her hand and pulled her back as the monster burst through the doorway: a thundering ball brighter than the sun, white-hot at its core, red-black around the edges. They dived to the ice, turning their heads away as the heat blasted past. Windows burst and shattered. Small pops like rifle fire—aerosol cans exploding. Bigger, more ominous explosions. If the fire reached the main fuel storage tanks . . .

She scrambled to her feet as Elliot had the same thought. They ran; stumbling, falling, getting up, stumbling and falling and running again.

They were halfway to the emergency shelter before they looked back. The entire building was in flames. Dirty white smoke poured from an inferno that rivaled Dante's. Zo put a hand to her mouth as the roof collapsed. The smell of burnt metal hung in the air. Soot drifted onto their hair and clothes.

Elliot slipped his arm around her and pulled her close. He brushed the hair from her face. She flinched.

"You're hurt." He turned her chin to face him.

She was hurt, all right: Black eyes, a swollen nose, a bloody ear, a slashed shoulder, burned hands, a chunk of meat missing from her thigh, but that was nothing compared to what she was feeling inside.

"I'm okay. What about you? You look—fine." Aside from a touch of frostbite on his nose and cheeks, he seemed completely well.

"I am," he said.

"Elliot, we figured it out," she went on. "We know why everyone's sick. The water—it's contaminated with insulin. Well, not really insulin, but something like it. It's hard to explain." She looked him over again. "You're sure you're okay?"

"I'm fine. While you were gone, I had plenty of time to think. Like you, I figured there had to be something in the water. I switched to orange juice, and right away I started feeling better. I was in the kitchen looking for more when the rats took over and I had to hide in the freezer. I wanted to tell the others what I'd discovered, but I— My God, Zo. The others."

She didn't answer. There was nothing she could say.

"Zo! Elliot!" someone called.

She turned around. "Mac!" She ran to meet him and grabbed him in a desperate hug. "I thought— I can't believe it. You're alive."

"So I am. Not feeling particularly great at the moment, but here I am."

"I gave him the honey just like you told me," Ben said. "It worked."

"So I see. What about Ross? Where is he?"

"Right here," Ross said, coming up to join them from the direction of the maintenance shed. "What's going on? Who started the fire?"

"Where's everybody else?" Zo asked. "Surely there are more."

"I'm sorry." Ben shook his head. "I checked all the men's rooms, and Mac and I had just finished the women's when we smelled smoke. Everyone was already dead."

"*No one* survived?"

"I'm sorry, Zo. We're it," Mac said. "Ben told me about the insulin. It's terrible to think that everyone could have been saved if we'd only known."

Everyone had died? *Twenty people* had succumbed? The loss was staggering. There was small comfort in knowing they hadn't been done in by the flames, but not much. And their research—the equipment, the station records— everything they'd worked so hard to accomplish was gone—Her eyes stung.

"We'll have to go back to the shelter," Ross said. "Now that the storm's over, the radio should be working again. We should be able to get an SOS out to McMurdo."

"Even if it doesn't, my people know I'm here," Ben said. "If they don't hear from me soon, they'll know something's wrong."

"Wait a minute." Elliot pointed to Ben. "Who's he?"

"I'll tell you everything after we're inside." Zo indicated his slippered feet. "Don't want you to catch your death of cold."

It wasn't much of a joke, but they laughed anyway and started for the shelter. Ben with his flashlight led the way, though they no longer needed it. Somewhere over the course of the past half hour, dawn had broken over the bay. The pinks were already turning to orange, the snow and ice a deep shadowed purple. A landscape Zo used to think starkly beautiful. Now all she wanted was to go home.

A tern circled once and retreated. Too much death, too much destruction. Zo squeezed Elliot's hand, reveling in its warmth, grateful to be alive and walking alongside her husband again. Still, it was going to be a long time before she could allow herself to be truly happy.

Then from the front of the line, Mac screamed.

Chapter 42

It was a terrible sound, more animal than human. "Get it off! Get it off of me!" he yelled again and again.

The rats swarmed over him, devouring him before he hit the ground. No back-and-forth dance like they'd done with her in the kitchen, no toying, no intimidation—just a full-out frontal assault.

The men waded in, Ben swinging his flashlight while Ross and Elliot grabbed Mac's shoulders. The pack turned on them, snapping and clawing. Elliot's pajama-clad legs took the brunt. He tried to knock them away, but more rats rushed in. Collapsing from the weight of them, he fell forward.

"No!" Zo screamed.

Ross and Ben picked him up by the arms and legs. "The Zodiac!" Ross yelled. They took off with Elliot dangling between them, his eyes closed, head lolling.

Zo ran after. The attack had lasted barely a minute, yet Mac was dead, and Elliot was gravely wounded. She glanced over her shoulder. The rats were following, pacing them.

Herding them toward the shore.

She understood as clearly as if she were one of them. Shaken, she ran faster, hardly noticing the wound in her thigh.

Then she stopped. These weren't demons. They were *rodents*. Fierce, yes; cruel, undeniably, but they were *not* going to prevail. As of this moment, the reign of terror was over.

She got down on one knee. Picked up a chunk of ice and threw it. Smiled when it connected. Picked up another and threw again.

The rats stopped; agitated, confused. She picked up another chunk.

"Run, Zo! Now!"

She glanced toward the beach. Ben was on his feet in the Zodiac, yelling and waving for her to hurry while Ross untied the moorings. She sprinted for the harbor. The rats took off, but surprise gave her the advantage. She pulled ahead. Ran out in water up to her knees, lunged for the handholds as the Zodiac bucked wildly. Caught one and hung on. Ben leaned over the side, grabbed her jacket, and hauled her in.

She lay in the bottom, gasping, then crawled to her knees and smiled grimly at the rats milling about on the shore.

Elliot lay on the floor beside her. The skiff of water beneath his legs was pink. He shivered violently. She took off her jacket and laid it over him as a wave broke over the bow. Without survival suits, they were in bad shape, but surely they wouldn't have to stay out long. The rats couldn't hold the beach forever. Once they went back to their lair, the humans could regain the shelter.

Then a rat leaped into the water and began to swim, followed by another, and another. Zo remembered Ross's students' rat facts, and her heart sank: Rats could swim for miles, tread water for days. "Miniature superheroes," the kids had dubbed them.

"Start the engine!" she shouted. "Get us out of here! Hurry!"

Ross turned the ignition key and pulled the starter cord. Nothing happened. He pulled the cord again. The motor caught briefly, sputtered, and died. He pulled out the choke, pumped the primer button, and tried again.

She smelled gasoline. "You're flooding it! Ease off! Hurry! They're coming!"

"I'm trying!" Ross yanked the cord like a madman until, at last, the motor caught. He revved the engine and they cut across the bay.

"Torgeson!" he yelled and pointed.

It was a good call. The Zodiac had such a limited range, they could never make it to another station. But the rats hadn't yet invaded Torgeson, presumably because it was too far. They could set up a beachhead on the island using the overturned raft for shelter. The Zodiac carried emergency supplies. Most important, it had a radio. If necessary, they could augment their rations with penguin meat until help arrived; maybe catch a seal or two; make blankets from the skins. Shackleton and his men had survived for two years with little more than a rowboat.

Then abruptly, Ross altered course. He pointed to a dark smudge on the horizon. "Check it out."

She strained to see, and broke into a grin.

It was a ship.

Chapter 43

Her grin vanished as a rat leaped into the boat. Before she could process what was happening, another scrambled up and over the side. It flopped into the bottom like a fish, swam over to Ross, and darted up his leg. He let go of the tiller to slap it away.

"Watch out!" Ben cried as the Zodiac angled sharply toward the shore.

Ross grabbed for the tiller, as Ben lunged for the rat. He pulled it off and flung it into the sea.

"Here comes another one!" Zo tore open the side locker and found an oar. Leaning over the side, she swatted the rat away. More rats swam up. "Help me!" she yelled to Ben as one after another scrabbled up the sides.

Ross gunned the engine and the Zodiac leaped forward, hydroplaning like a pebble between the ice floes.

"Slow down!" Ben yelled. "You're going too fast!"

Elliot raised his head. "What's happening?"

Zo hunkered beside him. "Stay down. Keep your center of gravity low."

The Zodiac slammed into an ice chunk. She threw herself over Elliot and fumbled for the handholds as they went airborne. They hit the water, bounced, and came down hard again, each impact snapping her head backward. She spreadeagled herself and dug her feet in.

At last, the boat slowed. She looked toward the tiller. Ross was gone.

"Jesus," she breathed. She scrambled to the pilot's seat as the Zodiac turned an aimless circle. "Where is he?"

"Over there!" Ben pointed.

She shielded her eyes. She could just make out a small red dot a football field away.

"Hang on!" she cried as she turned the tiller, even though she knew Ross couldn't hear. "We're coming!"

She cut around an iceberg bigger than a grand piano and nearly slammed into another. She detoured left, then left again. By the time she hit clear water, Ross was gone.

"Where is he! I can't see him!"

Ben leaned out over the bow. "I don't know! I can't—Wait! There he is! Turn to starboard! I mean port! Oh, hell, just turn right. Now left. *Left!* More . . . more . . . Slow down, you're almost there. I said *slow down!*"

Zo cut the throttle, and let the boat drift to where Ross was treading water. His head was barely above the waves.

Ben leaned over the bow. "Got him!" he cried and pulled Ross in over the side. Ross was shuddering so hard, he looked like he was convulsing. His face was blue.

Zo began to shake.

"Not yet, Amazon Woman," he said, and managed a wan grin. "You can fall apart later. Right now, just get us on the ship."

"Aye, Captain," she said as she aimed the tiller. "With pleasure."

PART THREE

We did not inherit the earth from our parents. We're borrowing it from our children."

—CHIEF SEATTLE

Chapter 44

Ben watched the litter carrying Elliot and Ross ascend to the deck while he waited below in the Zodiac. He hung onto the tie ropes, feet spread for balance. Only the rough seas kept him from dancing. He felt galvanized, alive. Despite all the tragedy of the past day and a half and the final unbelievably harrowing hours, he'd accomplished what he had set out to do: effected a rescue. The proof was right there on the side of the ship, painted in letters that viewed this close were as magnificent as they were impossibly large: *Polar Sea*. Soldyne's supply ship.

It wasn't only the successful mission and the multiple near-death experiences that had him feeling as invincible as a twenty-year-old (though facing down killer rats and deadly disease and surviving a helicopter crash did wonders for the self-esteem). The moment he'd seen the ship on the horizon and realized all was *not* lost, that he still had years in which to craft his legacy, he'd had an epiphany.

He'd looked at Ross shivering in the bottom of the boat and realized that meeting up with a man he hadn't seen or even thought of for nearly two decades hadn't been chance at all; it was providential.

For years Ben had thought he could have it both ways; that he could work for a company that was going to profit by turning icebergs into drinking water and still consider himself a good man who cared about the environment. Now he realized he'd overlooked the "for profit" part of the arrangement. There was too much money involved in a project of this size for hands to stay clean. It wasn't absolute power that corrupted, it was money, and Gillette was the biggest crook of all.

Finding out that his iceberg had been blasted off deliberately had been a stunner. And yet in hindsight, the news should have been obvious. The berg's near-ideal location wasn't coincidence, it was contrived. The business card in Quentin's wallet was there because Donald's flunky was moonlighting as an ecovandal. When Ben got back to L.A., the first thing he was going to do was hold a press conference. Knowledge *was* power, and it felt great to be the one in control.

Even so, he wondered how he'd gone so far off center. Ross's sister had fallen off the deep end with her radical, ecoterrorism tactics, but he'd sunk so low in the opposite direction, he'd ended up in bed with the enemy. Now his blinders were off. After he exposed Gillette, he was going to hand Soldyne his walking papers. Find a job compatible with his renewed sensibilities. Nothing as supersized and glamorous as turning icebergs into drinking water, but with more meaning. Maybe do some pro bono for an environmentally friendly nonprofit on the side. There had to be hundreds of ways he could use his engineering expertise that wouldn't impact negatively on the planet. Sarah deserved to inherit a working model.

"Going up."

Zo tapped Ben's arm and pointed to the descending basket. He held it steady, then climbed in after her and signaled the crew. As the winch lifted them higher, he looked out over the Southern Ocean. Below them, the Zodiac was a bathtub toy. The smoke on the shore, a distant campfire. As for the rats, they didn't exist.

The crane swung them around as they cleared the rail and lowered the basket to the deck. A man in a blue watch cap stepped up and offered a hand. Ben recognized Ed Halsey, the first mate.

Halsey raised two fingers to his forehead. A gesture of respect. Ben's chest swelled.

"Captain asked me to assist," Halsey said. "After you've cleaned up, you're wanted on the bridge."

Ben's chest deflated. So much for his happy sojourn on Cloud Nine. Of course the captain wanted to know what had become of his helicopter and his pilot.

Ben followed the first mate through an oval door, wincing as he stepped over the high flange. Halsey cranked the handle shut and Ben clattered after him down a flight of steep stairs. They turned left into a narrow corridor, left again, and then right, until at last Halsey opened a stateroom door. He stepped aside, then followed Ben in and opened a closet. "These are my quarters. You're welcome to anything in here that will fit. If you hang your clothes on the back of the chair, they'll dry in no time. We're next to the engine room."

Which explained the heat and the noise.

"If you need anything, I'll be on the forward deck." He touched his forehead again, and went out.

Ben looked over the rows of shirts and pants and selected

a pair of tan Dockers and a long-sleeved Oxford. Halsey's going-ashore clothes, he presumed. He laid them out on the bed, then went through the dresser drawers until he found a belt. He tried on a pair of loafers, then returned them to the closet and set his boots next to the heat to dry. He hung the rest of his things over the chair and stripped to his shorts.

There was a small sink in one corner. Luxury living, ice-cutter style. Ben turned on both taps to scrub the blood and soot from his face, then ducked his head beneath the faucet.

He filled a metal cup on a shelf above the sink, and took a long drink. As he put the cup back, he eyed Halsey's toothbrush, then ran his tongue over his teeth and reached for the toothpaste. In for a penny, in for a pound. Besides, beggars couldn't be choosers. Or was "what they don't know won't hurt them" the more appropriate proverb?

He toweled off and dressed. The fit wasn't as bad as he had expected. He sat down on the edge of the bed to turn up the pants cuffs, then closed his eyes. The adrenaline buzz was wearing off quickly, and no wonder. He'd used up a lifetime's worth during the last twenty-four hours.

Ten minutes, he told himself as he stretched out on top of the bed. Surely the captain wouldn't begrudge him that.

He opened his eyes twenty minutes later, smoothed his shirt, touched up his hair, and stepped into the corridor. No matter what approach the captain took, he decided as he retraced his path and started up the stairs, he wasn't going to let himself get beat up over what had happened. Cam's death was a terrible tragedy that would haunt him forever, but it was also an accident. Like most accidents, it could have been prevented if either he or Cam had been gifted with clairvoyance, but they weren't, and it hadn't. Recriminations (assuming the captain was planning to indulge) were a dead end. They needed to look forward, not back. As soon as they mustered a team to recover Cam's body, they needed to get back to the iceberg and to the crew.

At the top of the stairs, a deckhand pointed him toward the bridge. He knocked on the door, then entered at the captain's invitation. The first person he saw wasn't the captain, as he had expected. It was Gillette.

Chapter 45

"Ben," Gillette said.

"Donald."

Silence, while Ben processed the how and why. Donald matched Ben's restraint, using the silence-as-weapon tactic that now seemed childish in the extreme. Ben wondered that he'd ever found it intimidating.

He looked at his boss sitting smugly in the first mate's chair and was filled with disgust. Gillette was absolutely amoral, a man whose conscience had allowed him to destroy a section of the ice shelf that had been in place for centuries without remorse. That the destruction didn't have immediate and obvious global consequences didn't make it any less wrong. The ice shelves were *supposed* to be there; they surrounded the world's least understood continent for a reason. He clenched his fists, calming himself with thoughts of his upcoming press conference.

The captain broke the impasse. "If you'd like to talk in

private, you can go through there." He indicated a win-
dowed half door to a glass-enclosed observation room.

Ben trailed Gillette up a short flight of steps and sat
down in a swivel armchair bolted to the floor. He turned
the chair around to face the windows—ostensibly to admire an expanse of sky that would have done a Montana
rancher proud; in reality an excuse to turn his back on his
boss—and waited.

"You've made a hell of a mess," Gillette said at last.

Ben swiveled to face him. Gillette was glowering down,
brows beetled in a scowl. Too late, Ben remembered Gillette's second-favorite intimidation tactic. He couldn't very
well stand up after he'd already been seated, and even if he
did, Gillette's height would always give him the advantage.
He sat back and crossed an ankle over his knee, adjusting
his pants cuff while Donald launched his list of Ben's sins.

"One man dead on your watch. Abandoning your job and
crew for an unauthorized rescue. Twenty-four hours with no
word, forcing me to come clean up your mess. Now here you
are, alive and well and responsible for a second man's death,
along with untold destruction of property, including the
ship's helicopter and a scientific research base."

Ben picked at a spot of lint on his borrowed trousers.
When you put it like that, it sounded bad. He could only
imagine how much blacker Gillette would paint Ben's ac-
tions when he presented his case to the board.

"You're done," Gillette said. "Finished. Relieved of
duty, as our military friends would say."

"I'm fired?"

"Whether there's a position for you with the company
when you return or not is irrelevant. Right here, right now,
I'm in charge. I've instructed the captain to get under way

immediately. We'll arrive at the berg later today. When we do, you'll be staying on the ship."

Ben opened his mouth, then shut it. Fine. Let Donald think that he had won. Gillette wouldn't have believed him anyway if he told him that not more than an hour ago, he'd made up his mind to quit.

Chapter 46

With nothing for Ben to do, the minutes slipped by like the ice alongside the bow. He didn't know how long he had been standing at the rail when Zo joined him on the forward deck. Long enough for the wind to redden his cheeks and his snot to freeze as he shielded his eyes against the sun and admired the bergy bits and growlers the ship passed through. The formations weren't as impressive as Gillette's handcrafted berg, but they were awe-inspiring all the same with the morning sun lighting the ice from behind and a fresh breeze off the bow. He rested his elbows on the rail. During his first crossing he'd been so sick, he'd missed all the scenery. It was hard to say why this time he was fine. There were a lot of things about him that had changed.

He could feel Gillette looking down from the conning tower like a god. No, not a god; a messiah, his hostile takeover disguised as salvation. He just couldn't wrap his mind around Gillette's win-at-all-costs mentality. It wasn't simply a matter of too much testosterone; Gillette's over-the-top competitiveness was more indicative of a personality disorder or a brain dysfunction. A person could attain responsibility and power and still be mad as Hitler.

Zo hadn't spoken to him beyond a greeting, which was fine by him. He appreciated the company of someone who understood the art of silence. He stole a glance. She looked like she'd staggered out of a boxing ring the loser: black eye, swollen nose, angry red scratches along one side of her neck. The ship's medics had patched her up; there was a bandage across her nose and a row of neat, black stitches along the top of her right ear. But her clothes were a mess—ripped, scorched, and bloodstained. He sized her up. Maybe some of Halsey's clothes would fit.

"How's your husband?" he asked.

She blinked as if she hadn't realized he was there. "Stable," she said after a moment. "He lost a lot of blood. The doctor's working to restore fluids. He's concerned about infection. The rats really did a number on him."

No kidding. It had taken all of his and Ross's strength to save her husband from being eaten alive. Ben didn't really think the rats were by nature man-eaters, despite what he had witnessed. Most likely, they were acting out of character because they were freaked out by the fire. Still.

"He was lucky," Ben said.

She arched her eyebrows.

"I mean—because the rats didn't . . . well, you know. And because there's a doctor on board. With medicine . . . and stuff."

The cold coming from her shoulder was worse than the wind off the bow. He let the thought trail off. He'd never been fond of folks who tried to spin a ray of sun into a full-blown sunrise, either.

"Can I ask you a question?" he said after they had stood in silence for some minutes more. Several lines of thought had converged as he'd been musing at the rail, and he needed to know if the conclusion they led to was true.

She shrugged. "Why not."

"I've been thinking about what Ross said back at the station—that people got sick because of the insulin in the water. I'm wondering what their symptoms were."

"You should know."

So he *had* been poisoned. At least now she was willing to admit it. He'd hoped she was a person of integrity, because if he was right, he was going to need her help.

"Can you be more specific? I was a little out of it at the time."

"Sweating, dizziness, headaches; tingling in the hands and feet, drowsiness, mental confusion, personality changes, behavioral abnormalities, inability to concentrate, blurred vision. Then in the final stages, hallucinations and death. Hypoglycemia is extremely subtle. It can have its onset in minutes, but because of the mental confusion that goes along with it, even careful diabetics often don't realize what's happening until it's too late. Death from lack of glucose to the brain or cardiac arrest can happen within the hour."

Exactly as he had expected. "How come you and Ross didn't get sick?"

"I'm diabetic. So's Ross. Why do you want to know?"

He wrestled with the wisdom of trusting her, then decided he had no choice. "The iceberg water is contaminated, too."

"Really?" Finally, a spark of interest. "What makes you think that?"

"When one of my men drank the water, he got sick just

like you described. Headaches, dizziness, confusion—the works."

"Just one?"

"Possibly one other." Quentin had drunk two cups the day they turned the satellites on. Hours later, he was dead. Maybe the rats hadn't killed him at all; maybe they'd only found his body after he'd collapsed from insulin overdose. An autopsy could confirm it.

"You can't draw a conclusion from such a small sample. Besides, Ross and I believe the rats are the key."

"How so?"

"The rats harbor a virus that produces an insulin-like compound. The compound acts on human insulin receptors the same way real insulin does. When people drink the water, their bodies react as if they'd been injected with insulin. How sick they get depends on how much water they drink, and how much sugar they eat to counteract it."

Eugene's workstation was always littered with candy wrappers. Quentin, on the other hand, was a health nut.

"So unless your berg is overrun with rats," she finished, "I don't think you have a problem."

"But it is. Not overrun, but we do have rats on the berg. I haven't seen them, but my crew have and one—" He stopped. He didn't have to describe what had happened to Quentin's body.

"Of course," she said slowly, as if she were thinking out loud to herself. "My research camp was in the area where your berg was broken off. I knew about the rats, of course, but they didn't bother me—they just hunted out at the ice shelf's leading edge like they'd probably done for centuries. But when your boss blew up the ice shelf, they were cut off from their food supply. Some of them crossed the peninsula to Raney. The rest must have been trapped on your iceberg."

"So you agree our water could be contaminated?"

She nodded. "All the elements are there. You'd have to test the water to be sure."

He thought about his *Dummies* kits. Talk about sending a boy to do a man's job.

"Just how powerful is this compound?" he asked. "How many parts per million would it take to contaminate, oh, say, a tanker full of water?"

"Try parts per billion. You'd be amazed how little it takes to poison an entire ocean."

"Then we're in trouble. Because right now, there's a tanker full of contaminated water halfway to L.A."

Chapter 47

Zo stayed at the rail after Ben left and thought about what he'd asked her to do.

The tanker, he explained, was moving slowly. On a good day, a fully loaded supertanker could make 12 to 15 knots. At over three thousand miles, the trip from the berg to Los Angeles was expected to take weeks—a time frame that had frustrated him at the outset, but that was now going to work in their favor.

"Their favor," he had said. She'd caught his use of the plural pronoun right away. Apparently, he was operating under the misperception that confiding his concerns made her his partner.

The tanker would make port in around ten days, he'd continued, which meant they'd have plenty of time to obtain a water sample and get it tested before the water was discharged into the city's system.

The plural pronoun again.

She didn't want to partner with him. For one thing, she

doubted the situation was as dire as he seemed to think. Governments tended to act responsibly when it came to city services. Surely providing clean, safe drinking water for their inhabitants was high on their priority list. She doubted the iceberg water would be added to the public supply without thorough testing. Then again, most of the standard water-quality tests were designed to detect bacteria, not viruses. The insulin-like compound was even smaller. Conceivably, it could slip through.

The other reason she didn't want to work with him went deeper. Ben *claimed* to have seen the light, even insisting that he'd been about to quit his job when he was fired, but could you really come back so easily from the dark side?

Regardless, she'd pretended the role of compatriot and agreed to go along with his request, not because she wanted to help him, but because right now, there was nothing on earth she wanted more than a sample of the tainted water—aside from Elliot making a full and speedy recovery, of course. The discovery of the insulin-producing microbe was as potentially world-changing as the disaster Ben had laid at her feet. Somewhere between the time she and Ross discovered the microbe and the destruction of the station, she'd planned to bottle some of the water and bring the samples back for research. That plan had gone up in flames along with the rest of station, but now Ben was offering a second chance. Researching the microbe and publishing her findings wasn't how she had anticipated making her mark, but discovering a whole new class of diabetes medication was an adequate substitute. She and Ross would have to share credit when they published, but she was all right with that. She might even let him list his name first.

Ben had explained the layout on top of the berg and what he wanted her to do. It sounded simple enough. All she had to do was contrive a way to get onto the iceberg, get out to the melt zone, and fill a few bottles. Or, if the lake had already reverted back to frozen, chip off a few chunks and stick them in a Ziploc.

There was an element of danger. Ben's boss was on the ship—a competitive megalomaniac who would stop at nothing to get what he wanted, according to Ben. But Zo wasn't worried. The way to handle a narcissist was to play to their ego. She'd pretend to have an interest in the iceberg operation, even flirt a little if she had to. She wasn't bad looking beneath the bandages and bruises.

Besides, even if he caught her obtaining samples, nothing he could do could compare to what she'd just been through.

Chapter 48

Donald stood at the window of the observation room and looked down at the woman at the rail. She and Ben had been deep in conversation for a good half hour before Ben wandered off. What they were talking about, Donald didn't care. Nothing Ben Maki could say or scheme could touch him. Ben was finished, as dangerous as a castrated lapdog, the woman as intimidating as something the cat had refused.

He smiled. After Adam called him up in Alaska and Donald flew down to pick up Ben's pieces, he hadn't known precisely what he would find. That Ben was one of the four bedraggled survivors was a bonus. Dead, Ben would be a martyr. Alive, he was fair game. The *Times* story Donald had planted throwing suspicion on Quentin's death had gone a long way toward discrediting the microwave operation, but any publicist worth their fee knew it was hard enough to create a buzz, let alone sustain it. Now, Maki's Misadventures would make feature fodder for weeks to come.

His smile faded as he thought of his brother-in-law. Quentin had been a good man, devoted to the end. That kind of loyalty took time to cultivate. He still had one man on the berg, but Donald was a believer in redundant systems. Not knowing in advance which one of them he could turn, he'd brought gifts for them all: fresh fruit and vegetables for Toshi, exotic cheeses for Phil, and for Eugene, a case of fine wine.

He turned away from the windows and sat down at one of the small, fixed tables. The observation room wasn't the most comfortable place to set up his office, but nothing on the ship was. At least this room had the bank of windows he preferred.

He opened his laptop to review his notes. He'd spent hours researching the satellite interface program on the flight down. He was sure he had a handle on it, but when the stakes were this high, there was no such thing as too much preparation. Adam had faxed the site plans and schematics. The layout revealed a backup server in the pumphouse for off-site data storage. It wouldn't be difficult to contrive access now that Donald was the boss. Adam had also sent the password to Toshi's program. Donald knew exactly which keystrokes would disable the interface beyond repair. With Ben's reputation in ruins, his microwave process was as good as dead, but Donald never stopped until he'd buried the body.

There was a knock on the door, and a seaman came in carrying a lunch tray. Donald indicated an unoccupied table. He lifted the lid off a steaming dish. *Ostiones al pil pil*, with an order of *empanadas* on the side. He picked up the bottle of wine the ship's steward had thoughtfully supplied to go with it, and tsked.

Cabernet with scallops?

Chapter 49

Los Angeles, California

For ten years, the table in Rebecca Sweet's dining room had been set with papers. Yellow legal pads in front of each chair, stacks of major newspapers and scissors for cutting clippings in the center, cardboard filing boxes filled with more papers on the floor. An ancient PC sat on one end of the table; the telephone cord connecting it to a brand-new three-in-one fax machine on an antique sideboard snaked across the floor.

The family took their meals at a wooden table in the kitchen, or carried plates into the living room in front of the television, or when the sun wasn't too hot or the wind too strong, under the mesquite tree in the yard.

This morning, six people were seated around the dining room table. Rebecca's husband, Antonio, stood at the door. Trouble was more likely to come via electronic surveillance, but Antonio was older than her by a decade and had served in the Gulf War. His enemies were flesh and blood, not bits and bytes.

She looked at her people. Her own excitement was mirrored in their faces. She smiled. The electricity emanating from POP's executive committee could have lit up a ballfield. Tomorrow, at long last, Soldyne's tanker was due.

"Why so early?" Neil Walks-as-Bear, Rebecca's cousin and POP's treasurer, wanted to know. "I thought the tanker was going to take at least another week."

"It's only half full, so they made good time," the group's secretary and chief intel gatherer, Julie Walks-as-Bear said. Neil's sister.

"Too bad." Raoul, Julie's fiancé, shook his head. "If the water in the hold is below the waterline, the blast charges will have to be set underwater as well. Won't be much of a statement if no one can see the explosion."

Rebecca had been disappointed when she heard about this, too. Video footage of Soldyne's ill-gotten gains pouring out of the side of the ship would have played well on the news.

"Besides, Raoul continued, "an underwater blast won't even be effective. The iceberg water won't flow out; all that will happen is seawater will flow in."

"I agree," Sherry Kowalski, one of the few non-Diné in Rebecca's inner circle, said. "This stinks. I guess we can settle for contaminating Soldyne's water, but that wasn't the point. We wanted to make a statement. Something big that will get people's attention. Something dramatic and visual."

"It still might work," Julie said. "If the tanker's only half full, it will be riding high in the water, right? So some of the water in the hold might be above sea level. It's possible we can still have our big bang."

"We need to stop speculating about this and find out," Neil snapped. "Someone should talk to Ramon."

"I already have," Rebecca said. "He's on it. Don't worry."

She studied their faces, earnest, worried, but as always, sincere. These were good people. Loyal. Dedicated not to her, but to the cause. Self-sacrificing. Willing to put the needs of the many over the needs of the few. Like the 3 billion people all over the earth who lacked clean water and sanitation.

POP could have chosen any of a million other globe-threatening problems on which to concentrate their efforts: hunger, global warming, pollution, desertification, loss of wetlands, nuclear proliferation, ozone depletion, war. But the Navajo's respect for the spiritual quality and importance of water in people's everyday lives made water issues a natural. Under that umbrella fell still more issues: pollution, abuse of the aquifer, irrigation, sanitation. POP's executive committee had elected to focus on Soldyne as their target because, simply put, Soldyne was a thief. Access to clean water was a fundamental human right; water could not be allowed to become a commodity sold to the highest bidder. And yet all over the world, multinational corporations like Soldyne were buying up vast tracts of wilderness that included whole water systems, then reselling the water at exorbitant rates, sometimes to the very people from whom it had been taken. Tens of billions of gallons of precious groundwater stolen, bottled, and sold.

Soldyne's microwave process was their downfall. The image of a microwave beam shooting down from space and melting icebergs into drinking water was so compelling, it was the perfect vehicle for highlighting the problem. Big, romantic, and fresh. People were burned out on pictures of dusty landscapes and dying children.

"In other news," she went on. "I talked to Ross this morning. You won't believe where he called from." She looked around the table. "At this very minute, Ross is heading for the iceberg on Soldyne's supply ship."

The room erupted in excited exclamations. "How?" someone asked. "Do they know he's one of us?"

Rebecca held up her hand. "They don't have a clue. All Soldyne knows is that he's a microbiologist who works at Raney. I don't know how he managed to get on board. I'm guessing the supply ship detoured to Raney, and Ross talked his way in. I'm sure he'll tell us all about it when he gets home." Their telephone conversation had been brief. Ever since her arrest, she presumed Homeland Security had her phone bugged. "However, he did manage to tell me that he's going to make sure they give him the grand tour."

"Excellent," Neil said. "Does he have a camera?"

"No doubt. Ross is always on top of things. There's not much that catches him by surprise, but one thing did: He told me Donald Gillette is on the ship."

"Unbelievable," Julie said, and it was. That Ross had managed to contrive the opportunity to follow Soldyne's executive vice president around as he toured the iceberg was nothing short of miraculous. The intelligence he would bring back was beyond price.

Ahéhee, Rebecca whispered to the gods above. *Thank you.* Things couldn't have worked out better if she had planned them.

Chapter 50

Iceberg, Weddell Sea, 68° S, 60° W

Ben stood on the deck of the *Polar Sea* looking up. The stairs leading from the harbor to the top weren't stairs at all. The ledges looked more like bleacher seating for a ball game played by giants, a series of short, irregular, horseshoe-shaped plateaus that had been carved out by wave action over who knew how many eons of time. Some of the steps looked like they were going to be an easy climb, but most would require more effort. For the taller ones, they were bringing a ladder. Not the easiest route to access the berg, but now that the helicopter was no more, the amphitheater was the only way to get onto the berg—or off.

He stuck his gloves between his knees and tied his hood tighter around his face. The harbor may have been considered sheltered from a seaman's point of view, but the half-moon-shaped walls surrounding them chilled the air like a refrigerator. He glanced over at Gillette and noted with satisfaction that he was shivering, too.

He put his gloves back on and stuck his hands under his armpits. He'd known all along that Donald's threat to confine him to quarters was only posturing. No one knew the layout on top of the berg as well as he did, and Donald couldn't make the climb alone. The only reason he'd threatened to leave Ben behind was to massage his inflated ego, but even an egomaniac knew when to be practical.

Ross and Zo were coming along as extra hands. Ben would have liked to have had at least a dozen bodies; the amount of gear and personal effects that needed to be off-loaded onto the ship was substantial. But in view of what had happened to his pilot, understandably the captain was disinclined to involve his crew.

The crew lowered the gangplank and they set off, Gillette in the lead, Zo next, Ross and Ben carrying the ladder in the rear. As they reached the other side, they paused to regroup.

"One hundred seventy-five feet," Ross told them. "That's what one of the crew members said."

Zo put her hands on the first chest-high ledge and swung her legs up and around. She stood up, and looked down. "Make that one seventy."

Halfway to the top, they stopped for a break. Ben peeled the foil from an energy bar as he dangled his legs over the edge. The sky was gray, but not threatening. There was a black dot on an ice floe far below that looked like it might be an elephant seal. He wished he had his camera. He'd been chronicling his Antarctic adventures for Sarah from the beginning, but ever since the incident with the stolen picture book, he'd stepped up the pace. If she wanted pictures of Antarctica that badly, all she'd had to do was ask.

Behind him, Ross was setting up the ladder. Zo was behind an ice hummock relieving nature. Women definitely had it tougher than men. He'd read about a device women could wear in the field; an anatomically contoured funnel called the "piss-phone" or the "whizzomatic" that allowed them to unzip and urinate like a man. He wondered if Zo was wearing one.

Gillette was sitting on an ice boulder to his left. His backpack lay unopened at his feet. Donald was handling the climb remarkably well, moving from ledge to ledge with a fluidity that hinted at rock-climbing experience. Ben was surprised until he realized he had no context for Gillette beyond what he saw of him at the office. He probably worked out at the gym.

He stood up as the cold worked through his jeans. It wasn't smart to let your clothes get wet. His boots hadn't dried out before he'd had to put them on again, either, which worried him. When you were out in the cold, the most important thing was to keep your feet dry, Ben's dad had drilled into his head. Eino Maki had cut pulpwood for a living, jack pine in the summer and swamp cedar in the winter. Ben used to run pole for his dad during Christmas break. While his dad limbed the downed trees, Ben laid the measuring pole alongside so the logs could be cut to the correct length. It was piecework, fourteen cents a stick, and Ben had to hustle to keep up, wading through snow over his knees, stepping in and around the brush, the cedar boughs tripping him up or acting like snowshoes until a foot would break through. They'd stop only twice, at ten and at two, when Ben's dad would make a pile of boughs and light a fire. With the saw shut off, the air was cold and still. Ben would stand beside the fire eating his sandwich and drinking hot tea from his thermos, listening to the trees crack from the cold and the chickadees whistle. Once, a flying squirrel whose nest had been disturbed mistook him for a tree and landed on his shoulder.

Clear-cutting was the reason Ben became an environmentalist. The paper giants wanted the public to believe that trees were a renewable resource, but Ben had seen the results of cutting them down firsthand. The forests never grew back the same; scrub pines and poplar sprouted from the left-behind brush; once-rich, loamy soil turned acrid. The cut-over areas were hot, dry places that were only good for growing blueberries, and when you went out to pick them, you made sure to wear a hat and carry plenty of water. Trees in exchange for berries. What kind of trade-off was that?

He finished the energy bar and zipped the wrapper into his pocket. Idly, he brushed the crumbs off the ledge, then realized they were actually small, brown pellets, and frowned.

They made the top a half hour later and found four snowmobiles waiting. An extravagant number, in Ben's opinion; they could have doubled up and made the ride with only two. But Gillette was the boss, and if he'd ordered one each, then so be it. Ben supposed he was going to have to get used to someone else making the decisions.

Next to the snowmobiles was a staging area piled high with boxes. The crew had been busy. Gillette must have called ahead. Ben looked down at the ship and was glad Ross and Zo had come along.

"Everyone know how to ride?" Gillette asked.

They answered in the affirmative, Ben chafing at the way Gillette had managed to insult three seasoned pros under the guise of solicitation. Gillette in the lead, they took off for the op center, a small, silver glint on the horizon. The ride was uneventful, and fast. Granted, snowmobiles weren't difficult to drive; where Ben grew up, kids as young as six or seven rode their own; but Gillette managed his as if he'd been born to it. Ben wondered what else about his ex-boss he didn't know.

They pulled up outside of the op center. Ben hung his helmet over the handlebars and hurried inside. The crew welcomed him with hugs and high fives, then fell silent when Gillette strode in behind.

If Gillette noticed the change, he didn't let on, greeting everyone by name and making introductions, handing out compliments and presents like he was wearing a red suit. No wonder he'd risen in Soldyne's echelons; the man could charm the glow off a lightbulb.

Gillette explained the situation in a surprisingly accurate if sanitized rendition, then instructed everyone to pack while he went out to the melt zone.

"We've already shut things down out there," Eugene objected. "Everything's turned off and locked up tight. Well, in a matter of speaking." He grinned. "It's not like we have to worry about break-ins."

Gillette sent him a withering look, but Eugene didn't melt. Why was Gillette going to the melt zone? Ben wondered. Had he somehow gotten wind of Ben's plan? It hardly seemed possible. He and Zo had discussed it only once, outside standing at the rail. Even if Gillette had been watching from the conning tower, their backs had been turned toward him the entire time. If Gillette was on to them, Ben was going to have to add mind reading to the man's talents.

"I'd like to go, too," Zo said, shooting a quick glance at Ben. "I'd love to see what your operation is all about."

"So would I," Ross chimed in. "I've read about your process. Impressive stuff."

Ben frowned. If Zo had brought Ross in on their plan, she should have told him.

Gillette looked like he wanted to refuse. Ben supposed he could contrive to get the sample himself if he did. It wouldn't be easy with Gillette hanging around issuing orders, but he could figure something out.

"Oh, all right," Gillette finally said. "Anyone else? Ben? Everybody? We can make it a party."

"That's okay," Ben said quickly. "We've seen it all."

As the three headed for the door, Ben grinned. Not only were things going exactly according to plan, but Gillette had just given him the chance to tell his side of the story *without* Mr. Popular around.

Chapter 51

Too easy, Zo thought as she tugged on her helmet and turned the key. Ask "Can I come?" and the guy says yes just like that? She expected to have to argue harder. Ben implied that his boss was some kind of Machiavellian mastermind. Either Ben was wrong, or Gillette had something besides his arm up his sleeve. She opened the throttle and fell into line.

The melt zone was three miles north of the op center. The lack of a flag line made her nervous. At the moment the weather was clear, but what if a storm blew up? Three miles was more than enough room in which to get lost. Her snowmobile had a GPS on the dash, but when she'd navigated across the peninsula in the Hägglunds, there were plenty of times she'd needed both.

She thought about her camp, and her research, and her whalers' hut. *This is my ice shelf,* she whispered fiercely to herself. Somewhere close by, possibly right beneath her feet, were the boreholes she had made to measure its movement.

She'd spent hours, days, tramping the surface. She knew it intimately, the way a mother recognized her baby, or a woman her lover's contours. That raised area off to the right where the ice was piled up like alphabet blocks definitely looked familiar.

Gillette was riding blithely in the lead as though he owned the place. She would have known he was responsible for destroying her ice shelf even if Ben hadn't told her. Ruthlessness emanated from him like a stink. Men like him ruined everything—plundering the planet, piling up profits, their utter lack of a conscience allowing them to sleep like babies.

The kind of man the world would be better off without.

The thought came to her unbidden. Full-blown. Insistent. Gillette could have an accident and no one would be the wiser. Antarctica was completely outside the law. Remote, and inaccessible. A place where anything could happen, and often did.

She clenched her teeth and sped up.

"Easy, Tiger," Ross said.

His voice took her by surprise. She hadn't realized her helmet with equipped with a mike. She was glad she hadn't spoken her thoughts out loud.

Gillette stopped near a spindly-looking overhead grid. Beneath the grid was a lake of frozen water so smooth, Zo almost wished for a pair of skates.

"This is a rectenna grid," Gillette explained. "What you're looking at is a series of short, dipole antennas. When the satellites are turned on, a pilot beam shoots up from the center of the grid like the beam of a flashlight, then the microwaves follow the beam back down. That building"—he pointed to a red Quonset a half mile away—"is our pumphouse. We control the three submersibles in the middle of the lake from there. Over there"—he pointed to a large-diameter pipe leading off toward the west—"is our water hose. Runs out to the edge of the cliff and down to the tanker. It's black to absorb heat from the sun and keep the water flowing. Naturally it's insulated, too. Okay. That's the grand tour. Not much to see, as you can tell. The real action happens up in space." He picked up his helmet. "I'm going over to the pumphouse. Stay here or go back to the op center, whatever you want. Just remember we're leaving in half an hour. If you're not ready, we're not coming back."

Such a gracious host. As Zo watched him drive off, she wished a crevasse would swallow him up.

In fact, if she wasn't mistaken, there *was* a crevasse nearby. She tried to picture the scene without Soldyne's intrusions. Yes, the formation behind the pumphouse was the one that used to remind her of Mount Rushmore. On the other side, a dark blue line below the surface led to a crack that opened into a crevasse so deep, when she'd dropped in a handful of beach gravel, she hadn't heard them hit the bottom. God, they were such idiots. Setting up their microwave operation in the vicinity of a crevasse was beyond stupid. If they'd melted their lake just a little deeper, or located it closer, there was no telling what would have happened. Typical. Dream up a new technology, and before they even considered the consequences, they rushed to try it.

She waited until Gillette had attained the pumphouse, then walked over to the lake. There was a narrow band of open water along the edge where the ice didn't quite meet the shore. She took off her gloves, took a plastic bottle from her pocket, filled it, capped it, and filled another.

"If you're that thirsty, I've got a water bottle in my pocket," Ross said.

"You wouldn't want to drink this water. Or rather, the ninety-three percent of the population that's not diabetic wouldn't."

"What are you talking about?"

She handed him a bottle and grinned. "The water's contaminated, Ross. The same as ours at the station. Probably not in the identical concentration," she added, considering the frozen expanse, "but the microbe's in there just the same. Ben told me his crew showed signs of insulin overdose after drinking the water, and they have rats here, too. This used to be the ice shelf's leading edge. When it broke off, some of the rats that were out hunting must have gotten trapped."

Ross opened his mouth, said nothing, looked appalled.

"Come on, big guy. Smile. This is a good thing. Don't you get it? Now that we have a microbe sample, we can research our discovery, demonstrate our theory, publish a paper. You're the one who was looking for extremophiles. Now you've got one."

"It's not a good thing. This is terrible. Worse than you can possibly imagine."

"If you're thinking of the water in Ben's tanker, don't worry. One of these samples is for him. When we get back, he'll have the tanker's water tested. If the microbe shows up, he can get an injunction or whatever to make sure the water stays inside." Talk about a spoilsport. Here she'd offered him a chance for fame and glory, and he couldn't even see it.

"You don't understand." Ross's face was as pale as she'd ever seen it. "Keeping the water inside the tanker isn't going to happen."

"What are you talking about?"

"As soon as the ship docks in the harbor, POP is going to blow a hole in the side of it."

"*What?* My God, Ross! You POP people are nuts! What is it with you guys and explosions? I read about the stuff you do in the papers. Rebecca Sweet is out of her mind. I don't understand how you can condone her behavior, let alone be a part of it. There are plenty of ways to fight for the planet and stay moral."

"POP *is* moral—more moral than people like you who'd sit back and judge. They never hurt anyone, only property. At least they're doing something besides compiling statistics."

"Well, you're going to have to rethink this one. Do you have *any* idea what could happen if that water is released into the ocean?"

"Who's the microbiologist here? Of course I know. I'm not nearly as stupid as you give me credit for. We've got to get back to the op center right away. I need to call Rebecca and tell her to put her plans on hold." He pulled back his sleeve and looked at his watch. "We should just make it. The next satellite window opens in a few minutes."

"Why the rush?"

"The tanker's due in tomorrow."

"*Tomorrow?* Ben said it would take at least another week."

"Ben's wrong. POP has been tracking the ship. I talked to Rebecca this morning."

"You *talked* to Rebecca? You're that high up in the organization?" Zo remembered Ross's earlier e-mails. A spy. What other critical information had he been supplying?

"I'm nobody special. I'm not even a member. Rebecca is my sister."

Zo studied him for a long moment. For all his arrogance, his manipulative game-playing, his withholding of personal information while slyly extracting hers, she sensed that this time, he was telling the truth. She pulled on her helmet, then stopped.

"Wait a minute." She pointed toward the frozen lake. A thick, white mist was rising from the center, hanging over the surface like fog over a field. At first, she thought it was the wind kicking up snow. Then she realized what she was seeing.

Steam.

Chapter 52

"He *fired* you?" Toshi said. He and the rest of the crew were sitting in an interested circle while Ben filled in the gaps in Gillette's version. "Un-friggin-believable."

"Hey, I'm really sorry, man," Eugene said.

"Makes *me* want to quit," Phil said. "This is total crap."

"Don't worry about it," Ben said. "Really. Believe it or not, I was going to quit anyway."

"Why would you do that?" Toshi looked genuinely upset. Ben felt a twinge of pity. The kid was such an idealist. Wait till he heard what was coming next.

"I found out something about the iceberg that none of us were told. Zo—the woman you just met—was doing research on our side of the peninsula, measuring the movements of the ice shelf. She was there when the iceberg broke off. The iceberg didn't happen on its own. It had help."

"What do you mean?"

"I mean that someone blasted it off using explosives."

"No way," Eugene said.

"It's true. Zo took pictures and collected some of the garbage they'd left behind." Evidence which unfortunately had been lost when the station burned down. What Ben wouldn't have given to be able to wave her photos at his upcoming press conference.

"And you think Soldyne was responsible?" Susan asked. "It could have been the Australians. They got to the berg first. They were probably right there waiting."

"It was Soldyne. But you don't have to take my word for it. Quentin will tell you himself."

"Quentin?" Susan looked at him as though he were nuts.

Ben walked over to Quentin's desk, opened the middle drawer, and took out a business card. "I found this in Quentin's wallet. If Quentin wasn't involved, why was he doing business with an explosives expert?"

"Holy cow," Phil said. "Gonna be something when this hits the fan."

"No kidding," Toshi agreed.

"Who else knows about this?" Susan asked.

"Only the five of us, Ross and Zo, and Zo's husband, Elliot. He's in the infirmary on the ship. I imagine others at Raney knew, but they're all gone." He shivered.

"I'll bet anything the detonating cord leads right back to Gillette," Eugene said. "It's got to. He and Quentin were tight."

"I'm going to call a press conference when I get back to L.A.," Ben said. "Tell the world what Soldyne did. Then I'm through."

The others were silent. Probably wondering if they should do the same. Ben wouldn't have minded their support; multiple resignations would make a stronger statement, but he wouldn't fault them if they didn't quit. It wasn't easy to take a stand for principles when there were bills to pay.

Suddenly, Toshi's laptop began to beep. It wasn't a friendly "You've got mail" kind of chime; to Ben, it sounded more like an alarm.

"What the—" Toshi swiveled around and stared at his monitor.

"What is it?" Ben hurried over.

"It's not possible," Toshi muttered as he clicked the mouse and punched keys. "It can't be."

"What can't be?" Ben asked. "Come on, Toshi. Fill us in."

"It's the satellite beam. Someone turned it on."

"Impossible," Susan said. "No one's touched your computer."

"I know that, but look." Toshi pointed at the screen. The scrolling figures meant nothing to Ben.

"It's an anomaly," Susan said. "Something's wrong with your program."

"Or maybe it turned itself on by accident," Phil offered.

"No way," Toshi said. "There are controls to prevent that. The *only* way the beam can be turned on is if someone does so deliberately."

Deliberately. The word hit Ben like a punch to the gut. Just like someone had deliberately broken off a section of the ice shelf? Could Gillette really be that stupid?

"Then there has to be something wrong with your program," Susan repeated. "There's no other explanation."

"There's nothing wrong with my program. Numbers don't lie. I'm telling you the temperature's going up. Look! It says so right there. The lake is melting."

Eugene ran outside. A moment later, he was back. "The beam is on, all right, and you should see all the steam. The melt zone looks like a damn mushroom cloud!"

"What's up with that?" Phil ran for the door. "The lake didn't create steam the first time we turned the beam on."

Toshi punched in more numbers. "The beam's set to maximum power!"

"Goddamn," Eugene said. "Turn it off."

"I can't. The program's not responding." Toshi looked like he was going to cry.

"Okay, we're done here," Ben said. "We're not going to stick around and see what happens. I want everyone to head for the ship. Don't take anything with you, just get the hell off. I'll meet you on board. I'm going to warn the others."

"But—" Susan said.

Ben silenced her with a look. She didn't have to spell out the danger. If the beam really was set to maximum power, there were no guarantees it was confined to the melt zone. But did he have a choice?

"Get to the ship," he repeated. "On the double. Move!"

He picked up a helmet and went out the door. Apparently, fate had once again designated him the hero.

Chapter 53

When the lights in the pumphouse flickered, dimmed, and came back up ten minutes earlier, Donald had presumed a power fluctuation and gone back to work. Now, he wasn't so sure. The atmosphere inside the pumphouse felt strange. Charged. Crackling with static, as though the very air were on fire. He knew it was his imagination, but that didn't prevent the hair on his arms from standing on end. He hated dark, confined spaces, and the windowless pumphouse qualified on both counts. Too many unexplained noises; too many secret shadows.

Ten minutes earlier was also when he had gotten the call from Susan with the two ominous words that had changed everything: *"They know."* It was no wonder his nerves were on edge.

How Ben had found out about the explosion, Donald had no idea, but it was going to stop here and now. The knowledge couldn't be allowed to spread. The longer the situation went on, the worse it would get, like a gyroscope spinning off-center. Action was key. Immediate. Bold. Un-flinching.

Ben and the others had to be eliminated. It was that simple. If the news got out about what Donald had done, the environmentalists and politicians would have a field day. He'd done nothing wrong—the blast wasn't illegal; no one owned Antarctica and there were no regulatory agencies to answer to and no enforcement, but it wouldn't matter. Public opinion would crucify him. When they got through, no one on the planet would be willing to take his side except the lawyers he'd be forced to hire.

He took a drink from a thermos of water he had found in the pumphouse and smacked his lips. The water tasted good; pure, and cold as the frozen lake from which it came. Sweat beaded his brow. He took another drink and wiped it away. He knew what he needed to do. The problem was that for perhaps the first time in his life, he wasn't 100 percent certain he could carry it out. Could he really kill another human being? A drowning man, you could turn your back on; someone bleeding on the sidewalk, you could walk away. But initiate the act and commit cold-blooded murder? Not just once, but multiple times? Hard to say.

An accident would be better. People fell into crevasses, they got lost in snowstorms, froze to death, crashed their snowmachines. The possibilities were endless, especially when you helped things along.

He disconnected the laptop from the server and shut the lid. Sabotaging the satellite program wasn't the easiest task he had set for himself. The programming course he'd taken while flying halfway around the globe had given him the basics, but a thorough understanding of such an intricate level of information took years. Whether he had successfully corrupted the program beyond saving remained to be seen, but disabling the satellite interface was only extra insurance. Redundant systems.

As he slid the laptop into his backpack and stood up to leave, he heard a rustling sound, followed by a series of clicks. The wind, most likely. That, or his nerves and the darkness were getting to him again.

He turned out the lights and opened the door. Stepped outside into the sunlight, and blinked as he ran into Ben.

Chapter 54

"What did you do?" Ben would have shaken Gillette by the shoulders if he could have reached them.

"I have no idea what you're talking about." Gillette started to brush past.

Ben grabbed his arm. "The hell you don't! You're not going anywhere until you tell us what you've done."

Gillette glared. "I haven't 'done' anything," he said, his voice as cold as the ground beneath their feet. "I'm going back to the op center. I strongly suggest you do the same." He looked down. "And get your hand off me."

"Are you really that stupid? You turned the microwave beam on!"

Gillette paled and looked toward the melt zone. Steam was rising from the surface, forming a giant white cloud. He turned around. "Turn it off."

"We can't," Ben said. "You corrupted the program. It's not responding. Not only that, the lake is steaming because you set the beam to maximum power. We've got to get off *now*. I've already sent the others to the ship. Where are Zo and Ross?"

Was it Ben's imagination, or had Gillette's eyes glittered?

"We'll do no such thing," he said, his voice oddly calm. "Get on your machine and go back to the op center. Sit down at your desk, and stay there until this is fixed."

"You're crazy," Ben said. "Do what you want, but I'm leaving." What he wouldn't have given for another foot of height. It was hard to deliver an ultimatum when you were looking at your opponent's chin.

Gillette drew back his hand. Ben's eyes narrowed. Was Gillette really going to hit him?

When the blow came, Ben ducked. Gillette's momentum carried him around. He spun in a circle, staggered, and fell.

Ben bent over him. Gillette's eyes were closed. Sweat beaded his brow.

Ben was still trying to puzzle out what had happened when from behind him, came the sound of snowmobiles and Ross and Zo pulled up.

Zo looked at Gillette sprawled on the ground. "What happened?"

"I don't know. One minute he was screaming, and the next he passed out."

"You don't suppose . . ."

Ben shook his head. "I don't know. If he is suffering from insulin shock, it doesn't matter," he said. "We have to get off the iceberg *now*. Gillette corrupted the satellite program. He turned on the microwave beam to full power, and we can't shut it down."

"That's insane!" Zo said. "This whole area is riddled with cracks! The berg could split apart! We've got to get out of here!"

"Exactly."

Ben and Ross lifted Gillette onto Ross's machine. Ross climbed on behind and reached around him for the controls. Gillette's eyes fluttered.

"He'll never make it," Zo said.

"We don't know that," Ross said. "Come on. We've got to get him to the ship."

Ben looked back at the pumphouse. The door was open. Whatever Gillette had done, there was evidence inside.

"You go on ahead," he said. "I'm right behind you. First, there's something I have to do."

Chapter 55

"We shouldn't have left him!" Ross heard Zo's voice in his helmet say as they raced along. "We should stay together!"

"He'll be all right." Ross peered over Gillette's shoulder to check his speed. Sixty miles an hour; a mile a minute; ten miles to the staircase. Hopefully, Gillette could hang on until then.

A minute passed. Two. Ross struggled to hold Gillette upright and control the machine. He was a big man, almost as tall as Ross, and as dead weight, twice as heavy.

They drove on. Then from behind came a *craack* that was so loud, Ross thought his heart had stopped.

Zo screamed.

The iceberg shuddered and rumbled as explosion followed explosion, coming faster and faster like the ending to a fireworks display. Ross cranked open the throttle. The machine leaped forward, slewed, found traction, and jumped forward again. Gillette flopped to one side. Ross leaned to compensate as the machine bucked and tipped. He glanced over his shoulder. Zo was hunkered low a dozen yards behind, focused and centered, driving fast and well.

A crevasse opened on their left, and they veered right in tandem. Another yawned on the right, and they veered left. The cracks seemed to be spreading outward like a fan, beginning at the melt zone and running toward the staircase. If they could stay the course and avoid falling in, they just might make it . . .

Suddenly his machine spun in a circle. He glanced down as he fought for control. Water was spraying out from both sides of the track like a fountain.

There was only one source for water on the berg. Soldyne's lake.

Chapter 56

Ben grabbed Gillette's backpack from where it had fallen and looked inside. A laptop. He added a thermos from inside the pumphouse and stored the bag in the snowmobile's rear compartment just as all the thunder in the world crashed down on him. He covered his ears and dropped, expecting a supersized lightning bolt to come blasting out of the sky. The ice beneath him trembled as one terrible crack followed another.

He scrambled to his feet, and as he looked toward the melt zone, his jaw dropped. The ice between the pumphouse and the melt zone was completely gone—replaced by an ever-growing half-mile-wide crater. Chunks the size of the Empire State Building tumbled into the hole; crevasses shot out in every direction like fingers. On the far side of the chasm, the rectenna grid wavered, trembled, and collapsed into the void as if it had been stepped on by an invisible foot. The iceberg was imploding, a black hole sucking in everything in its path.

A crevasse raced off toward the op center. Seconds later, the op center disappeared. Fire shot up from the crevasse as the fuel tank blew.

He leaped onto his machine and gunned the engine. Glanced behind, and saw the pumphouse tip and roll into the hole. He aimed for the staircase, praying he could make it in time; praying the others were already there.

Then from behind came a new sound, a soft, sibilant *sshhhssstt* that grew gradually louder.

Water.

A flood.

He wrenched the machine cross-wise to the current and sped toward an ice hummock that formed an elevated rise.

Below him, a river was spreading out as broad as the Mississippi. Ice chunks the size of houses twirled as the floodwaters rushed toward the sea. He pictured the water pouring over the cliff—a man-made waterfall smashing into the ocean, throwing up salt spray and waves.

Man-made, *contaminated* water. Rushing toward the sea. Toward the staircase. Toward Zo and Ross.

Chapter 57

Zo slowed to a crawl as the water grew higher, her machine slipping like a ball of mercury. Her feet were already underwater, her legs drenched. Ahead of her, Ross was similarly struggling. They were still moving, but barely.

Suddenly his machine spun in a tight circle. Gillette flopped to the side. Zo gasped as Gillette's head disappeared beneath the water. Ross grabbed him by the hair and pulled him upright again. She wondered if he was still alive.

Then her snowmobile coughed, spit, coughed again. *Please, God,* she whispered. She'd used up a lifetime's worth of supplications over the past twenty-four hours, but surely He wouldn't mind one more.

The machine slowed even further. Stopped. Stalled.

She turned the key. Tried again.

"Ross!" she called. "I'm stuck!"

"So am I," came the voice in her helmet. "The water's too deep. My machine quit."

"Should we get off and walk?" They had to keep moving. Behind them, the iceberg was snapping and popping like an ice cube dropped in warm water. The stairs couldn't be that far away.

"No! Stay with the machine! The current's too strong. It'll sweep you away. As soon as the lake empties, the water will go down."

She hunkered down to wait, shivering as the water rushed past. She felt the ground shudder. Lifting her visor, she turned around.

In the middle of the river, a split was forming like the part in a head of hair. The split raced toward them, swallowing up the river as it ran.

She barely had time to loop her elbows around the handlebars and grip the seat with her knees before the ice opened beneath her, and she was gone.

Chapter 58

She didn't scream. Her mouth was too full of water.

There was a brief sensation of falling, and then the machine stopped. She coughed, gasped, fought for air as the water poured down on her like Niagara—freezing ice water pounding her head and back, pulling at her, trying to tear her off and wash her away. The noise roared in her ears. Chunks of ice smashed onto her helmet like rocks. An ice boulder rolled past. Another lodged over her head. The torrent eased, momentarily diverted. Then the boulder rolled off and the flood resumed.

Stay with the machine.

She tried to calculate the number of gallons. Whatever the amount, it was finite. The deluge couldn't last forever. All she had to do was hold on.

Something hit her helmet and dropped onto the seat between her knees. A rat. It darted up and sheltered in her crotch. Another dropped into the crevasse, and then another.

They scrambled up her arms, her neck, down her back, digging in, desperately trying to hang on, just as she was.

The flood continued, pounding, relentless. One by one the rats washed away. She looked down into the abyss and watched them land in the water with a splash.

The water was rising.

Despair washed over her. This was it. The end. The only option left was to wait for the water to swallow her— or let go.

She loosened her grip. The roaring faded. She thought of her husband, and of her unborn child, and suddenly, miraculously, Elliot was beside her. He took her face in his hands. His hands were warm, and she smiled, grateful not to have to face death alone. He kissed her cheek, smiled back. Then as abruptly as he had come, he was gone.

The water stopped. Suddenly and completely, it turned off like a faucet. She blinked, drew a breath. Lifted her head.

Water dripped off the walls, her helmet, her clothes. Below her, a dozen rats were treading water. The water was receding.

"Zo! Are you there?" came a voice in her ear. "Can you hear me?"

"I'm okay!" she called. "The water's stopped."

He laughed, a warm, human sound that pushed the wet and cold away.

She looked around. Her machine was wedged front-to-back in a narrow crevasse. The walls glowed from the sunlight pouring in above her head. The lip of the crevasse was within reach.

"I'm going to try to climb out."

"Be careful."

"It's okay. It's not far."

She drew one foot up onto the seat, keeping a grip on the handles. The machine didn't shift. She brought up her other foot, tested her balance, and let go. The edge of the crevasse was only slightly higher than her waist. Washed smooth. Slippery.

She ran the sequence through her head, visualizing the maneuver, then jumped and threw herself forward. Belly flopped onto the ice, scrambled away, and lay still.

A shadow fell over her moments later. "Well, what do you know," Ross said. "The Amazon Woman does it again."

She smiled past her chattering teeth as he pulled her to her feet.

"You sure you're all right?" he asked.

"I'm fine. A little cold and wet, but nothing a hot bath and a cup of tea won't fix. Where's Gillette?"

His eyes went dark, as he shook his head. Zo understood. It had taken all her strength to hang on. If Gillette had been on her machine . . .

The ice sparkled benignly in the sun, the cracks and explosions replaced by a musical tinkling as the skiff of water refroze.

"What now?" she asked, and shivered.

He took her hand. "*Now* we walk."

Chapter 59

Ben drove as fast as he dared, paralleling the path the torrent had taken. The explosions had stopped, but that didn't mean a crevasse wasn't about to open in front of him at any minute. He didn't know how long he had been riding, how close he was to the stairs—if the stairs were still there.

He veered to avoid a crack, jumped another, and tried not to think of the torrent waterfalling over the cliff, polishing and smoothing the ledges, engulfing the ship.

In the distance, he saw two figures, and angled toward them. Zo and Ross.

"What happened?" he asked as he pulled up alongside. "Where are your machines?"

Zo pointed toward a narrow crevasse.

"Jesus," Ben breathed. "Just when you think things can't get worse."

"You have no idea." She looked at Ross.

"Go ahead. Tell him. He's in it as deep as we are, now."

"We've got a new problem," she said. "Remember you

told me your tanker wouldn't make L.A. harbor for another week? Turns out that's not true. It's going to arrive tomorrow."

"How can you possibly know that?"

"Before we left the ship this morning, Ross talked to his sister by satellite phone. POP's been tracking your tanker."

"What? Why, so she can move her protest down to the docks?"

"No," Ross said, "so she can blow a hole in the side of your ship."

"What?"

"Obviously she doesn't know the water's contaminated. I only just found that out myself."

"You've got to stop her," Ben said.

"You think?" Ross pointed to Ben's machine. Ben slid forward. Zo wrapped her arms around his waist, and Ross piled on behind.

The iceberg began to rumble, a low vibration that seemed to come from its very core. Zo's crevasse opened wider.

"It's breaking up!" she yelled. "Go, go, go! Now!"

Ben gunned the engine. Nothing happened. He cut back on the throttle until the machine caught traction. Gradually, they picked up speed, flying over the refreezing river that was as smooth as a hockey rink.

At last he saw a thin, dark line in the distance where the berg dropped away and the ice met sky.

"Slow down!" Zo yelled. "You're going too fast. You'll drive right off the edge!"

Ben hit the brake. The machine continued. "I can't! There's no traction!"

He shut off the engine, but the momentum carried them on without slowing.

"Jump!" Ross yelled.

They leaped. Ben slammed into the ice, tucked and rolled, cut his hands, banged his shoulders, came to a stop and crawled to his knees in time to see the snowmobile power over the edge. It hung for a moment, then plunged out of sight.

The rumbling grew louder. They ran for the stairs as the ground shook. Ben stopped at the top and looked down, shuddering at the shattered snowmobile that lay three steps up from the bottom.

The *steps* from the bottom. The stairs were intact.

"Hurry!" he cried, and jumped. He landed hard, twisted his ankle. Got to his feet, ran to the edge, and jumped again, flexing his knees to absorb the impact. The next step was too high. He slithered off on his belly. Dropped. Ran to the next ledge, and jumped again. Down and down, faster and faster as ice chunks rained down around him.

At last, he reached the bottom. Zo and Ross hit the ground moments after. Together, they sprinted across the gangplank and onto the ship.

Chapter 60

Crew members hurried them across a deck littered with ice. Ben looked back at the berg. A piece as big as a piano broke off the lip and rolled down the stairs. Larger chunks followed as the cliff edge disintegrated.

"Anyone else?" the captain cried as they fell through the door.

"No one," Ben said.

"My God," Susan said from behind him. Her face was white. "What about Donald?"

Ben shook his head.

The crew fastened the gangplank in place and dogged down the door. As the captain raced for the bridge, an explosion rocked the air, greater than any they had heard, a sonic boom of epic proportions.

Ben rubbed the condensation off the porthole glass. A massive crack ran down the middle of the stairs as though they had been cleaved by an ax. The iceberg grated and groaned.

"Hold on!" someone yelled. "This is going to be bad!"

Ben grabbed the rail as the iceberg split in two. The halves leaned in toward each other, balanced for a long moment, and then slowly slid away until they crashed in opposite directions into the sea.

Spray hit the porthole as if shot from a fire hose. The lights went out. Someone screamed as the ship canted at a terrifying angle. It seemed to lift, then plunged down with a sickening thump. It rose, dropped, rose again and dropped again.

"Almighty God," Ben heard someone pray. "You bestowed the singular help of Blessed Peter on those in peril from the sea—"

He closed his eyes. "By the help of his prayers," he whispered as he lost his footing and tightened his grip on the rail, "may the light of your grace shine forth in all the storms of this life and enable us to find the harbor of our everlasting salvation." In the darkness, he heard sobs.

At last, the bucking slowed. The lights came on. The sailors cheered.

"Holy crap," Zo said.

"Just when you think things can't get any worse," Ben said, and winked.

She shook her head. "I don't know about you guys, but I've had enough. If you'll excuse me, I think I'll go check on my husband."

"By all means." Ben turned to a crewman. "And I believe my friend would like to use the phone."

Epilogue

Los Angeles, California—Five Months Later

Sarah Maki pushed her plate to one side and propped her elbows on her dining room table, staring at The Iceman while the grown-ups talked. She could hardly believe he was really here, at her very own table, eating the dinner that she and Cassie and her mom had made: spaghetti and meatballs (her favorite), garlic bread (Cassie's idea) a salad, (her mom's contribution), with Ben & Jerry's for dessert.

"WaterLife's a good organization," The Iceman was saying. "POP-approved." He smiled like he was making a joke. The Iceman had nice teeth. And a dimple. Sarah loved dimples. Beside her, Cassie poked her arm and grinned.

Her dad laughed. "We're a great fit. The big relief organizations don't serve rural villages with ongoing water shortages, but these communities represent the greatest need. WaterLife picks up the ones that fall through the cracks. I'm leaving next week to engineer a four-thousand-liter reservoir in Cameroon."

"*Nizhóní*. Excellent. One well supplying clean water to a community can make a hell of a difference."

Sarah's mom frowned. Sarah grinned. Her mom didn't like it when people swore. The Iceman looked at Sarah and winked.

"Sarah, Cassie, will you girls help me in the kitchen?" her mom asked.

"In a minute," Sarah said. "I have to go to the bathroom."

She went out into the hall and sat down on the bench beside the front door. Snatches of conversation: "*microbe couldn't survive in salt water*"; "*working at the University of Utah now*"; "*research*"; "*new drug*"; "*diabetes.*" Boring grown-up talk.

There were footsteps on the other side of the door. The mail fell through the slot. She picked up a big, square, blue envelope, the kind that meant an invitation or a card. It was addressed to her dad.

She carried the envelope into the dining room. "This is for you."

"Thanks." He smiled. Her dad had a nice smile, too.

She scooched onto his knee. "Go on. Open it. See what it says."

He slid his bread knife under the flap. "It's a birth announcement," he said. "From Zo and Elliot. Seems Zo had a baby boy."

Sarah knew all about Zo from her dad's stories. Her dad was a real hero. He'd saved The Iceman. She'd helped, too, after The Iceman accidentally sent his SOS e-mail to Mr. McMurtry instead of McMurdo Station. The Iceman told her so himself.

"What'd they name him?" she asked.

Sarah's dad passed the card across the table. The Iceman read it. At first he looked embarrassed. Then he grinned.

"They named him Ross."

Author's Note

While the microwave technology as depicted in this novel is only loosely based on fact, the world's water crisis is real. So is the WaterLife Foundation, a U.S.-based non-profit dedicated to providing clean, safe, affordable water and sanitation for children and families in disadvantaged communities around the world.

To learn more about how you can get involved, go to www.waterlife.org.

Suggested reading: *Blue Gold: The Fight to Stop the Corporate Theft of the World's Water*, by Maude Barlow and Tony Clarke

About the Author

After dropping out of the University of Michigan, Detroit native Karen Dionne moved to Michigan's Upper Peninsula wilderness with her husband and daughter as part of the back-to-the-land movement. For the next thirty winters, her indoor pursuits included stained glass, weaving, and constructing N-scale model train layouts. Her stories have appeared in *Bathtub Gin*, *The Adirondack Review*, *Futures Mysterious Anthology Magazine*, and *Thought Magazine*, where her entry won first place in their spring 2003 writing competition. She worked as Senior Fiction Editor for *NFG*, a print literary journal out of Toronto, before founding Backspace, an Internet-based writers organization with over 750 members in a dozen countries. She is a member of Sisters in Crime, Mystery Writers of America, and International Thriller Writers, where she serves on the membership committee and website staff. She and her husband live in Detroit's northern suburbs.

Don't miss the page-turning suspense, intriguing characters, and unstoppable action that keep readers coming back for more from these bestselling authors...

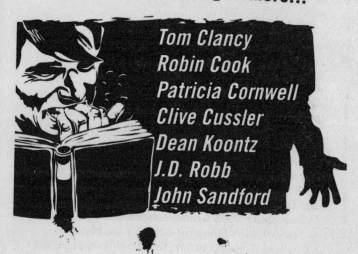

Tom Clancy
Robin Cook
Patricia Cornwell
Clive Cussler
Dean Koontz
J.D. Robb
John Sandford

Your favorite thrillers and suspense novels come from Berkley.

penguin.com

M14G0907

Penguin Group (USA) Online

What will you be reading tomorrow?

Tom Clancy, Patricia Cornwell, W.E.B. Griffin, Nora Roberts, William Gibson, Robin Cook, Brian Jacques, Catherine Coulter, Stephen King, Dean Koontz, Ken Follett, Clive Cussler, Eric Jerome Dickey, John Sandford, Terry McMillan, Sue Monk Kidd, Amy Tan, John Berendt...

You'll find them all at
penguin.com

Read excerpts and newsletters, find tour schedules and reading group guides, and enter contests.

Subscribe to Penguin Group (USA) newsletter and get an exclusive inside look at exciting new titles and the authors you love long before everyone else does.

PENGUIN GROUP (USA)
us.penguingroup.com